FAR FROM THE TREE

ROB PARKER

THIRTY MILES TRILOGY
BOOK ONE

RED DOG
UK

Published by RED DOG PRESS 2021

First Edition

Hardback ISBN 978-1-914480-43-0
Paperback ISBN 978-1-913331-74-0
Ebook ISBN 978-1-913331-85-6

www.reddogpress.co.uk

PRAISE FOR FAR FROM THE TREE

"A superbly-written, taught, gritty and visceral thriller."

— *Howard Linskey*

"I started this book with a 'Wow!' followed by a gulp, and it carried on from there!"

— *Nick Oldham*

"A dark, powerful and utterly compelling tale of Northern gangsters tied together by blood. It just drips with real life."

— *Tony Kent*

"Proper noir. Proper gangland. Proper excellent."

— *Judith O-Reilly*

"Taut, tough and darkly enthralling. Loved it."

— *Chris Whitaker*

"Foley and Madison are a great duo. I was pleased to see it's the first in a trilogy."

— *Elly Griffiths*

"A taut, immersive story with a big emotional heart."

— *Chris McDonald*

"A superbly crafted dark descent into the depths of a family on both sides of the law. Takes dark and gritty to another level."

— *Robert Scragg*

To Mum and Dad, for everything.

And to Becky, for everything else.

PROLOGUE

THE GARDEN HOSE was peeled from the open rear door of the transit van. It snaked at speed across the glistening black top. At 1 a.m., the moon had long since been choked out by thick cloud, but a couple of street lamps gave the quiet suburban street a sharp, amber profile.

'Quick, go on, right up to it,' urged a hushed voice, as two figures dragged the hose and dumped the end on the ground in front of the cash machine at Bargain Booze. A third person exited the driver's side and joined them, leaving the van's engine quietly rumbling. He was taller than the other two, and held a crowbar in a gloved fist. He jammed the iron into the frame of the machine, jarring and prising.

It wouldn't budge.

'The hammer,' the man said. 'The big one.'

The two younger guys ran back to the vehicle, their breath staccato gasps. One returned seconds later with a rubber mallet.

'You do it,' said Fitz, still bracing and pulling down on the crowbar. 'When I say.'

Connor held the hammer, feeling nervous, terrified, euphoric and very fucking alive.

'Now,' said Fitz.

Connor whacked the end of the metal shaft with a dull thunk.

'Put your back into it, lad.'

Connor held the mallet high with two hands, and heaved it down, forcing a meatier, metal clunk. He checked around him. That noise would not go unnoticed in a tight-knit suburb like this—and it was only going to get noisier in just a couple of seconds.

'Good. You know what to do,' said Fitz, swapping the hammer in Connor's hand for a small squirt bottle of Durex lube. He jogged back to the van.

Connor took the end of the hose and shoved it into the small hole that had opened in the frame of the cash machine. It was tight, so he coated the hose casing in lube. With extra effort, he managed to get about a foot of the tubing inside.

He waved to the van and heard the soft hiss of the oxyacetylene mix pouring down the hose, filling the frame of the cash machine with gas.

He ran back to the van, where Fitz and Moston were leaning out of the open rear doors, watching the shop.

'It went in all right?' Fitz asked.

'Yeah, just about,' replied Connor, in a voice on the cusp of breaking—not quite a boy, not quite a man. 'Here's your bottle.' He held out the lube.

Fitz smiled. 'Keep it. You're gonna need it when this is done.'

They waited.

Silence.

Moston shuffled on his feet and said, 'How lo—'

The street was shredded by a deafening boom and the uneven clatter of disturbed metal and brick. The front of the cash machine was propelled outwards on a trail of white-grey smoke, landing noisily in the road, as notes fluttered to the ground like downed paper planes.

'Go, now.' Moston started pulling the hose back into the van, as Connor and Fitz ran to the hole in the side of the shop, the former with a couple of hold-alls, the latter dragging a hydraulic trolley.

Connor grabbed a wad of cash from a puddle. It was soaked, streaked dark by the rain. More money than he had ever held in his life.

In the distance, a door opened. There was shouting, although he couldn't make out what was being said.

He smiled. *Time to go.*

PART 1

THE GODFATHER

ROB PARKER

CHAPTER 1

THE SUN BROKE cover hard beyond the thick tree line, for the first time that day. The forest floor still crackled beneath the footsteps of Detective Inspector Brendan Foley. Aided by the stubborn chill in the air, the atmosphere in the woods was as cold as ice with a grudge.

He stopped. 'How many?'

'Twenty-seven,' replied Detective Sergeant Iona Madison.

Foley's breath danced just below his nose. His heart banged beneath a white Tyvek all-in-one suit. 'This must be up there with some of the biggest in the country, right?'

'Not sure, but I haven't heard of many others,' Madison answered. Her eyes were on a clipboard, pen scratches punctuating the whistle of the breeze through the tree trunks.

She was also dressed in a full bodysuit and Foley could just see her cold-pinched cheeks and that criss-cross scar on the end of her right eyebrow, which had gone pink in the chill. She seemed contained, controlled and *with it*.

'Anyone?' he asked.

'There was one that had forty in it. Found under a Sainsbury's car park, a couple of years back.'

Foley looked up at Gavigan, who was peeling back the hood of his coverall. He removed his eye protectors before speaking again. His gaze flared with excitement. 'But they were put there by Richard the Third.'

'Present day – anything?'

'Nothing. Nowt like this.'

'Well,' Foley said, stepping forward. 'History it is, then. One for the grandkids.' He stopped on the edge of the pit, his eyes narrowing as he took it all in. He swallowed hard. 'Or maybe not.'

In front of him lay a hole six feet wide, twenty feet long and three feet deep. It was filled with human bodies, vacuum-packed. Their skin was visible through the plastic sheeting. Some were opaque with condensation, others looked like they'd been factory-packed just hours earlier. Others, at the far end, were green, brown and indistinct – just a long package of rotten meat. One, really close down near the front, had thick, deep maroon matter strewn about the plastic.

Jesus, thought Foley, at pains to keep his racing mind to himself. 'The super?' he asked.

'Monroe's on his way down. He's already talking about it going outside,' said DS Tom Christopher, joining Foley on the pit-edge. He was in a coverall like everyone else, only his face visible; jagged cheekbones and purple bags bold as war-paint under his eyes. He tilted his head, only glancing at the pit intermittently as if he were duty-bound to look at it, which of course he was. 'We'll need all the manpower we can get to shift this lot. IDing them won't be simple. That'll need time and space I'm not sure we have.'

'Agreed. Best get our house in order for Monroe getting here then. Time of discovery?'

'Call came in at 6.48 this morning,' Madison said, reading from her notes. 'Anonymous female. Reported freshly moved earth in the woods in the south-east corner of Peel Hall forest park. PCs McMonagle and Flynn attended the scene. Took them a while to find the spot. McMonagle, bright spark, brought a shovel with him, and found the first one. After parting with his breakfast, he stopped there. 8.12 a.m., Flynn called it in to the nick.'

'It's a long time between 8.12 a.m. and now. What was the hold-up?'

'We didn't realise the extent of it at first. And we tried our best not to disturb your day until… well, you know.' She nodded at the hole and the bodies within.

Foley pursed his lips. 'I appreciate the effort. But in future, next time a mass grave opens up on our patch, do feel free to give me a call.'

'Yes, sir.'

'Hoyt?'

'Sir?' A man stood back from the scene, beyond the police tape, clutching a coffee. He had a thick pointed beard, and the top half of his bodysuit was bunched about his waist, displaying a navy fisherman's jumper.

'Head back to the station and hit the databases. Both public and in-house, PNC and PND. Look for all missing persons reports for the last… let's say five years. Keep it local to start with, then widen the circle. See what we get. If you think anyone in those reports could even remotely be in this damn hole, keep onto them. We need a head start for IDing. And while you're at it, put in a tech request for the station phone log. We need to know who tipped us off and where from. It has to be local. We need to find where that call came from, ASAP.'

'Yes, sir – although it might take a bit of time with it being a Sunday and all.' Hoyt had a soft, Irish cadence.

'Then do lean on them a bit, Detective Sergeant.'

Foley began to stalk the edge of the trench. Looking towards the opposite side, he could see ten scene of crime officers, Gavigan included, standing waiting for his word. He checked his watch, a thick, scuffed G-Shock at odds with his suit. Eleven thirty in the morning.

'Christopher, get an OS map of the woods and circle every single possible access point to this spot, both by road and on foot. Go check them out in person. If you're wearing that Harrington under there, you're gonna freeze, so take my mac before you go.'

'Thank you, sir.'

Foley's phone rang in his pocket. He checked the caller ID, took a second, stepped to one side and answered it.

'Hi, love.' He couldn't pull his gaze from the extinguished humanity all around him. He didn't have time for this.

'Where are you?' came the voice on the other end of the line. He could hear the anxiety in his wife's tone.

'We're having a bit of a do at work.' That was all he could say.

'I guessed. Are you coming back?'

'I don't think I can.'

She blew out a breath. 'Then do you have the cheque book? I can't find it to settle up.'

Foley patted his breast pocket, immediately feeling the pressed oblong that had taken him ages to find that morning. 'Yes.'

'Can you bring it back? They're being a little funny about it, worried we're all gonna do a runner.'

Foley could picture her, baby on her hip, trying to balance the demands of her guests – *their* guests – and felt guilt press up. 'Are they really insisting we pay by cheque? Does anyone even do that anymore?'

'Village halls and all that.'

He sighed. 'I'll be there shortly.'

Stepping beyond the scene cordon, he undid his coverall to reveal a dark full-length mac over a blue wool suit, pressed white shirt and a gaudy skinny tie with glitter-blue floral stitching. He shouted over to his DS as he shrugged the coat off.

'Madison, you be my eyes here. Control the scene, keep an eye on the crime scene log. Take the notes, answer the questions, defer to me if need be, for as long as the scene is still ours. And give this to Christopher, please.' He handed her the mac.

'Yes, sir… If asked, where do I say you are? What about Monroe?'

'I've got to settle up with the caterers, then I'll be back. I won't be long.'

'Was it all going to plan before we called you in?'

'Yeah, vicar showed, family showed, nobody drowned in the font – went as good as these things can.'

Madison nodded curtly, her blue eyes focused on her clipboard. The abrupt movement caused a fringe of peroxide to fall from her hood and over her thick black glasses. She brushed it away hurriedly. Foley watched her, feeling a rising empathy for his assembled colleagues. This was going to be tough. His team were young – hell, at thirty-six he wasn't exactly an old hand either, but this was a test the likes of which you could never really expect.

What in God's name were they up against here? This was as high-profile as serial murder got.

'Any press involvement?' Foley asked.

'Not yet. I'm guessing Monroe will want to have a say in that, but there's nothing public so far. The remoteness of the location is about the only thing that's helping us here.'

'It won't last long,' Foley replied, glancing back over his shoulder. 'Small towns and all that. It'll be out before we know it. I'm going to have a word with the SOCOs, then I'll see you back at the ranch. And depending on how long it takes, get on to the White Horse in Padgate to see if they've got any of the Sunday roast spare – we'll need to keep spirits up any way we can on this one.'

'Will do, sir. I'll give them a buzz now.'

'Cheers, Madison.'

THE SUIT WAS itchy, but Madison still felt grateful. It was like a shield, a barrier, keeping her from contaminating the scene, as much as it kept the scene from contaminating *her*. What unnerved her most was the lack of smell from the trench. Before her lay twenty-seven corpses, in various stages of decomposition.

She couldn't smell a thing.

She noted everything on her clipboard with a meticulousness that bordered on mania. If she looked too thorough, that was preferable to looking like she couldn't handle it. She watched the SOCOs assess how to get the nearest awful bag out. Anybody would struggle with handling it – but that wasn't how she wanted to portray herself. She wanted to be ironclad, unflappable, reliable; not just equal, but more than equal. *Better.*

As the first bag was lifted, the sure outline of the person inside appeared. As the horror took a human shape, she felt a quake pass through her. She had a mechanism for hiding that though: a sharp intake of breath that she'd honed to perfection throughout her career. She could do it any time and nobody would notice – a quick gulp through her nose, lips pursed tight. It reset the balance. She'd been taught, as they all were, that it was normal to feel this way. But that didn't mean she had to show it.

One of the SOCO's hands on the corner of the bag suddenly slipped, and he whispered, *Shit,* through his face mask. The body dropped, landed on another with a wet slap, and suddenly Madison had to do her secret gulp again.

She looked away and immediately caught eyes with Hoyt. She thought he'd gone but he was behind the scene tape, watching her. He was bent, pulling off his own Tyvek suit over his ankles, revealing skinny jeans. Combined with the dense brown beard and thickly framed glasses, his clothes had made him known as the constabulary's only hipster copper. His gaze was earnest, seeing straight through Madison's careful self-portrayal. His eyebrows rose in question. *You OK?* Madison raised her chin in response, a silent *Yes,* and made herself look back at the bodies.

FOLEY EMERGED FROM the forest on the dirt path. In his pressed suit, he picked his way through the mud churned up by SOCOs and dog walkers. His loafers were ruined – he should have worn his trusty work boots instead – and dirt streaked up his trouser legs in fine ribbons like shitty pinstripes. He hopped the low stile and scrubbed his shoes on the grass verge before nodding grimly to the two PCs guarding the entrance. One of them noted Foley's exit on the scene log sheet.

The street was quiet, with woodland pressed tight up to the road. Further up the street was a cul-de-sac of five houses. Red brick new-builds, sore thumbs against the surrounding greenery, looking as if they'd been dropped in ready-built by a higher power. Nobody visible.

Scratch that... There *was* someone there. A woman dipping between two of the parked cars, looking towards him. She was short, with a dramatic blonde bob.

Foley made a mental note of which drive she was standing on. Second house from the left corner. He had a feeling she was their mystery tipster.

He pulled out his car keys and unlocked the mint-green mini-van his family called 'the Toad'. As he slumped into the driver's seat, he caught a glimpse of all the christening presents on the back seat and the balloons dancing in the rear window. Foil baby bears, blue hearts, circular discs of helium-filled congratulations.

'Fuck *me*,' he said, and allowed himself a long, deep breath.

CHAPTER 2

WHEN FOLEY PULLED the Toad into the car park of the Legion, he couldn't find anywhere to park. He checked back and forth up the potholed rows, cursing his luck. He pulled in front of some bursting industrial-waste units, which hunkered tight up to the cricket nets, and jogged to the entrance. The Legion Sports Club was a sixties shell of faded grey brick, which somehow managed to contain a hall big enough for a party. It had hosted every major party his young family had ever put on, mainly because it was cheap, the rules were relaxed and they kept the bar open as late as anyone wanted to drink.

As he entered, he caught his brother going the other way. Ross Foley was only two years younger than Brendan, but carried himself like a teen. He had the relaxed gait of a man not overly arsed with anything, a head full of thick black hair (unlike Brendan's with its titanium dusting), and a set of baby blues so vivid a paint company marketing team might call the shade Blazing Azure.

'Here he is, Mr Popular – dossing out of his own kid's christening,' said Ross, pulling a crumbled packet of fags from his inner jacket pocket.

Brendan went for severe underplay: 'Bit of a do at work, that's all.'

'Sound.' Ross thumbed his lighter and looked at his feet, the unlit cig now in the corner of his mouth. 'I can't talk. I'm embarrassed too, about… you know. I'm sorry, it's doing my head in.' His own son – Brendan's nephew – hadn't shown for the christening, instead opting for whatever teenage boys did on Sunday mornings. This wasn't the first time he'd let the family down either. A pattern was emerging.

'Not your fault, mate.' Brendan thought it was entirely his brother's fault. The lad was on the cusp of becoming a full-on tearaway, whereas Brendan had a stricter relationship with his children than Ross did with his son. He nodded at the entrance. 'How is it in there?'

'Fine, the rellies haven't murdered each other, and Mim's got it covered.'

'Good to hear. See you in a min then.' Brendan walked inside, leaving Ross to spark up alone.

The lobby was bare, but once through the double doors to his left, the heat and noise of the party hit him.

The high ceiling was lined with ancient strip lights, the floor was scuffed parquet marked by lines of coloured tape denoting various playing areas. More blue balloons had been taped to the walls, and a tinny old CD player streaked with blobs of white paint jangled in the corner.

A handful of tables were dotted about, mostly taken by children ferociously colouring. Mim had had this idea that if they bought some ready-made packs of cheap crayons and paper from a wholesaler, that would occupy most of the kids. Nearly all the adults stood – the men in shirtsleeves with their pints never far away, the pastel-clad women loitering with wine glasses in groups overseeing the children.

Brendan made straight for the bar. It was governed by a stout woman who carried the air of a bullshit-proof northern matron.

'Everything all right?' she asked.

'Yes. I'd like to settle up with Anne if possible.'

'I'm Anne. You lot finishing?'

'No, no. I just need to get paid up in case I have to go.'

Anne eyed him as if he had made a very unnatural request. 'Cheque made out to Legion Sports Ltd. for £462.32.'

Brendan couldn't remember agreeing such a precise and strangely arbitrary amount. 'Is that what we said?'

'Mad how all them sausage rolls add up.'

He took that as a *yes*, and, to be honest, with the events of the morning, he could barely remember anything agreed anyway. He scrawled a cheque, ripped it and passed it over. 'It's all been great, thanks.'

Anne turned away without a word. Brendan scanned the crowd, looking for his wife. As he took in the faces, he was a bit surprised that he didn't really know a lot of people. But his wife's family kept themselves largely to themselves, and while his family were smaller, they did, well, just the same. There was also a bunch of local people he didn't know – school mums and their husbands, he guessed, and various women from Mim's community efforts.

There was Mim – he could never miss her, statuesque and topped with a ragged, bronze bob – talking to that woman who he knew only as a village fair busybody. He wished he was better with names in his personal life, but he had grown so separated in his work and home personas. His attention to detail was dynamite as a detective, but like a sieve as soon as he got through his front door.

He caught Mim's eye and waved her over. She excused herself and strode towards him. Little Mick rested on her hip in his white christening gown, which was plastered with orange goo around the neckline, carrying that little comforter he called Bun Bun, which was a small soft rabbit with a square of plush fabric attached – both of which were now entirely minging.

Halfway across the hall, her face softened as she saw his expression.

'A bad one?' She was wearing heels, which brought her eye to eye with him. No escaping her scrutiny today.

'You have no idea,' he replied. She hugged him side on, with her free hip against him.

'I've settled up,' he said, 'but it looks like you'll have to hold the fort. I'm so sorry but… I've honestly never seen anything like this, Mim.'

Mick reached for his father's tie with a dribble-soaked mitt, burbling contentedly.

'You OK?'

'Yeah. We've found some bodies. A lot of them. We don't know what we've got yet. Seriously. This is going to turn the constabulary upside down. I've got the team organised and holding it together until I can go back but…'

He was saying all this for his own benefit, he realised. Working through things. Mim didn't need to know what his team were up to; her glance had drifted back to the party, and she was probably wondering how she was going to manage the baby, a teenager and almost a hundred guests. He could see what she was thinking: she was the wife of a detective, she knew the role, and he guessed she hated it. What made it worse was what he knew about her – what he had always known about her since they had decided to start a family. She was a go-getter on hiatus, rather than a stay-at-home mum, a fact that inspired regular guilt.

'Let me go and find Mum and Dad, get them to give you a hand,' he offered.

She said nothing. He hadn't mentioned her parents. They had a four-hour drive back to Bath and didn't see their northern grandchildren so often. He didn't want one of their rare visits up north marred by any additional sudden responsibility.

'Or I could send everyone home?' he suggested.

'No, no. I'll be fine. Do you have any idea when you'll be back?'

'No idea, darl.' He didn't have much scope to say anything else. His mind had drifted back to that one plastic sack with deep viscera smeared all over the inside, and all he could think of was the horror they'd find when they opened it up.

'Keep me posted?'

'Yeah.' He kissed her, pinched Mick's cheek and it reset him. 'Dan about?'

'He's round here, somewhere. I gave him some money to keep the little ones topped up with Fruit Shoots, but I don't think he appreciated the responsibility. Last I saw he was hiding around the fruit machines.'

'OK, tell him I said hi. Love you.'

'Love you too. Keep me in the loop, OK?'

'Yeah. Got to go. Please let everyone know I'm sorry.' He pecked Mick's fuzzy blond hair, and got moving. He didn't want to get caught in conversation with anyone, but as he left the main hall the door to the Gents swung open with an oil-starved screech, and out walked his father.

'It's been a good one, son,' he said, smiling crookedly at his elder boy. His voice was a harsh scratch, years of ale and fags having cheese-gratered his vocal cords to nothing more than dangling fleshy rags.

Arthur Foley looked like he'd inhaled every moment life had to give him, and had gone back for seconds. He was tanned an orange that was not so much healthy as phosphorescent, with thick grey hair swept to the back and to the side, a stubbled goatee and the original set of vivid blue irises that had eventually reached his son, Ross. His girth made walking more of a waddle, and he continued wrestling with his belt.

'Good to hear,' said Brendan. Other sons looked to their fathers for guidance and support, but Brendan could never see Art in that way. That just wasn't their relationship anymore – and hadn't been since Brendan had become a man himself. 'Look, I have to shoot off. Could you keep an eye on Mim and the kids? You don't need to do anything, just make sure they're all OK and get off all right?' He didn't like asking this.

'Of course, course,' said Art, his belt finally fastened. 'Work, is it?'

'Yep. Not much I can do about this one either.'

'Well, you look positively anaemic over it. Have a Guinness before you go, that'll settle you.'

'I can't.'

'I'm serious,' Art continued, his palms outstretched as if to emphasise how serious he really was. 'Look, every time you hear of some old dear dying at one hundred and ten years of age, you find out later that she always had half a Guinness every lunchtime in her local Labour club.'

'Thanks for the dietary tips, Dad,' Brendan replied, softening.

'Now we both know I'm in no position to be giving out dietary advice.' He patted the furthest point of his belly. 'Off you go, I'll handle it.'

'Thanks.' Brendan felt that the moment cried out for maybe a handshake, or a pat on the shoulder, but he knew neither of them could do it. Maybe one day.

'Another time with the black stuff,' Brendan said – the biggest gesture he could make.

'Atta boy,' said Art.

As he left his father, Brendan's phone buzzed in his pocket. He pulled it out, nerves jangling in anticipation of a bollocking for leaving the biggest crime scene the region could remember. So, he was momentarily relieved to see it was just a text from Madison.

Meet at the mortuary.

CHAPTER 3

MADISON MET FOLEY at the entrance to the mortuary at Warrington Hospital – the hospital where she'd been born. As morgues went, even for an underfunded northern hospital, this was a weird one.

It was situated in a low slate-roofed brown brick building separate from the faded sixties construction of the main hospital wings. The recently deceased had to be wheeled out of the hospital and around the edge of a car park to get them there, a daily sight that cheap vinyl screens and scrappy foliage could do nothing to hide. The one bonus in this case, however, was that the bodies exhumed from the pit didn't have to be traipsed through the main hospital, and before any unwitting members of the public, twenty-seven times.

'Your wife didn't kill you, then?' she said as he approached. She'd run home to change before coming to the morgue, and felt much more at home in her black boots under a dark trouser suit, a roll-up in her hand, the first she'd had in a fortnight, which she'd tossed and stamped dead. She'd feel terrible about it later, it being so close to a fight, but today was definitely a *fuck-it* day when it came to depriving yourself of your vices. Whatever you needed to scale the obstacle. *Life was definitely too short.*

'I think I escaped with a lucky win on points. All square at the scene?'

'Yep. Monroe's holding court, running SOCO ragged. Hoyt's still crunching the numbers. Christopher gave me this for you.'

Madison handed him his coat, which he swung on and began buttoning tight. She pulled out her clipboard, gave it a once-over, even though she knew just what was on it.

'The first five are here, from the front of the trench.'

'Is that what we're calling it? Not pit?'

'Gavigan said a pit is usually much deeper. At just a few feet, he said trench was more appropriate. Since he's writing the forensic reports, I thought he could have that one.'

'They told us never to piss off your crime scene manager. Trench it is, then. Mackie here?'

'As per. Not happy about being disturbed mid-sherry.'

'She'll get over it.'

'When she was told there were twenty-seven to sort through, she did.'

They entered the cool corridor of the mortuary. The walls were a faded blue tile, the floor more Victorian in its slab-work. All wipe-clean. After signing in at the desk, they took the only corridor that led anywhere, the lights still shut off and the steady darkness giving the false sensation of descent.

The first door they saw in the distance spilled blue light through a frosted-glass panel, with dark shapes moving beyond.

'We in room one?' Foley asked.

'As always,' Madison replied.

Always was a bit much – this was only Madison's third visit, and Foley's fourth. Murder rates were not high in Warrington. Crime, yes – assaults, burglaries, theft, public order offences a constant. But you didn't often have people killing each other. In fact, before today, Foley could only count the number of dead bodies he'd seen on one hand. After this morning, he'd need a further five hands to count all the corpses.

Foley knocked on the door and was greeted by an uncompromising bellow.

'Come in.'

THE ROOM WAS laid out like a war triage before the main fighting had started, with rows of empty tables beneath unforgiving light. In the lower near corner, closest to the door, five were occupied by plastic cocoons.

'We're ready, thank Christ,' said Mackie, walking over from the far wall, where a handbag, a thermos emblazoned *Caffeine'll kill ya!* and an open laptop rested on a stainless-steel counter top. A heavy-duty Canon DSLR hung around her neck, lens cap off.

Denise Mackie was the region's Home Office pathologist, called in to undertake the post-mortems of Warrington's suspicious deaths. She was in her early fifties, tall, built like a heptathlete, with short feathered hair in flecks of platinum and blonde. The younger PCs of both genders called her a GILF, a word Foley had reluctantly and disastrously had to Google. She had gone all-in with a full Tyvek suit herself, albeit minus the hood, and her hands were already encased in the usual latex.

'I must admit, Foley. I don't envy your position on this one,' she said. Foley could have taken this the wrong way but didn't. He had known Mackie for a long time. She had lectured Foley a number of times during his inspector training. And she was right: at thirty-six, suddenly to be the senior investigating officer on a case like this was daunting.

'If you're going swimming, be ready to get wet, right?' he replied.

Mackie smiled the least humorous smile possible and walked past them to the cadavers. Around the tables were a couple of assistants, a middle-aged PC Foley recognised from the nick called Hossein, and a photographer.

Hossein stepped forward. He was earnest, the sides of his shaven head dusted with grey. 'Good afternoon, sir. I'm the appointed evidence officer.'

'Sorry about your Sunday, Hossein. Thank you for making yourself available.'

Hossein nodded in reply. The other assistants were mortuary officials, no doubt on overtime, and were busy assembling a wheeled cart full of sterilised tools.

'I could have given you all this in the report, you know,' said Mackie, removing her camera.

'I wanted to be here, at least for the start,' Foley replied. The discovery had hit him, without question. Seeing those rows and rows of the baleful, vacuum-packed dead, tossed aside like carpet off-cuts in a landfill, had really affected him. He took his responsibility seriously. In his gut, the responsibility was growing.

Shallow grave, he thought. Very shallow, to his mind. It was the first time the depth had occurred to him. Why so shallow?

'I suppose, in lieu of anything more definite, we have to label the whole body an exhibit,' said Mackie, at the head of the nearest corpse-bundle.

'The whole thing?' asked Hossein, ready to note it down.

'The whole thing. So, this is Exhibit E, making it the fifth victim pulled out.'

Mackie took a scalpel from the tray, examined it with a frown, then swapped it for something that looked like a steroidal bread knife.

The body in front of them was wrapped, like all the others, in tight clear plastic, wound so strong and so many times that the film had become opaque. What was visible beneath it, however, was a dark bottom half and a clear pinkish top half. The person inside appeared to be topless.

With the serrated blade, Mackie made a sawing incision across the chest of the deceased, careful to split only the layers of plastic and not the flesh itself.

'No wonder they hadn't been discovered. Not much odour was ever going to escape wrapped like that.'

The room seemed to hold its breath as the last layer was split with a popping sound. As the hole opened, the cadaver seemed to spread out and relax.

'Rigor mortis is long gone. This one has been dead a little while.'

Even the mortuary assistants watched in fascination as the layers were carefully split away, revealing more and more of the person inside. A smell began to make itself known – not exactly pungent, but no doubt of death in nature.

Before long, the layers of plastic lay spread out on either side of the body like low-budget angel wings. The person on the table was male, thin, once white but now grey-green of colouration, and had had his face cut off. The flesh that remained was grey, compressed and ragged. This wasn't the delicate first stage of any surgeon's transplant either – it was a hack job, nose cartilage and all, the remaining teeth bared, gums fleshy and eye sockets hollowed.

Time held fast.

Everyone took a moment, as if to retrieve their professionalism from where their shock and revulsion had dropped it.

'How long dead?' asked Foley, his voice a booming echo in the cavernous space.

'Given how it's been preserved, that'll be rather hard to say. Quite when the body was sealed up is difficult to pinpoint – and with it, the precise time of death. For the purposes of your investigation, I'd suggest it would be both quicker and more accurate to find out when he went missing.'

'No facial recognition algorithms are going to be able to help us here either,' Madison said, transfixed by the shapeless mess that had once been the man's face.

Foley thought fast and spoke faster. 'Before you open him up, can we do a quick spot check of discernible features? Better to do it now when he's in one piece.'

'That's a good idea,' replied Mackie. 'I'm concerned that, while the exterior doesn't look too badly decomposed, the inside will be a different story.'

'How so?'

'When a living organism dies, decomposition is something that happens regardless, no matter where said organism is stored. The external flesh, as you can see here, can fare better. But internally, the bacteria of the stomach and intestines will continue to digest anaerobically – eating the tissue from the inside out.'

Foley's stomach seemed to do a backflip. These were only the first five pulled from the trench – what state would the rest be in? The image of one of the bags near the back filled with a muddy sludge made him want to gag. 'Would you mind having a nosey about him then please for me, Denise?'

'Nothing would thrill me more.' Her voice was full of sarcasm.

'A record please, Madison.'

While Mackie examined the body, having put the knife down and picked up a rubber-tipped pointer instead, Foley's eyes drifted to the other four bodies lined up. He couldn't get over the loss of life, the scale of what was facing them – and the enormity of evil that had perpetrated it.

What kind of person was capable of this? What kind of devil was out there?

It wasn't just the death here that was nagging him – it was the whole practice surrounding the deaths. They were all wrapped in plastic, but would they all have their faces hacked off? Would they all be a skin-bag of fermenting sludge?

They all looked largely the same size – would they all be men?

Actually, one of the corpses looked a shade smaller. Possibly a short man or woman. The card at its feet marked 'Exhibit A' identified it as the one nearest the front of the trench. The most recent. The one whose hasty burial had been spotted during the night and started all this. If the case was going to be solved off the back of forensic evidence, their best chance lay in that bag.

He was so transfixed that he barely heard Mackie say, 'Tell you what, let's open them all up. Get a proper look at all the discernible features so you can get IDing them before we move on to the real grizzly stuff.'

Mackie repeated the process on Exhibit D. The plastic layers made a snapping fizz as they loosened. This one was dressed in a roadman's outfit. High-vis jacket, black jumper, bright orange trousers. No boots – and no face either. Same as last time, only the meat left where the cheeks should have been was less grey, and even had a touch of pink to it.

'No obvious cause of death, like the previous one,' said Mackie.

Foley looked at Madison, who had breathed in sharply but was now back in clipboard mode again. He got the impression she was using it as a convenient diversion to the horrors around her.

More power to her. Whatever you needed to scale the obstacle.

'Something's got at this one,' Mackie said, now at Exhibit C. She used her pointer to direct her image specialist to a small frayed hole on what was left of the right collarbone of the corpse. Pictures were taken, the flash popping bright.

'Vermin?' asked Foley.

'Possibly. There's dirt inside the plastic. Something got in. Either the hole was made accidentally before burial, and was eventually used for access by whatever got in, or indeed, the opportunistic bugger made it himself.'

The layers came away quicker now, Mackie clearly having warmed to the task. At the last pop, with the sagging of the corpse's shoulders, something rolled out and thunked softly onto the floor.

'How fun,' said Mackie. 'Hossein? He can be exhibit C-1.'

Hossein edged around the table, Foley watching him. 'Oh, *God.*'

On the floor, a rat – sleek, unnaturally elongated, and very much dead. Madison sucked in a lungful of air again.

'Must have got stuck on its way in,' said Mackie, motioning to one of her assistants. 'Put it in one of those kidney dishes there, please.'

'Could you get a timeframe from that?' asked Foley.

'I'm sure I can get something from it.'

Now the rat-drama had ceased, they could focus on the body itself. A nattily dressed man in cream chinos, boat shoes, a red jumper – and no face, as was becoming expected.

More camera flashes.

Exhibit B was opened up. A black guy, suit and tie. No face again, but they were getting numb to that now. Not dead all that long, it seemed, but obviously still hard to tell.

'How long will decomposition be slowed by them being wrapped like this?' asked Foley.

Mackie paused a moment and, lost in thought, brought the tip of the rubber pointer up to her mouth before realising it wasn't a pen and lowering it.

'They've been wrapped well, but not well enough to make each one in an identical condition. The discovery of our friend exhibit C-1 simply shows that each instance will most likely be different. I should imagine that the rate of decomposition will therefore be unique to each body.'

They moved as a unit to exhibit A, the one Foley thought might be a woman, and Mackie got to brisk work. A snip and pull here and there, and in a flash, the corpse was free. As the body settled, something seemed to take over Foley. A severe, grave tremor.

The loose trackies, the Converse sneakers, the hoodie. The shape. This was no woman at all.

Foley's chest seized.

His blood seemed to stop in his veins.

Something was off.

This was no man, either.

Now freed from the plastic, the corpse's blond hair had sprung out, still with youthful lustre. Foley could see a nose and chin. This one *had* a face, and it was smooth, with just a couple of acne bumps at the corners of the mouth.

It was a boy. A teenage boy.

The tremor in him gave way to a tide of gushing horror.

Foley managed to edge forward. As he moved, he saw more of the shape of the body, the bruised and cut hands, and the *face*.

Features he recognised.

The features, unmistakably, of his nephew, Connor Foley.

AS HE RAN from the mortuary, the cold air hitting Foley was the worst thing that could have happened. That musty sweet smell of skin and meat going rancid, only to be suddenly purged by bitter, icy oxygen. The shock went straight to his stomach.

He chucked up hard into the skeletal frame of a barren rosebush, odd bits of buffet, cake and that half of lager decorated the branches, heave after heave, until there was nothing left, just yellow strings of dribble from his chin.

Madison appeared behind him. 'Can I get you anything, sir?'

Foley couldn't speak yet.

'A water? Coffee?' Madison continued.

He gasped for air, tucking his St Christopher back inside his shirt where it had come loose with the violence of his body's purges. 'Just a minute please, Iona.'

Madison clammed up at her superior using her first name, the line between the professional and the personal erased for the moment. It wouldn't be what she was used to, but Foley had no time to worry about the line between professional and personal right now.

He straightened up carefully, and moved from the shrubbery, thoughts crowding his brain.

His nephew, Connor, was dead.

His nephew, Connor, had been murdered...

Buried in a shallow grave, wrapped in plastic, on a crap piece of woodland in east Warrington.

His brother, Ross.

His sister-in-law, Siobhan.

His father.

This investigation, and his link to it.

Who did this?

Who fucking did it?

Stay. Stay on the investigation.

Find who did this.

My responsibility. All mine.

'I need you to take this information as you find it, Iona,' Foley said as he pulled himself up. He looked through his pockets, found a blue napkin from the christening in his inner jacket pocket and dabbed his lips.

'Sir.' Madison straightened and took a step back.

'The boy... Exhibit A. That's my nephew, Connor.' Saying it out loud made it suddenly so real, and a single sob burst from Foley's mouth.

Madison stood frozen. Their relationship was work, work, perfunctory polite question about each other's weekends, work, work, rinse and repeat. 'Sir.' Her tone said more than any words could.

'I'm all right. I'm all right.' Foley breathed out hard. 'This is going to be tricky for me to continue the investigation. I'm going to have to be upfront with the super, and CID, but I need to see this through. I need to stay on. Are you OK with that?'

'You're sure, sir?'

'Yeah, really sure. I won't rest if they take me off it. I have to do this... for my family.'

'I'm... I'm so sorry, sir. So sorry.'

'Thanks, Iona.'

'Take a few minutes. I'll finish here and follow up. I won't tell anyone, unless I know you've spoken to them.'

'I'd appreciate that. But you can tell the team. In fact, I think it's probably better if you do.'

Madison took an extra moment, then walked back inside. Foley was left outside in the cool early evening, the lights of the hospital blinking on behind him.

He felt at sea, adrift in every possible sense – but also crushed by responsibility and sadness. The weight of everything he'd seen today, topped by *this*, was almost too much.

He had some calls to make. His super... and his family. His brother.

He had to tell his brother that his son – his only son, his beloved son – was dead.

He took another minute before doing anything, watching the dusk birdlife darting over the parked cars, knowing that his life had changed forever.

CHAPTER 4

ROSS WAS EXHAUSTED. Family parties did that to some people, and he was one of them. He always felt some errant pressure to perform, to hold it together, to be a certain useful category of family member. The kind that adds something to the overall pride in the bigger picture.

Now he was home, back to the house he shared with his wife Siobhan and their son Connor, wherever the hell he was. His antics had piled the pressure on too, the daft sod. 'Where's Connor?' everyone was asking with that condescending *knowing* in their eyes. His answer was always some derivation of mock despair at teenage unreliability: 'Teenagers... you know what they're like with family events. Too cool for school,' and so on, with an OTT sigh and panto eye-roll.

He took his tie off, left on his formal shirt. Slung some joggers on. Grabbed a beer from the fridge. Asked Siobhan if she wanted a cheeky takeaway, save either of them having to mess up the kitchen with a half-pissed attempt at cooking. She said she'd rather have egg on toast in a bit, as she curled up to watch *Wife Swap* on repeat with a bag of chocolate mini-eggs. He'd pecked her on her tousled hair, half of which wasn't hers because of the extensions she'd put in for the christening. He briefly contemplated trying to coax her into a quickie, with the house being empty and all, but decided against it and moved through to the little downstairs snug where his PlayStation sat. He'd conquered three of the four lands in his latest fantasy role-play game and was halfway through the last. A good stint tonight, even with a break for a Chinese, could see him finish it. Then he could start on that first-person shooter, which had been waiting on the sideboard since Christmas. He needed a little palate cleanser between RPGs – all those dragons and breasts got a little repetitive after a while, even though they always pulled him back before long.

He flicked the console on and slumped on the black torn couch that was once a kind of suede but now felt more like sun-beaten leather. He pulled out his phone. A slew of Facebook notifications cried for his attention, but he swiped them all as *read*. A text from his dad to give him a call in the morning, which he rolled his eyes at. *Yes, Dad, same as every Monday.*

He checked his Instagram account, and scrolled through the glossy feed of aspiration and jealousy. The accounts he followed were all centred on things he didn't have but dreamed of attaining – luxury cars, watches, lifestyles… and rich models. Lots of rich models. He scanned through, liking as many snaps as he could squeeze in before his game loaded. Every now and then, he direct-messaged some of the women privately. Told them what he'd consider doing to them. His account was anonymous, nothing to do with himself, and he never posted anything. The only thing that could be learned from his words in those messages was that he was a very horny male – which was the only truthful thing about his usage of the app.

Satisfied that he wasn't missing any responses, he did the same on Twitter. No replies, which meant there was nothing from the one he'd sent an artfully composed shot of his manhood to. Even with the decent use of lighting and in monochrome. He was happy at home with Siobhan in all the necessary ways that promoted a pleasant enough coexistence. He loved her, and was still pretty sure she loved him. He just liked to dream a little, that's all, and social media gave him enough of a window to let his dreams stretch their legs a bit.

They'd been together years. Originally, they were just friends with benefits, fond of each other because of their mutual attraction and the convenience of their close proximity. Those days were crackling, exciting. Until her belly got big.

Baby coming along had chucked a hammer through it all, but they'd agreed to get their heads together and see it through. Pressure from Siobhan's parents had been the fuel for the shotgun wedding and the urgency with which Ross fell into working with his father at the garage. He suddenly had a family to provide for, and working for his dad wasn't necessarily the best bet, but it was definitely the quickest.

From that moment on, they were in each other's pockets, day in, day out, both only seventeen when Connor was born. Kids having kids is rarely a good combination. The stresses on young love had been huge, especially considering that, at the time Siobhan had got pregnant, they weren't even properly together.

The game was finally loaded. Green goblins gurned at him while he selected his saved game, when his phone started ringing. He grabbed it – Brendan. He sighed, having had about enough of family for one day. He and his brother usually kept themselves to themselves; besides, Brendan was everybody's favourite, the high-flying bobby. Ross was just the family fuck-up, lolling along behind their dad like a thick-headed terrier.

Tilting his head and tucking the phone between his shoulder and cheek, he simultaneously answered the call and pressed start on his game.

CHAPTER 5

MY GOD, SHE needed this. It had taken three attempts to wrap her hands, tying them too tight on the first two goes, cutting off circulation to her fingers. She was taut as a cobra and it was obvious.

'Bad day at the office?' Joel was sitting on the boxing ring steps, adjusting his own hand wraps. His were nothing more than strips of old bandage left over from his fight career in the eighties, all held together with silver duct tape. Madison knew he had at least three rolls in his bag – a guy down in the building security office had a connection that kept Joel in steady supply. What type of underground connections dealt in just the right type of duct tape, for heaven's sake? Madison often wondered who supplied Joel.

It was 1.30 a.m. The gym, situated on the fourth floor of an old cardboard box factory on the edge of Warrington town centre, had been pitch-dark and freezing until the strip lights had been switched on – and then it was just glaringly bright and still freezing. It was usually locked and dead at this time, but Joel had a key and was good enough to squeeze in Madison's workouts around her job. Money was money, either way, and it was a tenner a session. A tenner's the same in the dead hours as it is in the waking ones – just shy of three pints in Joel's local Labour club.

'Challenging.' Madison was in no mood for chit-chat. Coming here was pure escapism, like going to watch a dumb popcorn movie at the cinema – a chance to leave her brain in a jar at the door.

After her shift had ended, she'd changed into the training gear she always kept in the boot of her car. She now sported compression leggings, a pair of Nike cotton shorts over the top, her electric-blue Everlast ring boots and a padded sports vest. She'd tied her long blonde hair up into an even higher ponytail. Blue sixteen-ounce boxing gloves completed the look.

She wasn't the usual candidate for boxing. At the start of her fight career, that had helped. It meant she'd never been taken seriously when the bell rang, so when she marched across the ring and banged like she really damn meant it, it would come as a sharp surprise to her opponents.

That didn't happen anymore, though. What with her being lightweight champion of the region's police forces, boasting seven consecutive successful defences, the word was out. In the ring, she was a demon. There was a lot of competition on the job – especially now with performance targets and collar rates constantly under scrutiny, the CID promotion talk that had the office abuzz, and the next big government budget cut never far away – but add sport into the mix and it was a killer. It had carved her into a winner.

Most nicks had their own gyms but Warrington Police was not like most nicks. Underfunded more than most, it was viewed as nothing more than an offshoot of the larger Cheshire Constabulary. It had a weights bench and a squeaky treadmill wedged into a glorified cupboard off a corridor – *get fit here, folks*. Recognising the need for the force to get some proper exercise, the desk bods had seen fit to grant free off-peak memberships at the local PureGym.

But Madison wasn't in for any of that. She didn't go to the gym to preen or take posed selfies for social media, even though most people who heard about her fitness antics thought that for such a pretty bottle-blonde there'd be some vanity involved. Wrong. She had a fight mentality, a winner's make-up. She enjoyed getting hit, only to hit back harder. You didn't find that flexing before a mirror in your lingerie.

'One minute,' Joel said. He walked around the outside of the ring apron to the far wall and flicked on the plug to the ancient timer. After a few reluctant beeps, the numbers began to count down: 59... 58... 57...

Madison rolled her shoulders twice and flexed her knees, then climbed the steps to the ring. She'd be doing the same in a few days' time, just in a different ring in front of a lot more eyes. Inter-job tournament and she was defending her belt for the eighth time. She'd earned that role through battering all the other lightweights in the north-west. No gifts, no sentiment. But, like all her fights, it meant everything to her. The week had all been carefully measured meal prep, protein shakes and definitely no roll-ups. Well, apart from the one earlier.

She tested the give of the ropes, leaning back against them with a practised push, then did the same in the opposite corner. It set her, gave her the dimensions of her workspace.

She often wondered if she was like this because of the lack of support she was saddled with. Her mum and dad didn't approve of her career, and definitely didn't approve of her boxing. She had grown up in the more affluent end of Warrington, in Stockton Heath, among the gastro restaurants and upwardly mobile professionals. But the lure of crime, and the study of its causes, had pulled her into the town centre. Her parents moved with her sister to Knutsford, in an upmarket relocation, but she had opted to stay and got a small flat in town. Now she was embedded, fighting crime from the inside out. She revelled in it, and all the adversities it posed. Her family were miles away, reluctantly leaving her to it.

34... 33... 32...

In the ring, a couple of hops to get used to the spring of the canvas, then a few throws to get blood down through her forearms.

'You sure you want to do this?' Joel said, climbing into the ring himself. Madison had trained with Joel long enough to know that he didn't advocate any heavy hitting the week of a fight, but he seemed to be making an exception tonight. Good trainers innately understood the needs of their fighters.

'Just hold the pads, will you?' Madison bobbed on the spot, head weaving from side to side. Joel smirked and flexed his broad shoulders. An ex-northern area amateur champion, his physique betrayed every one of the training sessions held over a stubborn thirty-year career. He'd boxed well into his late forties. Now in his sixties, he'd lost nothing of his reflexes and his love for the fight game, but he'd added a bit of a belly to his armoury.

3... 2... 1... The last three counts were marked with beeps, before a buzzer went and the clock reset to a two-minute counter, to resume the countdown.

'One,' Joel commanded. Madison stepped forward with her left foot and thrust her left fist out with a harsh jab. The snap of the shot brought a smacking thud from Joel's offered pad. 'One-two.' Another jab, followed by a solid straight right.

'One-two.' The brief combination was repeated.

Madison breathed out with each shot, throwing a hiss with each flying fist. She could feel her shoulders unknotting, and the blank distraction of an occupied mind.

'One-two, left cross.' The combination was lengthening, but to Madison this was still simple.

'All together.' That was the signal for a longer combination. A one two, followed by a left hook, followed by another straight right.

'All together and follow it.' Same again, but with a head bob to the right to slip the pad that was thrown at Madison's face, then another right, left hook, right. The fists were sailing, the combinations flowing.

Every police officer, from a PCSO right through to the super, had their own habits of downtime – to leave the job for a while, and banish its stresses and pressures. Following Joel's instructions, focusing on her timing, her breathing, had become Madison's primary method of decompression.

But today, she wasn't sure it would be enough.

'Step, slip, one-two.' Again.

'One-two, roll, left cross.' Again, but rolling under a horizontal pad.

Then it caught up with her. It was something from today, but not what she expected. Today had been horrible, just the fucking *worst*. And she'd successfully got through it by thinking of anything – of her recent desk change and how it wasn't like her old one, of how unexpected Hoyt's civilian clothes had been but how they somehow suited him, even of how smooth her chosen pen was that morning as it sailed across her crime scene log – anything, *anything* possible, to stop her looking at the wrapped shapes in that horrible trench. She had shoved it aside, and intended to keep it that way for as long as it took to get the case resolved. It could have taken years for her to get her head around what she'd seen that morning, or before she allowed herself an emotional reaction to it. Normally, the job kept you screwed shut like that; you couldn't function if you let everything inside run riot.

But not this case and not tonight.

Tonight, under the halide glare of the cheap strip lights over the ring, with Joel's pads sailing at her, it suddenly hit her.

When Joel had swung his pad horizontally over her head, for her to roll under, the crucifix around his neck had jiggled on its thin gold chain, sending out the tiniest hiss as it slid over links. That's all it had taken to sweep her back to the morgue, to the sight of her boss crumpled in grief. His own St Christopher had sent out a similar whispering hiss as he'd tucked it away beneath his shirt.

Her mind blanked for an instant and she missed the call out. It came to her too late, must have been an all-together, slip, straight right, because she missed the slip and the pad sailed straight into her face, the stitching scuffing her nose and upper lip.

She put her guard up again, to reset for another combo, as was the norm for a mistake, but Joel had stopped short.

'Shit,' he said. 'We've got to stop.'

Madison looked flummoxed – he never cheated on a session, not for a second. She shrugged and he pointed to her nose. She ran her glove across it, and looked down to find a bright red smear across the blue thumb guard. She understood now why she had to stop – it was fight week, and you couldn't go into one already dinged up.

'I'll be fine,' she said.

'Shit,' he said again.

'My fault.'

'You said it.'

They climbed down from the ring, and as the adrenalin began to flow from Madison's body, her pulse resetting, she was suddenly flooded with emotions. She was too strong to crumble, not in front of Joel, not here in the gym. She jogged to the toilets, switched the shower on, and cried angrily in the shower stall for five full minutes. Snot and everything.

When she eventually emerged, Joel was long gone. He'd left his keys on the ring steps for her to lock up, next to her tenner – he'd refused to take payment. He was one of the only people at the gym who knew her life outside those four walls. Him and Dean Mason, the gym owner. They both knew because the former was in her corner for all her fights, many of which had been attended by the latter, and the belt she held was kind of a dead giveaway to her vocation.

They kept her counsel, and she was grateful. They respected her privacy, just as Joel had done now. It meant that in the gym, despite it being all about physical combat, thrown fists and the spray of claret, she felt safe. And in that safety, she sat on the ring steps, and stayed alone in the dark for a while – until she picked up her phone, took a deep breath, and composed a text to the team.

She didn't know whether texting the team about a death in a colleague's family was the right thing to do, but nothing was right about any of this. Given the hour, she gave herself a break – and quietly thanked the gods of Nokia that she didn't have to speak to each team member, one at a time. DS Iona Madison, North-West Forces Women's Lightweight Champion, didn't know if she could have managed it.

CHAPTER 6

THE SILENCE ON the other end of the phone would live with Foley long into the future. When his brother had finally spoken, his voice had been hauntingly remote.

'What do I do now?'

That's all Ross had had to say – all he could say.

Now, Foley kicked back against the mortuary door, and waited. He was still in his christening gear. With time to kill, he'd walked over to the petrol station across the street from the hospital and bought a lone can of draught Guinness – ironic that a pint of the black stuff had been his father's suggestion, hours earlier. He popped the tab, took a deep pull, then raised the can in a silent toast.

To you, Connor. My godson.

A couple of tears salted his upper lip. He'd made the relevant arrangements – all that was needed now was for Ross to identify Connor's body - their first named victim.

It was an unavoidable formality, one that would hang over the brothers' relationship.

Now, Ross arrived in a taxi with Siobhan. As the bereavement counsellor emerged from the building, Foley went ahead of her to pay the driver. Then he took Ross by the shoulders.

'I'm so sorry, Ross – but it *is* him.'

At his words, Siobhan wobbled on the other side of the car and the counsellor joined them just in time to catch her.

Foley took his brother, while the counsellor, a woman called Dobbs, guided Siobhan. Connor had been transferred to a smaller viewing room (*Connor's body*, Foley reminded himself), so the four took a right turn at the now-unmanned desk and walked to a small waiting area. A handful of armchairs, two plastic ferns and a couple of battered magazines.

They sat silently, Ross and Siobhan oddly apart, at least to Foley's eye. He'd seen grief in different forms before, but this was too close to home for him to view dispassionately.

Dobbs checked if anyone wanted a cup of tea, but each refused.

Foley worried about his brother. One glance in Ross's eyes showed the depth of his grief. No specialist training was required to deduce that.

At the far end of the waiting area was a pale blue door with opaque glass. A shadow passed on the other side, and Foley knew it was time. Mackie exited, her post-mortem whites replaced with a cream trouser suit and blue blouse. She would never ordinarily undertake formalities like this herself, but had agreed when the late hour meant that there was nobody else available.

Ordinarily, they could have waited until the morning, but Foley had been informed by command that a press conference had been convened for 9 a.m. – which meant that the body needed to be identified urgently. Monroe hadn't said why it was so urgent, but Foley read between the very faint lines. If the police already had one body identified in time for the press conference, it would make them look like they were making headway, that they were on it. It was a PR-friendly move that pissed him off, but if he wanted to stay in the frame, he had to go along with it.

When command had got in touch, he'd also been told that prior to the conference he was to present himself at 8 a.m. in Superintendent Monroe's office. Foley was sure his future involvement in the case would be the first thing on the agenda.

Mackie nodded once to Foley, and he went over to help his shell-shocked brother to his feet.

'You don't have to go too, Siobhan,' he said.

'Yes, I do,' she replied, eyes glassy.

He nodded. 'I'll be here if you need me.' Torn between offering support as a family member, and the need for professionalism, Foley let them go on without him. They didn't need to see him, stony-faced and mute.

Breathing hard, his brother and sister-in-law walked across the threshold. Dobbs followed the couple, shutting the door behind her, and Foley sat back down again. He couldn't imagine what was going on in there, and all he could think of was his own perfect, very *alive*, kids at home. Just thinking of what his brother had lost made him feel sick to his middle and dizzy everywhere else.

From behind the door, a long howl rang out. It came from a sub-human place, as if the owner's guts were being dragged from their throat, one hot fistful at a time. Identification had been completed. The crime had its first sure victim, and Foley had heard the second

34

sound from this investigation that would stay with him until the day he died.

FITZ WAS RUNNING.

In every sense.

He had a blue canvas duffle bag over his shoulder, a beanie pulled down to his eyebrows, a long peacoat on over his jeans. As he jogged across the industrial yard, he ran through the plan again in his mind.

Borrow his mum's car.

Drive through the quiet side roads of Warrington, avoiding the main artery of Winwick Road, which tunnelled the motorway traffic into the town centre.

Park out on the industrial estate by the indoor go-kart centre.

Go on foot through the industrial estate, avoiding roads.

Emerge over the fence by the back of Bank Quay station.

Use his phone app to buy tickets to Bangor.

Catch that train.

Christ, *catch that train.*

He'd already done most of the checklist – it looked like he was going to make it. Dawn was breaking, rendering the old husks of the abandoned factories in the industrial quarter an unnatural shade of pink-brown. This part of town was quiet, dead, mostly abandoned. He'd picked it for his approach because it was close to one of the town's two stations. The other one was too close to the lights of the town centre, the all-hour throb of the bus station and the constant pulse of the main roads. But this one was in a part of town that was mostly forgotten, and he hoped he'd be forgotten – or at least not noticed – too.

Weeds grew up through the cracked concrete. He jogged to the end of the courtyard and lightly hopped the fence into the next. He was always alert for dogs but was pretty sure that the buildings on the route he'd picked were all long since abandoned. The factories loomed over him as he walked, windows smeared with grime. Even though he was fairly confident he was alone, he couldn't shake the feeling of being watched.

He'd felt it since the moment he heard the kid had gone missing. Moston, the other lad, had shared the news in a panicky text after Connor hadn't shown at his house this morning as they'd agreed. Fitz had called him and warned him that if he told anyone what had happened, or anything about anything for that matter, Moston would end up going missing too. The tears on the end of the line reassured Fitz that Moston wouldn't be talking.

That cleared up, the next problem was erasing his own involvement. So he set up a hasty cover story. Called his mate Lloyd at Bangor University, and said there'd be a hundred quid in it for him if he could swear Fitz had been over visiting him since Friday at least. Fitz was going there now, armed with a couple of changes of clothes, to stage some photographs that would suggest they'd been on a string of benders since the end of last week, and that Fitz had never been anywhere near any North West cash machines at any point in recent memory.

He could see the station lights coming up over the hedges. One more fence, then a quick sneak up onto the platform.

He was only aiming to be in Wales the one night, but every minute that had gone by, right throughout that awful Sunday, had worn his nerves more and more threadbare. His composure was running on empty, aided by all those stories he'd heard. In truth, he didn't know when he was coming back.

Over the fence, emerge from the hedge, head down, walk steady.

Past the taxi rank.

Through the station's automatic doors.

Phone out, app loaded, ticket ready.

Barcode scanned direct from his screen.

Through the barriers, and he felt that first taste of safety. In the musty pedestrian tunnel beneath the tracks, the rumbles of one of the early trains juddering above him, he checked the overhead screens for his platform.

Platform 2, 6.07 a.m. Destination: Bangor.

Relief started to prickle.

But then he caught sight of the next screen. Sky News, the graphic in the corner proclaimed. It was an aerial shot of a woodland, taken by a drone or helicopter. Though obscured by trees, it showed a host of white suits buzzing around a large square object. He couldn't make it out. Rows of something white.

The ticker tape flipped by at the bottom, announcing the main takeaways of the news bulletin. His heart skipped with every bullet point.

Mass grave uncovered in Warrington.

Twenty-seven dead.

The Warrington 27: Who Are They?
The biggest mass grave in modern UK history.
The first victim has been identified as sixteen-year-old Connor Foley,
Warrington.
Fitz ran, despite the loosening of his bowels.
His plan had changed.
I'll never come back, he thought.

WHEN FOLEY GOT home the birds were singing, and for a brief and beautiful moment it reminded him of being a student again. Usually, an occasion like that had the strange tang of mischievous happiness, but nothing could brighten how he felt, nor dilute what he had to do next.

He opened the door as softly as he could, having kicked his shoes off outside, the dawn chill on his toes immediate and unpleasant. The house was quiet and warming, the heating pipes ticking into life from beneath the floorboards. He padded up the stairs, still in his coat, for fear any rustling material would wake Mick. Not Dan. Dan's sleep was that of the typical teenage shutdown.

Connor.

Brendan opened the door to the master bedroom and crept in, sending a column of light from the landing shooting along the wall to the dressing table. In the bed, squeezed up against the dressing table, Mim stirred. Brendan put a finger to his lips and sat on the edge of the bed.

'You're still in your coat,' Mim said, her voice alert and crisp. She hadn't been asleep at all.

Brendan breathed out.

'What's happened?' Her body snapped upright.

He couldn't really see the expression in her eyes, which made talking easier.

'We found a huge grave out in Peel Hall woods. Twenty-seven bodies.' His voice became distant and tinny in his own head. 'Connor was one of them.'

Mim's reply was incredulous. '*Our* Connor?'

'Our Connor.'

Mim seemed to cough in the darkness, wet and rasping. Brendan couldn't tell if it was a retch. He reached for her with one hand, the other left limp in his lap. Never mind Mim short-circuiting, he felt like his own systems were shutting down.

'Ross and Siobhan have identified him,' he said. 'I saw him too. It's him, sweetheart. It's Connor.'

A short burst of breaths fell from Mim, a sudden bout of hyperventilation, and she reached for him. Within seconds, they were wrapped around each other in a shaking tangle of coat, suit, pyjamas and tears.

CHAPTER 7

THE STORY HAD gone national. It dominated every single channel in the news category of Madison's satellite TV guide, both domestically and abroad. It was even making a decent showing on God TV, the Christian news network. The big man upstairs must have taken an interest, along with everyone else.

Madison had crawled in close to 3 a.m., and hadn't left her sofa since. She was still in her post-workout gear of joggers and hoodie, with her legs tucked up beneath her as she flicked between the different news outlets competing for her attention with the same scant set of facts.

Mass grave.

Twenty-seven dead.

Warrington.

The *Warrington 27*.

Hoyt was there when she got in, as had become the norm since she'd given him a key. He'd stayed up with her, pawing at her hopefully until, realising she was in no mood, he'd retired to bed. Madison understood, knowing that everyone dealt with life's tougher moments in their own ways. Hoyt needed proximity, closeness. But Madison couldn't face being touched by anyone – not after what she'd seen that day. Fortunately, he'd understood too. Cops got cops, that's how it worked.

She'd been unable to sleep at all, feeling the weight of responsibility press heavy, which was joined by the pressure of national scrutiny as the rolling news channels started catching up. She watched the distant images, as threadbare facts began to circulate. Someone had chartered a helicopter to fly over the scene and get some pictures, which were promptly sold to the press.

From that height, the pictures made the scene look like a half-completed kids' craft project, all bits of packaging lined up, white boxes and mess. She saw herself, a white speck on one side of the trench. She remembered the thud of the helicopter overhead and how she'd kept her head down.

'Bastards, aren't they.'

Hoyt's voice snapped Madison back into the room.

'The helicopter?' she said, as she turned to look at him.

His beard was flatter, less pointed thanks to how he'd been sleeping. It was one of those intimacies that she'd only recently learned about, the kind that you only get when you're sleeping with someone new.

He stood in the doorway to her room, its bare white walls beyond softly reflecting the lamplight glow. She could see the stack of fantasy books by her bed behind him – the books she'd kept hidden the first time he came over, when she'd made him wait in the living room while she got rid of anything he could deem embarrassing.

They were past that now, and her books were left wherever she last closed them. Hoyt was fast becoming a part of her life.

'Just the media in general,' he replied. 'We haven't even identified most of those people but when we do, don't fret, their lucky families will always have grainy aerial footage on bloody YouTube of their loved ones being hoicked out the ground.' His voice exposed more of his Irish heritage the more passionate he got. Even though he hadn't set foot on the Emerald Isle since leaving for university at eighteen years old, his roots were still rock-solid green.

Madison smiled pensively. He had a point, but there was a benefit. 'National outrage will probably help here. Everyone will be so vigilant, the net will feel tighter to the culprit.'

'I hope so, the rat. And who leaked Connor Foley's name to the press?!'

Madison didn't answer, because she couldn't. She had no idea how that had got out.

'What's the time?' she asked instead.

'Five thirty, I think. Was gonna get moving. Coffee?' He started walking back towards the kitchen.

The flat was simple yet offered exactly what Madison needed. A place to crash between training sessions and shifts at the nick. It had one bedroom, one bathroom and an open-plan living and kitchen space – all white emulsion and appliances – which was separated by a breakfast bar that served as dining table, desk, the works. She'd toyed with opting for the two-bedroom version but thought her parents and sister wouldn't be caught dead at the town centre development, so she decided to save her pennies instead.

'I'm a bit caffeined out.'

'Juice then?'

'OK, thanks.' Madison brought a knee up to rest her chin on. 'We really have to go back to this today, don't we?'

'Yes, we've got to go in. Nobody else is going to sift through the paperwork on this one, and, my God, there'll be a lot of that.'

She watched him rattle about in the fridge. He was a man of activity, only still when he was sleeping.

'How's the gaffer? Reckon he'll get to keep the case?' Hoyt asked, his voice muffled by the fridge door.

Foley. His nephew. She'd texted the team the news, and elaborated to Hoyt a bit more when she got in. The horror of yesterday was bad enough, but the tilt it had taken since then was what had stolen the sleep from Madison. The look on his face. That *sound* he'd made outside the morgue. Every life has moments tougher than others, and every family goes through loss, grief and all the processes that accompany both. However, she had never heard a man go through the wringer like that before and it left her feeling lucky and guilty all at once.

'I'm sure he'll try. You know what he's like,' she replied.

'I bloody do. All guts, all glory. Stubborn bugger. He's the best we have, like, but he's got a head like a pissed mule.'

Madison kept quiet. She felt her superior's loss keenly, and his dilemma even more so. Could he really keep the case if he was related so closely to one of the victims? Would he have a clear enough head to pursue it dispassionately, even if he could keep it? These concerns couldn't be voiced. He'd selected her personally for his CID unit and, because of that, she had a loyalty to him that was granite despite its infancy.

'*This even-handed justice commends the ingredience of our poison'd chalice to our own lips.*' She remembered the line from her GCSE text – *Macbeth.*

'Hmm?' asked Hoyt.

'Nothing,' she mumbled. 'Just thinking out loud.'

CHAPTER 8

WARRINGTON POLICE WAS housed in the town's old converted Victorian baths, with changing rooms converted into interview rooms. The pools had been drained long ago and separated into American-style open-plan bullpens, with cold tile and dark wood everywhere. Office screens separated certain areas and departments, with high, green, skylit ceilings overhead. Access was by the two sets of steps at either side of the shallow end, with thick power cables snaking down their railings.

It was the most bizarre police station in the UK, and members of visiting forces couldn't believe what they encountered when they got there. When the public baths closed in 2004, having been open for well over a hundred years, the building sat derelict and empty until 2013, when the council was about to demolish it. Fate intervened in the guise of a budgetary dispute between Merseyside Police, Greater Manchester Police and Cheshire Constabulary, none of whom wanted to claim Warrington as being fully in their jurisdiction. Warrington sat directly between them all, but no one wanted to devote budget to its management.

The fall-out led to some bright spark with a pen decreeing that Warrington should have its own police force. Once that was confirmed, it would need a home and a staff to fill it. Fast-track police courses, from detective inspector to PCSOs, twinned with some old hands drafted in, and an empty Victorian baths that had almost the precise square footage required to house a constabulary, saw the birth of Warrington Police.

Foley's rise to detective inspector had been swift, thanks primarily to the void at such rank, which needed filling. Yes, he had been good at his job, and would have probably got there anyway, but even he was surprised to become a DI at thirty-five. As he walked into the main cavernous space that once held the empty twenty-five-metre pool, and approached the steps to descend into the bullpen, he felt too high, too exposed and too on show. Eyes were watching him from every angle of the drained pool below. He didn't know exactly how much they knew, but he didn't want to go there – he just got that cold, detached pity that rubberneckers give in spades. His 'office', as he was supposed to call it, was at the far end of the pool. It was partitioned by felt-clad screens that doubled as noticeboards, with four desks within each space – one of which was his. This was now the major incident room. Not ideal but it would have to do in the circumstances.

At the bottom of the steps there was a communal area, which housed a couple of knackered sofas, and a folding table carrying a hot water cafetière, a shoebox of coffee jars, a bowl of spoons, a row of UHT milk cartons in varying states of use, and three different makes of supermarket-brand toaster. There was a small congregation of people. Foley didn't have small talk in him, because he'd been rehearsing the big words all night, the words that really meant something, ready for his one-to-one with Monroe.

He was not going to be knocked off the case. He would say *over my dead body*, but the last thing they needed at the present time was any more of them. What he did need, though, was coffee. And something to eat, considering it had been yesterday morning, the morning of the christening, since he'd last eaten – and even that had ended up in a bush outside the mortuary.

Three men, each of them wearing a boxily cut supermarket suit, rotated to him subtly.

'Morning,' he said, reaching the table. 'Yes, it was tough yesterday, no, we don't have any leads yet, yes, that's off the record, no, I've not seen Monroe yet. We all caught up? Yes. Good.' In the time it had taken him to speak, he'd poured boiling water into a mug, added a dash of instant from some jar or other, and was heading off to take it black.

He wanted a quick check in with his team before meeting the super, so as to be armed with the most facts possible. He walked through the central open-plan spread of the office, which housed some plainclothes officers, and the odd DC. The rest of the beat bobbies had a mess hall fashioned out of one of the other empty swimming pools, there being three in total. Foley could hear a rhythmic thunk from the left-hand wall, behind which the mess hall sat. It was the thud of a football. There always seemed to be a kick-about going on in there, cops blowing off steam.

Passing between the remaining partitions, he found his unit. Madison, Hoyt and Christopher, all at their desks, paperwork strewn in front of them, computer screens in their corners. Their desks faced each other in two rows, Foley's being the only empty one. At the far end, three whiteboards had been positioned.

'Is this all we could do for a major incident room?' Foley asked, setting his coffee down and rubbing his chin. A meeting with the super and he'd forgotten to shave. Foley had been able to grow a half-decent beard at fifteen – he just had those evergreen genes – so if he ever forgot to shave, it wasn't something he could get away with. *Damn*. It didn't help his nerves.

'Monroe's orders, sir,' Hoyt said. 'Think he's got something special planned. Besides, the other conference rooms are full of the usual.' All four of them knew the *usual* was old Warrington files transported over from the outlying police forces, boxes and boxes of dusty paper and folders that hadn't been sorted and ordered yet. It was a task that resources still hadn't got round to, and five years down the line didn't look like they ever would either.

Foley paused before sitting at his desk and took a breath. He felt tired and weak, but somehow knew he'd be able to press on to wherever he needed to go. Waking up that morning had been hard, getting home at 4 a.m. even harder. Telling his wife that their nephew was dead was one of the hardest things he'd ever had to do. Getting up just hours later to face it all again would have been a challenge for anyone.

'Thanks for coming in so early.' He leaned on the desk, the frame creaking softly. His tie dangled loose and he looked down at it briefly, before untying then retying it as he spoke. 'I know Madison has told you the news. Yep, it's hard. I'm not going to doll it up any other way, or try to convince you that I don't give a shit. I do give a shit. I can't think of anything else. But… if you'll let me, I can use this. I won't rest until we find who did this.'

He looked at the team. Suited and booted now, their crisp professionalism restored since yesterday. Madison was focused, attentive and alert. Hoyt looked solemn but with grim focus. Christopher's eyes were filled with murder, fire and brimstone. He was intense, the veins of his shaven scalp visible. They looked ready for anything, and steeled for what was to come.

'I'm well aware that in two minutes Monroe might take the whole thing off us, and God knows he possibly should. At the very least, we need a pile of resources and manpower that I'm not sure we could even pull together at any rate. But I was the on-call DI, and that means it's still mine until I hear otherwise – and so far, I've not heard otherwise. Christopher, what have we got?'

Christopher cleared his throat briefly and ran a hand over his bristled head. His sharp cheekbones gave him a soldier-like quality, and his tough reputation had come hard earned: he was one of the only coppers of his rank who'd ever come from that bruising housing estate where he still lived with his mum, and he'd taken every hard lick along the way. Such was the life offered to a lad from a rough spot who dared to do something even approaching cuddling up to authority. But he'd survived.

'I walked the entire perimeter of the forest park,' he began now, 'and every possible access point, unofficial and official, has been noted in here.' He held up a battered, folded OS map with a pink cover, then put it on top of a pile of four other pristine copies resting on his desk. 'I'm about to copy my findings into each of these maps too, so we all have a common reference.'

'Very good,' Foley said. 'Anything stick out?'

'Four official access points exist to the forest park, each via stile or gate. Forensics examined them all yesterday afternoon but found nothing to suggest anyone entering with a body or two. Obviously, we need to establish time of death on the most recent victim so we can look at what time frame to focus on—'

'Between 3 and 5 a.m. yesterday morning,' Madison interjected, before her eyes drifted to meet Foley's. 'Connor's time of death has been estimated at between 3 and 5 a.m. yesterday morning.' Her voice dwelt unhelpfully on the word *Connor*, as if she'd found saying it difficult.

'That from Mackie?' Foley asked, trying hard to stop that acute melancholy clawing back in.

'Yes. I was there first thing. I thought we could do with all the latest details and she's been working through the night.'

'Good thinking, Madison. Anything else, Christopher?'

The DS stood and unfolded the top map, then refolded it down into a small square around one particular piece of woodland. 'There are a few areas where it would have been possible to gain access unofficially. Most promising is here.'

He took the map to Foley and placed it on his desk. Madison and Hoyt joined them. Christopher pointed to an area on the edge of a green circle.

'Here. There's a wooden fence that marks the boundary of the park, remember?'

'Yes,' said Foley.

'Well, in this section there's no fencing. Must have guessed the woodland was too thick to put it through, and they'd have been right – thirty years ago. Other side of the boundary was an even thicker forest on the edge of some private farmland, but through the farmer's expansion they've deforested quite a bit. Now, there's just a cursory tree line and then you're straight onto the farmer's property. I haven't looked, but there could be access via the farm. Plus, and it might just be dog walkers, especially when you consider the amount of shit I stood in yesterday, but the ground there had been tramped. There's a track leading through those trees.'

'Excellent. If it's still ours, follow it. Visit the farmer, see what's what.'

'Aye, sir.'

'Hoyt, thanks for setting up back here – how are we for the databases?'

Hoyt returned to his desk and grabbed a notebook. 'Last five years, we've had over 10,000 people reported as missing. After removing the troublesome ones who turned back up, and repeat occurrences involving the same people, we are left with 177 people gone in five years, across all demographics. I've got them all here.' He motioned to a stack of fresh paper on his desk. 'Shouldn't take too long to flip through.'

'That's if every one of them was in that hole… But it's definitely a start. Nice one, Hoyt. Again, if we are still in to bat, start working with the info coming in from Mackie. See if we can get any more IDs sorted. Madison, how are you getting on?'

Madison stood with her own paperwork. This morning, she was wearing a black trouser suit. Foley wondered whether she'd meant to look so funereal. A giant murder case had landed in her lap and her superior's nephew was one of the victims; it'd be a miracle of composure if any of his three detective sergeants knew quite how to act. She looked pale and tired, and her top lip swollen. If he didn't know what she got up to in her spare time, he'd have worried.

'Mackie is working as quickly as she can, but has sent some prelim findings, which I have here.' She briskly distributed two sheets of A4. 'Full post-mortems are being arranged for the first five, and of course the rest as and when they arrive – as, it happens, a further eleven bodies arrived overnight.'

'Gavigan have anything for us? Anything at all from SOCO for that matter?' asked Foley.

'Yes.' Madison consulted her notes. 'They are working on the assumption, based on the varying sediment and soil consistency across the distance of the trench, front to back, that the bodies have been placed in the trench during an extended time frame. We're talking over a decade. A Home Office-appointed geologist is coming up from the Midlands.'

'OK. I think that was what we all assumed, yes? I mean, we all saw the progressively worse condition of the bodies...'

Connor.

'...the further back in the trench you looked. This only confirms what we knew, correct?'

Nods from his unit, as the facts were starkly processed. A killer on a decade-long spree. Here, in Warrington.

'Any consistency with cause of death?' Foley held up the papers Madison had handed him.

'Yes.' She eyed him. *Are you sure you want to hear this?*

Foley nodded.

'Of the sixteen bodies exhumed so far, we have ten fatal knife wounds, two strangulations and four gunshots. Of those sixteen, four are women.'

'The guys with no faces?' Christopher asked. 'Their cause of death? Was defacing before or after they snuffed it?'

'Of the ones we've seen, two died via strangulation. Piano wire, thin cord, something like that. The grim stuff happened after.'

'Garrotted, then peeled – lovely,' said Hoyt, blowing out.

'The other two died of massive head trauma.'

'And Connor?' Foley asked. He braced himself.

'Two knife wounds. Spinal column,' Madison said, reading from the sheet, not daring to look up.

Foley simply nodded again. If anything, he was relieved. Pretty quick and painless, the severing of your spinal column. One minute you're there, the next you're not, although he didn't want to think about the fear that Connor might have felt. The cuts on his hands were classic struggle. His godson knew exactly what had been happening to him.

Foley's G-Shock beeped twice: 8 a.m. Shit, he thought. Monroe.

'I'll have to go, guys,' he said, pushing himself upright. 'Christopher, get on to the owners of that farm, see what you can get out of them. Madison and Hoyt, get to cross-referencing the mispers with the pictures from the mortuary. If any match, you know what to do. If we're still on it, I'll be right back and we'll crack on.'

They all offered affirmatives, as Foley made his way through the pool. His phone started to thrum in his jacket pocket. He fished it out, thinking it was Monroe, but was surprised to see his father's name flash up on the screen. His dad wanted a word with him. Foley could imagine it, the sharing of grief, the touching of base between father and son when the world had gone Dutch.

He hopped the pool steps. Art Foley would have to wait.

CHAPTER 9

ART TOOK THE phone from his ear and watched the last few rings play out. A distant prerecorded voice urged him to leave a message, but he shut it off.

He threw the phone back through the open window of his smart blue Audi RS6, and it bounced off the cushioned leather of the passenger seat and down into the footwell.

'Bollocks,' he murmured, before standing upright again, and taking a long sip from his strawberry milkshake.

He was in the car park of McDonald's on Winwick Road, the main traffic artery into Warrington town centre, comfort eating. Three bacon and egg McMuffins sat on the roof of the Audi, each with a hash brown perched on top, with a coffee, an apple pie and the milkshake to go with it. He zipped up the collar of his triple XL golf jersey, not that he was playing golf today, but it was the warmest top he had that still retained a touch of smartness to it. Pulling apart the wrapper of the first McMuffin, it released a miniature steam-cloud that caught on the cool breeze. He watched it sail away over the drive-thru.

Art wasn't just eating because he was upset – though he was, for sure. Completely heartbroken, and full of a growing black hatred, the kind of extremes of emotion he hadn't felt in some time. But he was also worried. He believed in luck, he believed in chance, he believed in coincidence. Life was too varied and full of curious happenstance not to. But that also meant he believed in the reverse of those things. He believed in fate and that things happened for a reason.

The questions had started. Who were the twenty-seven in the hole? What linked them?

What connected Connor Foley to them? Art was crushed by what had happened and was struggling to organise his thoughts. He wanted to believe that Connor had been the victim of bad luck, of wrong place wrong time, but he couldn't quite see it.

Connor. His grandson. The one who looked most like Art and carried most of his characteristics above any other male in the family, his own sons included. No more.

He cried a little then, his tears dripping onto the toasted muffin as he ate. He felt for his boy, and his boy's boy.

Before long, he'd made up his mind.

He needed to know what Brendan was going to do about it, now that he knew he was spearheading the investigation.

And he needed to know where that stupid lad had got to. The lad he had valeting and soaping cars at the dealership. The one who'd been getting proper nosey, asking all sorts. Where was that damn fool, Fitz?

CHAPTER 10

'FUCK-A-DUCK, Foley,' came a strong north Lancashire accent. 'You are aware how the spread and share of resources works, aren't you?' Chief Superintendent Monroe was red in the face.

'I am, sir,' replied Foley, sitting opposite him. 'But this happened on our patch, in our jurisdiction, right where we were specifically created to cover. Do you mind?' He motioned to his jacket, and Monroe waved with a nod. His was already off too, a fan flapping his white shirt in intervals as it oscillated.

The chief superintendent's office was created out of the third pool at the bath house – the smaller spa area. It was a hot pool, designed originally to replicate a hot spring – but considering Warrington had no natural geothermic activity and never had, they'd had to pump heat into the room and clad it to retain it. The end result was dark, dingy and oppressively hot. The pool had been drained like the others, and was now decorated with the usual office accoutrements: framed pictures and certificates, one of those clicking silver-balled physics toys, only the silver balls were painted with golf ball dimples, a plastic ficus as big as a small rugby player. The walls were lined with only a narrow strip of tiled walkway, and a concrete bench right the way around the wall. High ceiling, no natural light.

'You know how many murders we get here in Warrington, Foley?'

'It's about four a year, I believe.'

'Four a year is right. Since the department's inception in 2013, we've had nineteen deaths to investigate – total. I mean, this is hardly downtown Chicago. But this is something else. I've had some weasel from the Home Office on the phone asking whether we need help. Ready to come and take it off us.' Sweat was pooling above Monroe's blond moustache. Monroe was six foot five, ex-military, thirty years' hard street graft turned desk jockey. Now, his midriff was expanding, while he still retained the tight curly blond hair that Foley had always wondered might be a perm. He was still the somewhat belligerent big dog on campus, despite now being essentially an admin man in a sauna with a big fat pension on the horizon, calling him home.

'We have a good solve rate on those murders though, haven't we?' said Foley.

'It's fair, I'll give you that. But those cases all concerned single fatalities. Every last one of them. This is a multiple murder investigation. We're not just talking three or four, there's twenty-bloody-seven of them. We don't even have the staff to attack this properly without bankrupting us with overtime, and, more importantly, we do not have the experience. Nowhere near. I'm feeling we need to give it to the Home Office with a bow on top.'

Foley couldn't imagine some slick team from London coming up, with no knowledge of the area and how it worked, looking at this case dispassionately. Connor Foley would just be a number on a to-do list. 'No, sir. What about pride? What's the point of being a police force if you just pass the buck when something bad happens? And does anyone have experience with a thing like this? It'd be new territory for anyone taking over.'

Monroe leaned back in his chair, causing it to wheel back on the slick tile of the pool floor. 'You're talking to me like there's a chance I can keep you on the investigation – which you know I can't.'

Foley felt heat behind his eyes but urged himself to stay quiet. If he was going to stay involved, it would be by showing control, restraint and good measure.

'You *can*, sir. You remove a DI, never mind the SIO, then you *are* understaffed. Like you said, we don't have the manpower. The case would lose so much in terms of momentum and progress while it was effectively restarted.'

Monroe's voice lowered. 'My sadness for you, and compassion for your loss is not in question here, Foley. Nor will I ever forget that on my watch here, the on-call detective was summoned to a crime scene that involved his own nephew. That is chaotic at best. Any super in his right mind would have to remove the detective as an investigating officer, never mind the SIO in charge of the whole bloody thing. Surely even you can see that?'

Foley could, but he wasn't in the mood for logic this morning. He leaned forward and planted his fists on the desk. 'You've seen we've got leads,' he said. When he'd arrived, he'd filled Monroe in on everything they knew. 'We have lines of enquiry right now to be going on with. You'd have to tell your press conference that you're starting all over again, and you know how they'll take that. Highest profile crime story of the year *nationally*, and the police force playing pass the parcel at the beginning. And you, as super of this nick, would be the face of all that.'

Monroe's gaze darted away. 'You know my hand is forced here.'

Foley stood. 'No, I don't. With all due respect, sir, this is your nick, and you can do what you like in it. At the end of the day, it's really *your* investigation – not mine. So, if you want to admit to the country that Warrington Police isn't up to the task, and therefore not really fit for purpose, then go for it. I heard you've got a press conference lined up – I hope it goes well. But I was there yesterday, I'm here now, we've got lines of enquiry and you know I'm more motivated than anyone to get a result.'

Monroe thought a moment and looked at Foley hard. Foley wished he'd stayed calmly in his seat, but he also knew all his points made sense. There was a lot riding on this for his superintendent. Fucking this one up could jeopardise all sorts. Monroe was near enough to imagine sailing into retirement with that lovely fat pension. He had a nice caravan set up in North Wales. He couldn't imagine Monroe wanting to head off there earlier than expected, with the weight of dismissal and a career fallen in the closing furlongs.

'What we'll do,' he said, 'is we'll merge the two CID units available. Yours and Wainwright's will work together. Just take down the partitions between you, and we'll be away. Use whoever you need. Delegate any other business down the chain to keep them covered. I'll tell the Home Office we'll keep Mackie on as a concession to teamwork, and I'll offer twice-daily updates to keep them sweet. We'll try it for a couple of days and see how we fare. But believe me, you've got to get me results. If there's any kind of fuck-up here, we both know the media will put it down to the fact I let the case be investigated by a grieving relative of one of the victims.'

Foley felt a flush of relief. 'Yes, sir. And the position of SIO?'

'Yours, for now. God knows Wainwright won't like it, but he'll have to. Now, get to it. I'll handle the press conference. You go and bring me something we can show them for the next one.'

'Yes, sir.'

CHAPTER 11

MIM STIRRED HER coffee with one spoon, and scooped Mick's baby porridge with another, her mind anywhere but in the kitchen. Dan would be down any minute, and she didn't want to lie to him. She knew Connor's name had already been on the TV – maybe her eldest son already knew.

The kitchen was a perfect square with a strange mix of blue Formica worktops and pine cabinets. Old white appliances were stacked in one corner – a knackered fridge-freezer next to a washer-drier. They'd always planned to do up the kitchen, but after six years living there, it had always been *next year*. By now it was an open secret that *next year* had become *next house*, and Mim had settled on only having a new kitchen when they eventually moved.

Of course, if Mim was still in work, they could have probably got it sorted well before now – two wages and all that. But that was a question that only led down that well-trodden path to the same arguments. The record was so broken the needle wouldn't catch, but the walls knew the words anyway.

When Brendan had told her about Connor's death, she was immediately stunned and grateful that the kids were not just safely in bed, but safely above ground.

Mick yanked the spoon from her hands, so she reached across from where they were sitting at the small circular table opposite the white goods and grabbed an extra spoon from the drawer. He waved his trophy over his head, spraying porridge blobs all over Mim's fresh black trousers.

She'd not actually gone back to bed after Brendan came home in the early hours and gave her the news. This cup of coffee was her eighth in half as many hours. Instead of going back to sleep, she'd got up and got ready for the day, imagining the moments ahead. She always left as little to chance as possible.

A rumble on the landing overhead made her stomach constrict. She didn't know how to face her son, to tell him that his cousin was dead. Dead was bad enough, but the actual detail of the murder itself was beyond what she could comfortably articulate. Then the awful warning, parent to child – that there was a mass murderer out there who was killing people, gift-wrapping them and burying them in the woods not far from their home.

She managed to coo Mick into actually eating his food instead of spraying it, having bribed him with yet another spoon, and tried to stay calm.

Dan and Connor, with one year between them, had been inseparable growing up. It had only been in the last couple of years, as puberty began to strike, that they'd started to drift apart, in the early, uneven processes of becoming different men.

She thought of Siobhan, her sister-in-law. She couldn't comprehend the feelings she would surely be dealing with, the depths of the despair. They were extremely unalike, Mim and Siobhan, thrown together through circumstance and their love for men who were similar in certain ways, and diametrically opposed in others. They respected each other in that unspoken way that women who marry into male-dominated families do. They didn't compete with each other, seemed to mirror each other, despite how different they were.

They were not the kind of sisters-in-law who would seek each other out for support – but right now, Mim was almost overwhelmed with how much she wanted to contact Siobhan. They were both mothers, after all.

She took out her phone, Mick now burbling with the spoons over his head, baby porridge in his hair. Balancing the phone in one hand, she redrafted a text to Siobhan multiple times.

So sorry for your loss… Rubbish.

I just wanted to say… Garbage.

My heart is broken… True but so over the top.

God, I can't imagine what you're going through… Spoken like someone who's truly glad of that very fact.

Thinking of you… She's not got flu, her son was just murdered.

Jesus, she thought. Why was it so hard to say what you feel?

But what did she feel? It was such a complex malaise of emotions: grief, shock, extreme sadness, horror, nausea, relief, fear. How to articulate that to someone who's surely going through most of those multiplied a hundredfold? Why should Siobhan want to hear that her sister-in-law was feeling barely a hundredth of what she was experiencing?

That solved it.

Sending all my love, Siobhan. No words for what's happened. Here if you need anything. Anything at all. Mim x

She worried if that was a little cold, but pressed send. Nothing would be right, but she wanted to say something, and she'd done that now. In the process of creating the text, and raking over the hot coals of such fresh and desperate thoughts, she'd begun crying without noticing. She wiped at her cheeks.

'Mum?' a voice asked delicately.

Too late, she thought.

Mim looked up to see Dan standing there at the kitchen door in his sixth form uniform, concern writ large on his young face. There was an urgency and fear to the way he looked at her that betrayed he didn't know a damn thing.

'Oh, son,' she said, and crumbled good and proper. As words fell out – words that blasted her son's world to dust – she wished that her husband was there to help.

FOLEY STOOD BEFORE his newly-formed team. His usual members had been joined by Detective Chief Inspector Wainwright, DS Karthik, DC Dean and DC Billings. They rearranged their desks in the new space to face the whiteboards at the end, the floor a messy patchwork of duct tape thanks to all the cables Hoyt had diligently taped down when he set up the Major Incident Room.

DCI Wainwright, as Monroe expected, had not been happy to be second-in-command to Foley. He had sulkily dragged his desk near to Foley's at the head of the MIR and angled it so it faced the team. Foley had let him, watching the pitiful sight of a man in his late forties pull a table along the deep end of an empty swimming pool, table legs squeaking angrily against the tiles, while he tried awkwardly to stop his computer monitor from tipping over. Still, he'd known well enough to keep his mouth shut. Whatever rank you were, if your superior said jump, you aimed for levitation.

Now, Foley pressed on with his instructions, mindful to play nice. No point rattling Wainwright's cage even more.

He had called them together to bring the new team members up to speed, and to establish strategy.

'DCI Wainwright, sir, could you visit the crime scene, and liaise with Gavigan for the latest developments down there? And it'd be good for you to see this place, however terrible that sounds. Billings, can you get onto tech and get a direct phone line for the MIR – in fact, get on this right now so we can tack the number onto the end of the press conference.'

Billings, a beanpole with a permanently bemused expression, got up and jogged away, before Foley continued.

'Dean, when it's up, you help him on the line. Sorry it's not very glamorous, but we'll have every man and his dog ringing up as soon as that number's out, and I want a pair of reliable hands to sift through what comes in. You'll have the usual idle speculation and straight-up bullshit, but you'll know what's important and what isn't.'

'Yes, sir,' said Dean. She had wavy red hair, thick lipstick the colour of a squashed blackberry, and spectacles as thick and round as the bottom of a jam jar.

Karthik, a slight man with a crisp, neat haircut and intense gaze, sat upright ready for his direction.

Looking around at the team, it suddenly struck Foley like thunder. They were all young, apart from Wainwright. Too young for this.

'Karthik, go with Wainwright. Two heads are better than one. Get a feel for it. We'll meet back here for a debrief at 1 p.m. and take it from there.' They all got up, chair legs wailing on tile.

'Sir,' said Madison, who had sidled up next to Foley.

'Yes?'

'I think I've identified another body.'

ROSS LAY ON the hotel bed, flicking through the TV channels with a packet of vending machine crisps on his chest. He hadn't slept a wink, hadn't had a touch of booze, hadn't even wanted to. He'd just sat there, all night, propped up against the headboard, staring at the television, numb to his toes.

After they'd seen Connor, or the bits of Connor they were allowed to see –which amounted to his pale, sunken face – the last thing he wanted to do was go home. He couldn't face seeing anything of Connor's, or looking into his wife's face – it was all too clear where Connor's looks had come from. He didn't want to see anybody, talk to anybody, face anything. The grief counsellor, whose name he'd already erased from his mind, had set him up a room at the local Premier Inn on the edge of town, then arranged a car to take Siobhan to her parents. She'd reassured them that this was entirely normal, that they weren't the first couple to grieve separately, and that they shouldn't be alarmed by it.

Everyone deals with these things in their own way, and there's no right way to react to such news.

He'd like to challenge that notion, because all he wanted to do was kill whoever had put his son in that state. Wanted to rip him limb from limb and wrap *him* up in plastic and dump him shallow with the dirt and worms.

He had his rage on simmer, but he knew it would froth. Shock was his main state, as he brushed crumbs off his stomach. Despite the snacks, he felt hollow.

He hadn't called his wife, or even messaged any of his Instagram conquests. He just wanted to sit and wait until he could feel properly again. After that, he'd call around, get the boys together.

Then they'd get to work.

Brendan had said – no, Brendan had *promised* – that he would find out who did this and arrest them. But Ross had different ideas about justice, and a different way of getting it. As far as he was concerned, justice in this country always ended up with a functional cell, decent amenities, three square meals and a host of human rights laws keeping it all in place.

That wasn't enough for Ross.

It wasn't enough for whoever did this.

Ross wanted to wait until his head was just a little straighter, and then he'd put the feelers out on the street. He had connections, people he could call, rocks he could look under – all of which were the kind that his brother didn't have and couldn't access. He'd lean on his dad too.

He cycled through the channels, watching everything he could about the grave, which was easy because it was on every one of the multiple news channels. He couldn't help staring, he was transfixed. This giant, terrifying *thing* that took his son had come out of nowhere like a lorry through a picnic. And rather than hide from it, he found himself looking at it, wallowing in it, drenching himself in it.

He imagined what the grief woman would have said about that.

As he repeatedly thumbed the remote, looking for the next bulletin, one or two began to show a bare lectern and a microphone.

Then he remembered the press conference. Brendan had warned him about it. He'd said it was normal, to come out and confirm things to the public like this, and to show the public what the police were doing about it. Best foot forward, Brendan had said. Show the public and the media that they were off to a good start and already making progress.

His brother. He'd do things his way. And Ross would do things his. And if Ross was a betting man, he'd feel confident putting money on who was going to get the job done best.

CHAPTER 12

FOLEY FOLLOWED WAINWRIGHT'S car all the way back to the crime scene. They parked on the opposite side of the street from the SOCO vans that had been there since the day before. He wasn't in the Toad today. Instead, he was using the family's second car – a small, black, ten-year-old Audi A3 with 175,000 miles on the clock. It was Foley's work runaround, and it did exactly what it was supposed to with very little pressure on his modest DI wage.

He watched Wainwright and Karthik get out of Wainwright's Beemer. Late model. Grown-up kids and a paid-off mortgage allowed you to do that – and no small thanks, Foley was sure, to the bumper incentive package he undoubtedly trousered for moving to Warrington. Karthik's body language was even tauter than usual, and Wainwright still appeared to be bristling. Foley couldn't care less, as long as he did his job. He gave them a thumbs up.

The station phone log search had come back, and his business was not with the trench, but with a house in the cul-de-sac. He remembered the one. Remembered that woman. His hunch yesterday morning had been right. He got out, as an unseasonably warm lick to the breeze felt like a pat on the back. *Go on, son.* The houses ahead were quiet, but cars were still mostly present. It had just gone 9 a.m.

Passing between the two cars on the drive – a red two-seater sporty thing and a dark blue bubbly old Nissan – Foley wasted no time in thumbing the bell. He wanted to catch her off guard. Force the issue. In the house, an electronic singsong bounced about. The frosted glass of the white PVC door was suddenly filled by a pink shape, and the door was opened with a jangle of keys left in the lock on the inside.

'Yeah?' A woman stood there in a faded cotton candy dressing gown, her hair already made up for the day in a high wave held in place by what had to be some industrial-strength hairspray. Her mascara was as deep and heavy as the cleavage she appeared to have no interest in controlling. She was in her mid-fifties, weary underneath the faux-glam, with a purple drink in one hand and faded Marge Simpson slippers on her feet.

'Mrs Flint?' he asked.

'Ms Galloway these days,' she said, in a tone that left the door to flirtation queasily ajar.

He moved quickly on. 'Excuse me, Ms Galloway, could I have a word? My name is Detective Inspector Foley.'

'Call me Val and come on in.' She turned strangely demure for a moment, hiding her body behind the door as she opened it wider, and pointed with her tumbler down the hall. Foley nodded and entered, catching a whiff of her glass as he went past. *Strong.*

A sitting room appeared, and Foley entered but didn't sit down. The television was on, and he could see Chief Superintendent Monroe going about the press conference.

'This must be very difficult for you, Val – living so close to the discovery,' Foley said.

Val came in behind him, and took a seat on the sofa, kicking an iPad out of the way and crossing her legs beneath her. She'd ditched the slippers.

'I assume the name change from the electoral roll is a recent one? Forgive me, I just want to make sure I've spoken to the right person.'

'Recent but a long time coming,' she said, baring her teeth in a smile.

Foley felt as if he'd be lucky to get out of here in one piece. 'So, nobody else is in?'

'None,' Val said definitively.

'What about the second car on the drive?'

'My son – he's walked to college today. Please sit down. Can I get you something?'

'Thank you,' Foley said, sitting on the edge of a faux-leather armchair opposite her. The room looked like it was plucked straight from a fifteen-year-old Ikea catalogue, with swaying scuffed units and tired bouncy laminate underfoot. 'It's a bit early for me.' He nodded at her drink. Her expression dented. 'It's all right, I don't judge. Vodka Ribena at nine in the morning would have me set up for the day too.'

She placed the glass down. The control of the conversation was suddenly all Foley's.

'What I'd like to know – what we'd all like to know – is why you wanted to stay anonymous?' he asked.

She came back at him quickly. 'I don't know what you mean?' But the look in her eyes told another story.

'Come on. You're the hero of this piece so far, why wouldn't you want to let the world know? You don't seem the shy, retiring type, if you'll forgive me for saying.'

Val grabbed her drink and took a hefty swig.

'Let me rephrase the question, then. What were you doing that you shouldn't have been doing – you know, when you saw something that made you call the police?'

'You can rephrase all you like. I still don't know what you're talking about.'

'All right. I can leave you to it, if you're saying it's not you.' He leaned back in the chair and looked at the TV set. Monroe was being besieged by questions. Across the bottom, a graphic shouted, bold as brass: 27 DEAD IN MASS GRAVE HORROR. 'Look at this. I can't believe it myself yet. It was unbelievable, Val. What we saw yesterday. I don't think I'll ever get my head around it. This is one of the worst crimes the country has ever seen, and I have to make sense of it. For people like you, and for me. So, the problem I have is that if I uncover something while I'm doing that, something that *you* already knew, you suddenly aren't the hero anymore. Just another rum 'un wasting police time in one of the biggest news stories – one of the *worst* crimes – in recent memory. And those people don't tend to come out too well in the retelling.'

She looked at her Ribena as if she wished she could dive into it.

'And I'd only have to come knocking on your door again, this time a little more forcefully, with lots of uniforms. People tend to notice that.' He flicked his head at the window looking over the street. 'So, I'll ask you one more time. How did you find out about it?'

A long moment passed; Foley's gaze never wavered from Val.

'You have to understand,' she said. 'I was nothing to do with what you all found. I promise you, it was an accident, and… I'm not proud of it.'

'What are you not proud of, Val?'

She began talking but stumbled over her words. 'The way I did it, I mean. There would have been other ways, but this was the best.'

'Do what, Val?' Patience was key in an interview like this, but Foley's was being pushed.

'Spy on him.'

Foley paused. Then he understood. 'Are we talking about your ex-husband?'

'If you're going to shit in your litter box, you then get out of the litter box, don't you?'

'I don't follow.'

Val became more animated. 'When you destroy your whole life and everyone in it, you should at least have the decency to move away from it.'

'You're saying your husband is local? Did he have something to do with it?'

'No, no, you're not getting it.' Val put her drink down, got up and marched to the front window, tightening her robe. 'He's only gone off... there...' She jutted a finger at the forest on the opposite side of the cul-de-sac.

Foley remembered the maps from that morning, the forest. There were multiple entries and exits, lots of buildings that pressed up around the boundary. That farm he'd sent Christopher after, that was only one. There were others...

'He's on the Wellington Estate on the other side of the woods,' Foley said, finishing for her.

'He wanted himself a slutty young chav and he's bloody well got one.'

Foley finally understood. It was a sad story all by itself. The Wellington Estate was a sixties development thrust up on a farmer's land. Affordable housing for the growing warehouse boom on the edges of Warrington. Only it soon became obvious that the location, right at the furthermost point of Mulbeth, one of Warrington's most deprived areas, was not the most desirable spot for prospective buyers. The Wellington Estate soon became council housing – but like anything at the bottom, it only got what flowed downwards and didn't cling on. It was a natural home for the ne'er-do-wells. Funding, money and amenities all seemed to be worn out by the time they got to the Wellington.

'So, you went over there to confront him. And saw something you felt you shouldn't?' Foley ventured.

'No, I didn't go anywhere...' Val's whole body told a different story.

'Go on,' Foley said.

She looked suddenly anxious. 'Don't tell him. You won't tell him, will you?'

'I'm not interested in what you've done and I'm sure your ex-husband isn't either.'

She grimaced. 'I'm not bothered about that old fool! But my son. You mustn't tell *him*. It was his, you see, his flying camera thing. His... his drone.'

TRAFFIC WAS LIGHT, most folks having made it to work by now. Foley was almost back to the station, the drone on his passenger seat. He called Madison through for an update. He should have called Wainwright but, well, bollocks to that. Madison was on her way down to Birmingham, just through a stop-start dirge from Thelwall Viaduct to Holmes Chappel and was now passing Stoke-on-Trent.

'The press conference. How was it?' He shoved a carrot stick in his mouth. He'd grabbed something to eat from Sainsbury's, along with a bottle of Lucozade.

'When you got past the oohs and aahs, it went mostly as could be expected. Your nephew's name was released, but no causes of death yet,' Madison replied.

'And me?' Foley asked warily.

'You were mentioned. The link was made by that hack from the *Warrington Post*.'

Foley grimaced. 'Not that hard to make the link, I suppose. First victim's name is Foley, here's your senior investigating officer also Foley. Can't blame him.'

'Monroe vouched for you. Said it wouldn't be a problem. Argued that the fact that you're only the victim's uncle – and that your professionalism is beyond question – was enough to let you carry on as lead.'

Only the victim's uncle.

Foley was a bit stunned at that. He thought the only back Monroe had was the late-night barman at his golf club down in smart Wilmslow. He felt bad for doubting him – cop code came through. 'He's back on the Christmas card list. So, what have you got for victim two?'

'Heading there now. I've given West Midlands Police a courtesy nod. They're sending someone with me to visit the possible victim's wife.'

'Well played. I won't ask again, but you sure you're up to this one?'

'I've been part of the death message a few times, boss, if that's what you're asking. It might not even be him, anyway. Plus, we need to spread our resources as far as we can.'

Foley brought to mind that body they were discussing. It was the older man, the guy dressed for a Sunday carvery, the one holed up with the rat. One of the ones who still had a face.

'You've got pictures for the ID?'

'I have. Mackie sent me a new one this morning, now that his features have... settled a bit.'

Foley put his carrots in the cup holder, his appetite zeroed. 'What was it like?'

'In the early shots, when we were looking for unique features, there was a tattoo. A footie crest: Aston Villa. Stuck in my head because he didn't look the type. Underneath the crest were the words, Holt End. I assumed that to be not just random, but something only those who went to the games would get. I ran his main characteristics through PNC with addresses set to Birmingham. Specifically, a ten-mile radius of Villa Park. Got a match. I believe the pic of West Midland's missing grey-haired football fan is our dead grey-haired football fan.'

Foley was impressed. Smart. He felt the soft buzz of progress. He needed this. He needed to be involved, and it kept the bad thoughts at bay. 'Nice one. Let me know as soon as you get confirmation.'

'Should be there in half an hour or so.'

'Good. Catch you in a bit.' He took a deep breath. 'Got to go see a man about a drone.'

CHAPTER 13

AT 10.45 A.M., DS Madison pulled up outside an old steelworks on the edge of Bromford, three miles north-east of Birmingham city centre. It was quiet, this corner of the industrial estate, occupied only by a couple of banged-up vans and a scooter. The steelwork was made up of high, corrugated iron walls with a corrugated tin roof. It looked like a hasty erection of corrugated offcuts, rows of yellow steel girders poking out of the floor next to the factory. They were all about three feet high. Madison had no clue what they were for, but they somehow gave the building a distant purpose.

Wide loading doors stood shut. A drill sounded on–off from somewhere.

Madison got out of the unmarked pool Mondeo and crossed the gravel to the main entrance. She'd tried the victim's home address in Stechford, only a few short miles away, but no luck. Hoping for a chat with the deceased's wife, she'd found shut curtains, the sills beneath them dusty. The home may have been empty for some time. She'd met a PC from the local constabulary, but that was a courtesy move more than anything. When he'd gone again, she'd fought the obligation to go back up north empty-handed. This was *her* lead and she wanted something to show for it. The scrapper in her kicked in. She checked her files on the front seat and found a most recent place of work.

As she'd stridden towards the loading doors – locked – she'd realised two things. One, that drilling she'd heard was coming from inside. And two, there was a service door to the right of the loading doors.

Now, she approached with less caution than she should, aware of the pressing time, but also because she quietly loved the rush, the harm, the danger. She'd always been like this. Best foot forward with the biggest bollocks in the room.

She knocked on the door and heard it echo inside. She banged harder and the drilling stopped.

Silence. She tried the door. Unlocked. She pushed it open.

Inside, an office. Dusty, dark, abandoned. Concrete floor. Scuffed wooden desks and dented steel filing cabinets. No bullshit bric-a-brac. Another door led to a much bigger space beyond, with shafts of sunlight that captured swirling dust motes. Through the doorway stepped a man. He looked surprised to see a woman in a suit checking out the front office.

'Detective Sergeant Madison, Warrington Police,' she said. 'I don't care why you're here. I'm trying to find out about someone who worked in this building.'

The man was skinny and ratty, wearing a dirty grey T-shirt under a puffed gilet, with black joggers and grimy trainers. He glanced back to where he'd come from. Madison's first instincts had been right – he was up to something he shouldn't. Silently, his eyes darted around as though he were weighing up his options.

'Has the place been closed long?' she asked. Keep it benign, get him talking.

He ran a filthy hand though his hair. 'Umm, a while now,' he said, in raspy Black Country.

'How long?' She was thinking of the decomposition of the corpse. About a month had been Mackie's best guess.

'Month or so,' came the reply. *Tick.*

'I'm looking for a man who may have worked here,' she ventured. This time, Rat Bag stiffened. 'No, not in connection to anything he's done. Just looking for him. Did you work here when it was open?'

That hand through the hair again. 'I did, but not for very long. One of the bosses walked, and the place went under.'

Madison's senses burred. 'Where'd he go?'

Rat Bag held his arms out. His expression said, *beats me.*

'What was his name?' Madison persisted.

A shake of the head.

'Clive Mariner?' Madison asked, to an immediate involuntary response. Rat Bag's hands dropped to his sides, bunching into fists. 'I don't care what he's doing, or what you're doing, or what any bugger in Birmingham is doing,' she added quickly. 'I just want to know what happened.'

He took a few seconds, and surveyed Madison carefully. A smile broke across his face. 'You're a bit tidy for a cop.'

'And you're doing God knows what in an abandoned steelworks. One call from me brings West Midland's best and brightest knocking on this door, and one step nearer is going to result in a left hook.

And don't look at me like you think you can take me – I watched you walk in here. When the heat's on, you'll be no more than a cart-horse with liquid knees.' She'd been in enough pre-fight face-offs to know empty bravado when she saw it.

'All right, girly, shit me. You're a bloody firework.' Rat Bag tried to play it off as though he were humouring her, but she could tell he was only trying to settle his nerves. He sat on the edge of the nearest desk. 'Clive went off into the sunset. Left his two partners high and dry. Meant they had to shut this down. Couldn't cover the rent without him. No one's seen him since.'

'A month ago...' Madison looked through the door at the empty factory. 'Where's everything gone? They've cleaned up quick.'

Rat Bag's composure was returning, and he smiled. 'Well, I worked the front end here – some fairly basic presses and welding stuff. We didn't do nothing heavy. But you're not here for that, are you?'

He was getting cheeky. Time to change tack. 'Too right. Now, wipe that ugly fucking grin off your face and tell me.'

'Voice of an angel, mouth like a sailor,' Rat Bag said, and that was enough.

Two steps, dropped her left shoulder, dipped and rose with a left hook that sent Rat Bag sprawling over the desk. He spat, and a couple of teeth tinkled off the desktop. Nobody wanted that left hook. It was a serious problem-solver.

'Fuggin' bish,' he spat through the gaps in his teeth.

'Didn't catch that. You were saying how I didn't want to hear about the front end? What was the real sell?'

'Puleesh bootali-ee.' His hand was on his jaw.

Madison moved to loom over him and clenched her fist again. 'Yeah, you try it. Everyone'll love listening to your story of how the five-foot-five woman cop from up north came down and twatted your teeth out. Either they won't believe you or you'll be the laughing stock of whatever shithole you crawled out of. Choices, choices.'

Rat Bag had to consider that, and within seconds the words started coming out.

'It was a frun,' he croaked.

'A what?'

'A frun...t.'

'A front for what?'

He slowed his breathing and took care with his words, which

helped. 'Other stuff. Bit of weed, bit of stripping nicked cars, bit of this, bit of that. Nothing major, the steel just covered it up and meant we could have the tools about for the cars. Them three loved it—'

'The three bosses?'

'Yeah.'

'What do you think happened to them?'

Rat Bag leaned back and sighed so hard Madison could hear the whistle through his brand-new dental gap. 'Didn't come from me. I think they had a fall-out. They were trying new things, wanted to get bigger. I heard Clive was stepping on bigger toes cityside, or was at least trying to.'

'And you heard this despite you working on the steel front, right?'

Rat Bag looked hurt. 'That's right. I'm not shittin' you.'

'You hear what happened?'

'Nobody's heard hide nor hair of Clive, but nobody's seen Paul and Wandage neither.'

'They're the other two partners?'

'Yep. Asset strippers came in, everything else has been sold except for a few bits. Bad debt behind this place apparently, so it all had to go.'

'And you?' Madison had a clear direction for her line of enquiry but was still curious.

'I'm just moochin' about.'

'Do you always drill when you're mooching about?'

That hurt little look again, which didn't suit this urchin at all. 'I lost my job. I've got to do something.'

Madison eyed him, bullshit-meter cranked high. She had most of what she needed, and everything else she could now pick up with the local police.

'Keep your nose clean,' she said, jabbing a finger.

Rat Bag raised his hands. 'Aye aye, miss. And none of that came from me, if you don't mind.'

Madison picked up her clipboard and left. She heard Rat Bag utter, 'Bugger *me*,' under his breath as the door swung shut. Before heading back to the car, she checked out the loading doors. They'd been padlocked shut, but there was a small gap of about a quarter of an inch, which offered her a very tall, extremely thin portrait view of inside the factory.

It was empty, as she expected, but on the floor, next to a couple of toolkits with odd bits strewn about, stood two motorbikes in various state of undress. As she watched, Rat Bag came back in, rubbing his jaw, and sat on the floor looking at the two bikes. Madison went back to the car.

She drove for two minutes through the industrial estate towards the exit, until there were more people about, and more prosperous businesses littered the roadside. She pulled up at a greasy spoon trailer, ordered a large black coffee with two extra shots of espresso, then hopped back in her car.

She dialled and had a hot sip as the tone rang through the car speakers. While it rang, she pulled out a small Tupperware box from her bag in the passenger footwell and popped the lid. A handful of broccoli stalks, a couple of cherry tomatoes and a wad of tuna looked back up at her forlornly. Fight week meal prep. She was on weight and had to stay there, even with everything going on.

The phone was answered. 'Hi, this is DS Iona Madison with Warrington Police. I'm after DI Warren? We spoke earlier today.'

A baritoned Brummie came on. 'Yes, speaking. I heard you didn't turn anything up at Mariner's house?'

She tried to get a tomato onto the end of her fork by cornering it in the Tupperware and stabbing it. 'That's correct. But listen, I've got an easy collar for you if you can give me a bit of local info. I'm not familiar with the ins and outs of the area, but I could do with a nudge in the right direction.'

A pause. 'You didn't go straight home, did you?'

'Not quite. But I don't think you'll mind too much if you can help me out.'

A sigh. 'What do you need?'

CHAPTER 14

THE TRAIN JUDDERED to a stop. Fitz glanced out of the grease-streaked windows at the sea. Frustratingly, the train was waiting just a couple of minutes out of Bangor rail station. The journey had been one of the least relaxing in memory. He'd been up six or seven times for coffee and to switch seats, terrified he was being followed; he'd ended up bouncing around the train like the trapped white dot in Pong. He'd even walked up and down the five carriages of the Arriva Wales service, and given everyone the once-over. End result? He couldn't have looked more conspicuous if he'd tried, and he knew it.

Despite all this, he *did* finally feel alone, which was a relief.

He'd found a copy of the free *Metro* newspaper and pored over its contents, taking in everything he could about this incident that had claimed the lad Connor, but no amount of turning it over in his mind could shed any light on what had happened.

A mass grave.

Twenty-seven – *twenty-fuckin'-seven* – people killed.

Connor Foley being one of them.

The cash machine job and Connor's death couldn't remotely be connected. No way, surely? To Fitz, the deaths could only be the work of a nut-job serial killer who made stuffed toys out of his victims' skins.

But he couldn't shake that spectre of coincidence, and the growing fear that they shouldn't have done that machine. It had played on his mind when they planned it. He'd felt it at the time. And he damn well felt it now.

It was the timing, really. Connor's death, coming when it did, right after that bloody job, was just too coincidental for Fitz to take.

Maybe that idiot Connor had taken a wrong turn on his walk home after dropping the van of, and had stumbled into the grip of a sicko.

That had to be it.

The train started moving again. Fitz ran his hand across his head, as if to check he was still there and still in one piece.

You're losing it, lad, he thought.

Outside the window, the sea abruptly finished and grey buildings spattered with seagull crap closed in.

He took out his phone, pulled up his texts. Found his conversation with Lloyd, and typed in:

Just gettin in. Where you parked?

Pressed send, then placed the phone on the table.

He just wanted this slow, painful, fretful journey to end. His nerves could barely take any more.

The phone buzzed.

Parked in the side street next to the station. Just nipped into the pub opposite for a shit. Left it unlocked. The green Astra. Five mins.

Fitz almost smiled. Bloody Lloyd. Ever the unpredictable.

The train was suddenly in the station, and pulling to a stop, and before it was stationary Fitz was up by the door, bag over his shoulder, pressing the open button repeatedly before it had even lit up green, which attracted a few searching glances. They only added to his nerves.

With a hiss, the doors opened and he was out, striding down the platform, faking confidence. But then he realized everyone else was going in the opposite direction, and he saw he'd gone marching off the wrong way, towards the service units and bins.

'Shit, shit, shitting shit,' he said to himself, while heading back with the throng.

He was naturally taller than most, at just a shade over six foot if he was being honest with himself (six two he told everybody as a rule). His height put him at an advantage – he could get a good look at the crowd. Nobody stood out. It was looking promising.

Through the barriers, showed his ticket, having been a good boy for once. Smelling freedom. Tasting safety. Main entrance. Quiet. A weird station. Lost in time, with orange brick over turquoise paint. No real modern touches. The old station clock read just gone eleven.

Out from under the walkway, into the cool morning. The salt in the air reminded him of holidays as a kid and imbued him with a sense of calm. He was going to make this. He turned right, found the nearest side street and glanced down it. A green Vauxhall Astra sat there, and he felt a tidal rush of relief as he jogged over.

Lloyd wasn't there, so he cast his eyes about, and sure enough on the other side of the road was a boozer – the Waverley Hotel, its front door ajar and inviting. Eleven wasn't too early for a pint, not by much at least, and definitely not when Fitz was feeling this happy. He'd drunk much earlier than this in Magaluf. Yeah. He'd go in the pub and surprise Lloyd with a pint. Dump his bags first.

Fitz suddenly felt positive.

After a second's fumble looking for the latch, he popped open the boot of the Astra – to find Lloyd lying there staring at him. Only he wasn't staring at him. His gaze was fixed high over Fitz's head in a long, faraway look. His throat was gaping, ragged meat. Blood all over the boot.

In the immediate shock, Fitz almost didn't feel the knife in his back. But then it felt like a punch, and a hot pulse deep inside. His legs began to buckle and the knife scraped horribly against his spine as it was pulled out, only to be thrust back in at a slightly different angle. That heat again, deeper this time. A loose feeling all over. No time to be scared, just surprised, and strangely immobile.

He toppled forward into the boot, Lloyd rushing up at him. His feet were thrown in after him and the last thing he saw was Lloyd's lifeless eyes peering heavenwards as the boot was slammed shut.

CHAPTER 15

THE ODD SPOT of rain dotted the windshield of Art's Audi as he sat on the driveway of Brendan and Mim's house. The clouds were settling slowly in a vast grey blanket, and had that obstinate look that suggested they were in for the duration. He'd been there a few minutes already.

The front door swung open. Mim.

He climbed out of the car. Brendan and Mim lived on a quiet estate in Culcheth, a village about four miles from Warrington itself. Far enough for Brendan to feel like he was going home after a shift, but close enough to be back there in a heartbeat. The estate was predominantly occupied by the young and perennially busy – and that meant that approaching a Monday lunchtime, the place was deserted. Art could see why his son and daughter-in-law had picked this as their home.

He saw Mim on the bottom step of the stairs. She held a finger to her lips as he approached, but the rest of her body was rigid, clasped tight. As soon as Art made it through the door, Mim hugged him fiercely. Art wondered in an instant why it had been so hard to get out of the car and step inside his son's home. Grief was supposed to be shared; it was what families did.

'Oh, Jesus, Art,' she muttered, and he could feel her shaking with release.

'I know, Mim,' he whispered. 'I know.' He thought he'd cried himself out while driving around all morning. Art felt her tears stain his shirt. 'Brendan's out?'

She closed the front door and led him to the kitchen.

The kitchen table was covered with dirty dishes and empty, stained mugs. Art lowered himself into a chair, while Mim grabbed two mugs and began rinsing them in the sink.

'Sorry, Mick is asleep,' she said absently. 'He doesn't usually have a sleep at this time, but I think he's sensed something. They say babies are like that, picking up on things you try to hide from them. He'd got a bit narky, so I put him down.'

'Brendan isn't returning my calls,' Art said.

Mim dried the mugs with a frayed, checkered tea towel. 'I don't think he'd be able to return mine right now, either. I'm not even sure when I'll see him next. He's the lead investigator on the whole thing, and he's taken it... well, you know Brendan.'

'That's what I need to talk to him about.'

'Why?' She filled the kettle, dropped a spoon and tea bag in each mug, on autopilot.

Art struggled to find the words. 'It's not good this, he shouldn't be... he's too *connected* to it, too close. I worry about him.'

'I see your point, I do. But I can't do anything about it. You know what he's like, he'd argue the sky was green if it meant he didn't have to give in just yet. Besides, it is his job, isn't it?'

'Not this. Not' – Art spread his hands – '*this*.' His voice fractured. 'I couldn't persuade him even if I wanted to.'

'Would you want to?'

He watched Mim think, filling the mugs from a dented chrome kettle.

Art pressed. 'Would you try?'

Mim turned. 'I don't see what it'd achieve—'

'It isn't right. He should be home, with you. Look at you! I mean nothing by that, darling, but his family needs him. He doesn't need to be looking at – *Jesus* – crime scene photos of our Connor. A man shouldn't have to. A man shouldn't want to. This will undo him.'

'Art, I *can't*. His job means everything to him, and now he's so involved, he couldn't step away. Come on, you know him, you know he'd never let it go.' Mim's voice dropped to just above a whisper. 'He wants to find Connor's killer. And come to think of it, wouldn't you rather have family in charge of that?'

That's exactly what I want, thought Art. Just not Brendan, and not the police. 'I think he should be at home. Looking after his children, and his wife.'

Mim tried to smile.

'How's Dan?' Art asked. 'Those grandsons of mine were close.'

Mim remembered the conversation at breakfast. Mim blurted out something about Connor being in a better place, but she'd seen the morning news and she knew for a fact that the place he'd ended up was emphatically *not* better. The last time she'd had to tell her children about a significant death in the family was a beloved turtle, but that was when Dan was ten, and went by Daniel.

Helplessly, she found herself resorting to glossing over the detail as she had done back then. But Dan was no slouch. He knew this was bad. He knew this was one of those things in life that didn't happen to everyone, but when it did, the seismic aftershocks would resonate through the family for generations to come. In the end, she'd had to tell him almost everything she knew.

Still, he'd insisted on going to school. He wanted to press on as normal. So, as he was on his way there, Mim had rung the school office with the news, which she recounted numbly. The staff, most importantly his favourite teacher Miss Hoyle, were going to try to intercept him and get him to a quiet room to give him some space and privacy. It seemed like a half-decent idea but Mim had wanted to do nothing more than to pull him as close as possible and mother the damn horrors away.

'I don't know, Art. Truthfully, I don't know.'

Art stood and motioned to leave. 'Brendan should be here. I mean that. He should be supporting you.'

'I'll give it some thought,' replied Mim, tossing their undrunk tea into the sink, spoons, bags and all.

'Please do.'

Art left, after another rush of tears on the front doorstep.

He got into his car, waited for Mim to shut the front door, then pulled out his phone. He sent a text to his son – his other son, Ross.

Let's meet. Usual place. Asap.

His sons. At least he could rely on one of them.

CHAPTER 16

'SO, WHAT AM I looking at?'

On the left-hand screen in front of Foley was an aerial view of thick forest, in various soft shades of grey. The right-hand screen was an interface with a list of file names.

22.10.19–23:21:56

22.10.19–23:44:14

23.10.19–00:50:22

23.10.19–04:17:03

And above those, many more. About thirty of them.

As absurd a place as Warrington Police Station was, the staff had to find a way to make it work. Sometimes, whispers would seep downwards through gobby cracks suggesting that there might be a new 'super futuristic' police station in the works on the outside of town, with all the latest conveniences like high-tech, fully automated office spaces, even reliable parking. All that felt worlds away to Foley as he sat in the present nick's audio-video suite – if you could call this Victorian changing cubicle a suite.

It was a small cave of dark wood, six foot by six foot, not unlike a Mexican drug lord's personal cigar thermidor. A couple of screens sat in front of Foley on a metal desk, with two Mac towers on the floor underneath. Wires snaked around the back of the screens in thick coils, held together by cable ties, and the right-hand wall was hidden by a bank of data servers, from floor to ceiling, making the space even smaller.

'They're the files on the right, you click them, they play on the left,' said a voice from behind him. The accent was pure Scouse. As there was only room for one chair in there, Jordan Seebaruth hovered in the cubicle doorway. Foley had taken his usual seat.

Known as Seabreeze – 'Just call me Seabreeze. Everyone else seems to think that's my surname' – he was young, lithe and mentally agile. At the last two work Christmas parties, he'd also proven to be chatty, sociable and horny as a dog with double the standard number of reproductive organs. His escapades were bordering on legendary, and the power of his dark eyes twinned with his mischievous persona had the gossip circles churning.

'And it's grey because?' It wasn't even midday and Foley's tie had been loosened. He had the horrible feeling that he could smell himself.

'Night vision,' Jordan replied. 'Or at least low-light vision. Most of the files were taken at night.'

'So, potted history, what's been going on?'

'This is just one night's work, across the two dates on the file time stamps.'

'The file names?'

'Exactly. The son had been using a 128gb SD card, with decent compression rate on the drone's onboard CPU, so there are hours and hours of this. I've just brought up the important stuff for you, and a bit for flavour.'

Foley, being a modern man with a young family and a camera that was always in his kids' faces, understood exactly what Jordan was talking about. Memory cards, processing units… long story short, they had a lot of footage.

'So, she's been doing this for a while, then?'

'I think it's any time she hits the sauce – which is often. You can even see that she peaks at ten to about half eleven at night, in terms of how pissed she is, because the drone's flight gets… wayward. And in terms of wading through how much there was – I just went to the date she called it in and worked backwards from the time of the call. Found it straight away, but I'll go through the lot just to be sure there's nothing else.'

'Good man. She said she just flies it over the woods to the Wellington Estate on the other side, that tallies?'

'Yes, absolutely. Number 45 Nelson Street. Nobody's ever come out of it, so I don't think he's seen the drone or is even aware of it.'

'Gotcha.'

'If you ever catch me spying on an ex with a drone, have a word, will you?'

'I would imagine you couldn't even remember all your exes, Seabreeze – you'll probably be all right. Where's the big reveal? What made her call us?'

'I've cued it up, just press play.' Seabreeze seemed nervous.

'OK, how do…'

'Just tap the space bar.'

The greys on the left screen suddenly started shifting in silence.

'No audio?' Foley asked.

'Nah, it's just a small camera about a hundred feet up. The only audio would be the buzz of the propellers. No mic.'

The treetops were clear, the darkness of the forest floor intermittently visible. It had been a clear night, thank goodness.

It only took a couple of seconds of that swishing, churning grey palette for him to feel seasick, and his eyes closed to slits.

'There, see them?' Jordan said.

Black shapes in the grey, like solid dark blocks moving through thick cloud.

'There's more than one?' Foley asked. 'Two of them...' He was shocked, but he couldn't quite say why. Maybe because it was proof that there was more than one total sicko in their midst.

The drone tilted hard to the right, then corrected itself in such a way that it needed a hard tilt right again just to get close to being straight.

'She was on the vodka when I saw her at about nine this morning,' Foley said, more to himself than anything. The poor woman had problems, but it was not in his detective's remit to go wading through them. He could always refer her on to the social outreach team but, again, that was a bit of a meddler's move. His role was clear: find the killer, not fix every damn shortcoming he uncovered along the way.

The figures came back. Two men, clearly now. Burly frames, dark clothes. It appeared that, at this point in filming, Val had noticed them on her iPad monitor. The drone seemed to pause. With a gradual jerkiness, the camera panned down to get the two men fully in shot.

'Attagirl,' murmured Foley.

'She's quite good with it,' mused Seabreeze.

'I think she might be well practised.'

The men, still fuzzy thanks to the camera's low-light sacrifices and image noise enhancement, were using a couple of gardening tools. One had a spade, the other a fork. The first was packing soil into a small hole, while the man with the fork was tending to the area around it, spreading dirt, and fallen leaves and branches. Covering up. They worked with brisk precision.

'They're meticulous,' said Seabreeze.

'Like they've done it before.'

These guys didn't fit. Foley had been ready for a strangled, desperate struggle to locate a lone psychopath – a serial killer with a clear manifesto for the horrors he wanted to create. That's what he had seen when he looked into that trench yesterday. But now, he was thrown. This didn't look right, a pair of guys doing some midnight gardening.

His phone rang in his pocket and he pulled it out, hoping it wasn't his bloody father again. He needed to work, and he needed the space to do it. It was a relief to see Madison on the caller ID.

'What have you got?'

As she began to talk, Foley's eyes drifted back to the drone's footage. He felt his skin turn cold. Suddenly, those two shadowy figures – two, not one – made the best sense in the world.

CHAPTER 17

AS SOON AS Art crossed the threshold of the farm club, the bad vibes seemed to press in on him out of every corner. The old sensor above the door triggered a loud *bip-boop* as he passed beneath it, which was a pain in the arse come seven on Friday nights. A super-cheap bar, right in the middle of working-class suburbia? The constant footfall sounded like Johnny-5 was having a prolonged seizure on the doorstep.

He walked along the threadbare carpet, deftly dodging the farm club cat's food bowl, and pushed through the big chipboard door into the main bar.

At 1 p.m. on a Monday afternoon, the place was busier than normal, one table in particular. The usual booth, which just so happened to be the only one in the place.

Art had called it, Ross had enforced it, and the others had diligently responded. Buzz, the proprietor, was vacuuming with a crooked back, trailed around the bar stools by an obedient Henry Hoover unit. The farm club was an old farmhouse that sat in the middle of nowhere in south Warrington. Buzz had got it for a song, patched it up and opened it as a social club. So... farm club. It was a fiver membership with zero eligibility criteria, and you could always go there for cheap beer, spirited karaoke or a quiet moment.

Two out of that three were just what Art needed today.

Ross was at the bar, at the tail end of ordering a round of six Guinness, and was now negotiating with Pam, the landlady, for some peanuts. Art nodded to the other men, who were sitting at the only booth. They nodded back. He pressed on to the bar, cheap fairy lights above him twinkling amid all sorts of souvenir tat – American license plates (mostly from Florida), postcards, fridge magnets, bath ducks in various location-specific outfits, even a Billy Bass, battery-less and decommissioned after becoming even more annoying than the *bip-boop*.

'Jesus, son,' was all Art could say as he got to Ross. 'You look desperate.' He'd seen his son after the news had broken, when his parents had insisted on seeing him at the hotel in the middle of the night. They'd had the hugs and howls then.

Ross was wild-eyed, hair standing up on end, shovelling nuts like hibernation was coming up fast. 'We all here?' he said.

Art considered what his son must have taken, but he didn't ask. The grief Ross was going through was something Art couldn't fathom. Last thing he wanted to do was make things worse with accusations. 'All here, I think,' he said. 'Save for Gary because he couldn't get out of work.'

'No loss there, then.'

'If you say so.'

'Let's get on with it.' Ross was up and heading to the booth, carrying the drinks on a tray. Art motioned to pat him on the back, but Ross was already gone, leaving Art hanging. He grimaced and squared up. Business time.

The booth housed four other men, and the black pints were passed in front of each – then one for Ross, and one for Art, who hadn't sat down yet. They all reached out, the other four all staring into their drinks. One at a time, they looked to Ross expectantly, but Ross's eyes had glazed. This was the moment for someone to say a few words, but they all knew words wouldn't make a damn bit of difference. The moment crystallised, until Art intervened.

'Save your thoughts and prayers, and drink up,' he said, and took a deep draught. The others did too, and Art patted his son on the shoulder.

'Time is short, gents,' Art continued. 'I'm not going to labour it, because that won't do one iota of good for anyone. Simply put, we need this fucker finding.'

He paused a second, remembering that Buzz was about. Buzz was onside and had always been looked after for it – it was one of the reasons they still kept meeting at the farm club – but Art knew better than to discuss something like this at volume. Thankfully, Buzz was dragging Henry Hoover over by the fruit machines, the aspirated drone of the vacuum persisting.

'Use whatever you need, whoever you know, whatever you can think of,' Ross said, suddenly articulate and fiery. 'Who's killing people and dumping them here in Warrington?'

'Where's the lad – Fitz?' asked Murray. Murray was a balding man with a Costa Del suntan atop a navy golf shirt emblazoned with the name Galvin Green. He wore cream slacks, and a face that screamed of a recent escape from mid-level corporate management.

'I don't know,' replied Art, lowering his glass to reveal a creamy froth moustache.

'Is he in that hole too?' This time, the question had come from Earl, a clear gym-goer clad in the tribal outfit of garish Lycra and too-tight, sweat-wicking, form-fitting top. An earbud dangled freely, the other still left in, and his hair gelled so fiercely it would still look like that next week, and after the week-after's nuclear holocaust. At odds with this, he was in his mid-forties, with good bulk across his chest and shoulders, and bad bulk around his midriff.

'Let's not jump to conclusions,' replied Art.

'But the fact you've not heard owt from him all weekend doesn't look great, does it?'

'No, I'll give you that.'

'Shite,' swore Murray.

'And that other kid, what's his name? The one Connor hangs around with?' asked Steadman, a thick-set skinhead in a yellow and blue striped rugby top and one of those scalps that was wrinkled and ribbed like a basketball.

'Moston,' Art answered, without looking up.

'And he's where?'

'Same story. No word.'

'Jesus Christ.' The men sipped their pints in unison.

'I know this might not be the right thing to say,' began Guppo, the last at the table, a tall, coiled pillar of a man who was mostly white but exhibited a dash of more distant heritage. 'But if they all found their way into that fuckin' hole, what is the chance that they can be linked back to us? Are we on some psychopath's hit list? I mean, them lads have been in here enough times for us to have been seen together.'

Art saw Ross's shoulders flex. Still, as insensitive as Guppo's comment was, Ross, a few stone lighter than Guppo, wouldn't try anything. 'Steady on, Guppo. I understand the need to cover all bases, but let's not lose sight of the task at hand. We've got together to discuss what needs to be done to find whoever did this to Connor – my fuckin' grandson – not how we can keep our own noses out of the shit.'

Guppo nailed half his pint in one belligerent, showy go. 'With respect, are you sure it shouldn't be the other way round? What's done is done.' His eyes flared with challenge.

'Is there any truth,' said Steadman, 'that this had something to do with what I heard happened over Culliford way on Saturday night?'

'What happened?' asked Art.

'A cash machine was done. Nobody's claimed it yet.'

'I've no idea. What does matter is this trench. Where was it found?'

'Peel Hall woods,' said Murray.

'Right fucking *here*,' seethed Ross, jabbing a finger into the chipped table. 'In Warrington. Right under our fucking noses, and–'

'And no one,' interrupted Art, placing a restraining hand on his son's shoulder, 'would dare do that here. Not in their wildest dreams would anyone do what you're suggesting here.'

'Yet here we are,' said Guppo, before chinning almost the rest of his stout.

'So, what we've got,' Art said, 'is a psycho who's bit off so much more than he can chew. There's a fucking sicko out there in this town, in *our* town. *Here*. Now between us we have plenty of contacts. Use whatever you can to find this sick shite before the police do.'

'You mean, before your other lad does,' said Guppo.

'Whatever the police can do will never be enough for this person. We'll decide how he gets dealt with, because if you fuck about here in Warrington, you answer to us. This group. You're accountable, to this group here. And don't worry – I'll handle the policeman,' said Art.

'This ain't the eighties,' Guppo sighed. 'We offing people now?'

Henry Hoover finally shut off, leaving a charged crackle.

'Find him, lads,' Ross said. 'Do whatever you need to make it happen. Shake down whoever you have to, kick down whatever doors you think need opening, look at everyone in the past who may have been less than happy or you think might have foolishly grown a pair of bollocks. But final say goes through me, no alternative.'

'Ross, *Jesus*,' sighed Murray. 'I know things are shit and what happened to Connor, it's just—'

'I'm going to see Brendan now,' interrupted Art. 'So get started. Phones on.' He patted his breast pocket with a slight nod. The other men nodded back, one or two slower than the others – except for Guppo, who didn't nod at all. 'Back here at 8 p.m.'

'Can we make it nine?' asked Murray. 'Gives the kids more chance to get to sleep before I dip out.'

Art sighed. Childcare, for Christ's sake? Guppo was right – this definitely wasn't the eighties anymore.

CHAPTER 18

FOLEY WAS NERVOUS. A break, no matter how grand or small the case, would do that to you. He wanted to chuck himself into it headlong, but as senior investigating officer, especially on something as big as this, he knew he had to do everything with protocol and caution. Monroe was over his shoulder, and he didn't have any leeway even for just a spoonful of fuck-up.

By the time Madison got back to the station, he was waiting for her and followed her into the Ladies locker room.

Her eyes flicked up. 'You're in the Ladies, boss.'

'So I am.'

'Bit of privacy?'

Foley turned around and faced the lockers, leaning his forehead against the metal with eyes shut. 'Start talking.'

She gave him a quick rundown of her visit to the steelworks front in Stetchford detailing the chat she'd had with a 'bloke she ran into', swerving the whole sweet left hook thing that had got him chatty in the first place.

'It does look like organised crime is the right way to go, however unlikely that seemed yesterday,' she said, grabbing a pre-made protein shake from her locker.

He banged his forehead against the locker, as if stamping the plan. 'We need CRB checks on every victim as soon as they are IDed, and to look for markers of organised crime involvement.'

She closed her locker door. 'You know that will ask questions of your nephew too?'

He nodded. He was nervous about that, but he was a realist.

They headed back to the main pool, where the investigative team was reassembling, but before Madison had even sat down, Foley was out of the traps.

'Sir. Karthik. The trench. As you expected?' he said.

Wainwright was sitting with his legs crossed, nursing a polystyrene coffee cup. It was emblazoned with the name of a national coffee titan, as opposed to the station's plainer offerings –

he'd obviously had to stop for something stiffer on the way back from the crime scene. He nodded without conviction.

As for Karthik, his entire energy had changed. He slouched, but gave a thumbs up, with a determined look in his eye. Foley was impressed and gave him a nod in return.

'Right,' Foley continued, 'I'll get to the phones in a minute, because I think what I'll say next might throw any news you have through a different lens.'

The team stilled.

'Madison went to check up on that second IDed victim down Birmingham way, and has come up with a very strong organised crime connection.'

His team were rapt.

'And I managed to get a video from the witness who called in the tip about the trench. Long, sordid story behind the video, best saved for over beers when we've put a big shiny bow on this one, but what I saw on it does strongly suggest a further organised crime involvement – namely that there were two men at the scene, covering up the grave. Seabreeze is working on getting the clearest image of them he can for use in enquiries.'

Hoyt shot his hand up. 'You have any idea of IDs? The footage suggest anything?'

'No, but that might just be me. If they're known in Warrington, someone here in the nick might recognise them, you lot included. We'll know when Seabreeze has something for us to circulate. Failing that, at the very least we'll have a nice parting gift for the Home Office guys and their facial recognition toys. Anything extra from the scene today, sir?' He looked at Wainwright.

Wainwright pursed his lips before speaking. 'Not that you don't already know. Gavigan says it's been hell wading through that scene.'

'I bet. That reminds me, when we get the pictures of our grave-diggers, we need to get a look at where they're standing – might be able to point Gavigan after prints.'

'Did the video show which way they headed out?' asked Christopher, pointing with a chewed HB pencil.

'Good thinking but no – it cut out beforehand. But you might be able to make the odd inference. At least enough to point Gavigan in the right direction for prints in the wider vicinity.'

A voice echoed under the high ceilings, drifting towards the incident space. 'Detective Foley?'

Foley saw Morgan, the station desk sergeant, imploring him to come over.

'Madison, please could you fill everyone in on Birmingham? I'll be right back.' He dropped everything and left – not before catching an eye-roll from Wainwright, who clearly hadn't got his head around his current position in the investigation's chain of command.

Foley ascended the steps.

'I'm sorry, Detective Foley. I wouldn't intrude if I thought it could wait,' Morgan said, splaying her hands across her uniform trousers. Foley could see her discomfort. 'It's a family thing, and considering the… day your family must be having, I thought I'd make the exception.'

'I appreciate that,' Foley said, without really appreciating it at all. Morgan was only trying to do the right thing, but Foley didn't want the interruption, and the word *family*, considering the turn the case was taking, made him uncomfortable.

They left the main hall and dropped into the much cooler, darker corridors.

'Interview room two,' Morgan said. 'I'll keep it free for as long as you need.' She placed a hand on his shoulder before leaving. However misguided her sincerity was, he was somewhat touched by it.

Room two was only a few yards away, another broom cupboard converted, this time into something resembling a meeting place. As he got there, the frosted glass of the door window revealed nothing, but he had a feeling…

There was someone he'd have to face sooner or later, and he tried to change his mindset into accepting that now was as good a time as any. He opened the door.

'I thought it might be you,' he said, as he saw his father sitting on a plastic chair.

'Brendan,' Art said, rising, his features soft with compassion. He opened his arms to embrace his son. 'I haven't seen you, not since… I've been calling you—'

Foley put a rigid hand up to halt both his father's words and his proposed embrace. 'Just… hold it, Dad.'

Art looked surprised and hurt. 'I don't understand. I thought—'

'The way things are shaping up, I was going to have to pull you into an interview room sooner or later. This is saving me the effort.' Foley pointed at the chair. 'Sit back down please.'

Art bristled. 'I'm your father – some civility wouldn't go amiss.'

'You'll get civility when you've explained a few things.' Foley took a seat on the other side of the table, and again motioned to the empty chair opposite. 'This conversation is unofficial – so far. I hope we can keep it that way.'

'You're treating me like one of your suspects here, Brendan.'

'How honest are you going to be, Dad?'

'I'm not following, son. I came here to ask you to step down from the investigation.' Art sat down and looked imploringly over the tabletop. 'Looking for the killer of your nephew. For God's sake, it's not *healthy*. It's not good for you. Mim agrees.'

'You've been to see my *wife*?'

'Of course I have. You're supposed to be at home, Brendan, supporting your family! I found your wife crying on the stairs at your place. Your kids are exhausted, she didn't even know if Dan had made it to school... That's where a man's place is when the world goes to pieces – at home, looking after his family.'

'I *am* looking after my family. I'm in charge of finding out who killed Connor.'

'You have a lead?'

'Organised crime, Dad. Your nephew was murdered, and our strongest lead is organised crime. You have anything to say about that?'

Foley could only hope his father was not the man he used to be.

'Brendan, what are you asking me? You can't possibly be suggesting...'

'Are you clean? Today, right now. Are you clean?'

'I've never taken drugs in my life.'

'You know that's not what I'm talking about.'

'Brendan—'

'Are you responsible for Connor's murder?'

'Jesus *Christ*, Brendan!'

'If this grave turns out to be a dumping ground for organised crime hits, what will you say?'

'Enough!' Art shouted, before looking at the door. There was something there, Foley caught it. He knew it well enough. *Fear*. The kind of fear Foley had carried his entire career: that someone would tap him on the shoulder and bring the past into the present. 'Enough... I can't help certain things that happened a long time ago, but *family*... everything's changed. I've always been clean, Brendan, despite what you may think.'

'We both know that's a lie.'

'I cleaned up my act, and everything has been above board since.'

'What about those greasy muppets you hang out with at that farm club?'

'Friends, Brendan. I'm not a man to turn his back on his friends. Me? I'm clean as a whistle and have been for nearly twenty years.'

Foley thought about this, searching his mind for early memories of his father. The late-night visitors at home, waking up to find his dad out, birthday parties with lots of attendees who he hadn't seen in years. The stories he knew of what his father had got up to, told to him by his brother and his father himself, but never voiced in any other circles.

His career hung on those stories staying in the past. Memories and nothing else. When he applied for the police force fast-track inspector programme, he had kept his fingers crossed the whole way through the process, through every exam, every last interview, that nothing would come up in his family history. It never happened, but he was always expecting to be hooked into a side room and given his marching orders. That feeling had only receded a couple of years ago. Now, here they were, investigating murders with an organised crime flavour, where one of the victims was the grandson of a supposedly retired crim.

When Foley thought of it in such stark terms, it didn't sound remotely good.

'What you claim you are, or what you used to be… The idea that Connor's death has nothing to do with you, I mean do you know how fanciful that sounds?'

Art flushed ruddy. 'What are you accusing me of?'

Foley pushed his face close and hissed words he'd long thought of but never truly dreamed he'd have to say. 'Do you have any idea how hard I've worked for this career? To get here, against the odds of what my dad used to do in his spare time?'

Foley abruptly rose from the chair opposite his dad. 'I've heard you. I've heard you protest your innocence, but the fact you're here says a lot to me, and it's not good. I think you're here because you want to see whether you're implicated, and I can tell you, you *are*. From here on, never mind every bugger else, I'm investigating you.'

Art laughed. 'You're not investigating me. I've done nothing wrong.'

'Well, we'll find that out, won't we?' Foley was out the door, looking for Madison – the surge to come clean to somebody blooming in his chest. Her professionalism was both impressive and intimidating. For some reason he couldn't quite place, she was the only person at the nick he felt he could trust with something like this, something so sensitive, especially when the topic was family secrets. He could maybe go to Hoyt, possibly Christopher, but nobody else. Not Wainwright – Wainwright would fucking love it, and the investigation would be his.

Art paced after him. 'Brendan, this is a family issue. You've got to stop!'

'Son, you know your family needs you. You know you need to leave this case behind. You're not seeing clearly! Accusing me – *me!* – of having anything to do with this. Can't you see how wrong you are? Let's sort this out at home like fathers and sons do.'

But Foley was through the door into the main hall, his father in hot pursuit, even though he knew he shouldn't be there. Art's voice crashed into the space, and heads popped up above desks. Foley saw his colleagues' gazes switch from surprise to pity, assuming they were watching a senior detective's family crumble under the pressure of grief.

They didn't know the half of it. Nobody did.

He signalled to Madison, tried to call her over, but he stopped on the top step, when Art grabbed him.

'Son, stop! Listen to me, stop what you're doing and listen—'

Foley suddenly felt a rush of bitterness and resentment fresh and hot. He threw his father's hand away. *How hard it had been to cast off this man's shadow.* 'Get the fuck off me, you fucking disgrace.'

'You—' Art grabbed his son, and Foley could see the panic and fear in his father's face. Of being outed, right in the middle of the cop shop. Foley shoved him off, but Art quickly came back at him, despite the older man's size. Somehow, they were on the top steps, and in between Art's panic and Foley's anger, they began to scuffle – and slowly lose their balance.

They tumbled from the top step, Foley banging hard off the concrete floor, while Art rolled down the steps. They landed in an undignified heap at the bottom. An excited murmur broke across the hall, the atmosphere cranked up a notch.

Foley reached over to his father, his ribs screaming in pain, his shoulder not much better, and tried to pull his dad's arm around and up his back. His mind primed the words – *You're under arrest* – when other hands pulled him roughly away and dragged him back. His father's crumpled form made the disgraceful scene more stark with every backwards step. The last thing he saw before he was whisked around and marched back up the steps was his team staring at him, frozen with incredulity.

He shook off the hands that held him, turned and walked away, leaving his dad alone and in pain, spread out on the floor.

CHAPTER 19

MONROE'S OFFICE WAS warmer than usual, even more so when Brendan had just had a rumble with his father. Brendan felt hot in the face. He'd buggered right up. The extra personnel in the room didn't help his composure. Brendan, Art, Wainwright and Monroe were all present, the three settling on one side of the desk facing the super on the other, who was on the cusp of aneurysm. As they'd sat down, Brendan had caught Wainwright's smug expression. *Opportunistic dick.*

'Mr Foley Senior, I fully recognise that this must be a hugely difficult time for your family, but a police station is no place at all for family discussion – not least when we are clearly at the outset of a very demanding and sensitive investigation.'

Art stayed silent, listening with thick blankness.

'As for you, DI Foley, I just…' Monroe sighed heavily. 'I was worried about letting you persist as SIO, you know that. I was worried that the added strain would be too much for you – that managing an emotion as charged as grief while trying to conduct a clean, impartial investigation would be a bridge too far. But this *fiasco* has turned out worse than I feared.'

'I understand your concern but if you'll just listen—' Brendan appealed.

'I listened the first time, and I gave you a chance. You've had the case a matter of hours and look at *this*.' Monroe glanced heavenward but only found the cracked ceiling tiles overhead, before bringing his gaze back down. 'Foley, I am *so* sympathetic to your position, I really am. Christ knows, I'd want the same chance to do right by my family if I were in your shoes. But this scene you two caused should never have happened, and it is on my head that it did. The only positive I can think of is that it didn't take place in the public eye.'

Brendan ran a hand across his hair. 'Five minutes, just give me five minutes, DS Madison and an interview room.'

'No. Wainwright?' Wainwright looked up at the super with a sleek innocence. 'Are you up to speed?'

'I am, boss.'

'Then it's yours and I'll extend the same advice I gave your predecessor: don't fuck it up.'

'Will not, sir.'

'You're making a huge mistake here,' interjected Brendan.

'I've already made one mistake in this investigation. I don't intend to make another.' Monroe's voice was firm, clear, devoid of anything resembling compromise.

'Why did you want to interview your father?' Wainwright asked.

Brendan looked between the super and the new SIO, then at his dad.

Wainwright was a detective of old pedigree. You didn't get twenty years in his position without having the nose for it – and he certainly smelled something off. Monroe caught where Wainwright was going and looked at Brendan questioningly.

Brendan had to think fast, scrambling quickly for a silver lining. He was never going to let this go, but if he was off the case he could go in a different direction. One that didn't follow the same rules.

'What's my position here?' he asked.

Monroe answered almost immediately. 'Suspension doesn't have the right sound to it.'

'In a PR sense, right?' Brendan quipped cynically.

'You're bloody right. *Force suspends grieving detective* is not a great headline. It's leave. Compassionate leave is what we are going to call this, and it's in place until further notice.'

The corner of Wainwright's lip curled.

'And this conversation stays in this room, and I mean, *this room*,' Monroe barked, before pointing at Wainwright. 'Any leak, I'll know where it's come from. Jesus, Foley – *Brendan* – go home, get your head right, be with your family. They need you.'

'That's what I've been trying to tell him,' Art said.

Monroe considered him for a moment, then looked back at Brendan. 'Usually at such times, families are united in grief. But you two… What are you falling out about?'

Brendan looked at his dad, his head swimming.

Should he tell Monroe to investigate his father, not as a murder suspect but as a person of interest? Tell him about his father's past?

But that would surely turn this suspension into a sacking. *Leave* would become *left*. And Brendan had worked too hard to lose everything now. He couldn't give up. Not yet. Not on his career, and not on his nephew Connor. He could still get a result if he played this a certain way.

'Nothing,' he said. 'I was just angry and trying to get rid of him.'

Art looked at Brendan, trying desperately to suppress his surprise. 'I shouldn't have come in,' he said. 'We're just such a mess. His brother is in pieces, the whole family needs him.'

'Well, now you've got him. Go on, off you go,' Monroe said, dismissing them all, before adding, 'Wainwright, 4 p.m., I'll be over to the MIR for a full report.'

'Yes, sir,' he said, before standing up.

Brendan breathed out, said, 'I'm sorry,' and left, without sparing his father a glance.

FOR THE PAST ten minutes Madison had sat unsure at her desk, breaking only to ask Hoyt and Christopher what was going on, but they were as baffled as she was.

The case was gaining momentum and direction, but when the SIO was involved in a fracas like that, she knew something had to be afoot.

She listened to the gossiping voices from outside the separating walls and heard the word *dad* used more than once. She tried not to jump to any conclusions.

Finally, her phone buzzed in her pocket.

She pulled it out to find a text from Foley:

I've been binned. W now SIO. Keep it quiet but can u meet tonight? The plough, hg – 8 p.m. BF

What on bloody earth was going on?

PART 2

THE OLD KING

ROB PARKER

CHAPTER 20

MOSTON HAD SACKED off school before, but never all afternoon. He'd got through the morning, but by lunchtime his hamstrings were tired from nimming – or at least, that's what his gran called that endless leg jiggling when a person has too much nervous energy and nowhere to put it. When he sat down in the college café for a bacon butty, he felt like he'd run the Great North Run twice.

His sixth form college didn't have a uniform, so blending in with the general public on a bleary Monday afternoon wasn't going to be a problem. He didn't even have to take off a tie, not like at one of those posh ones, not like North Weston where Connor went.

Went.

That's how quickly it kept rearing up in his mind.

That's why he'd run.

When his classmates had all started filing back into the corridors, he'd put his rucksack in his locker and gone out the fire escape the cool kids used as a secret fag exit. After lunch, nobody was there, everyone fed and nicotined, so it was a clean break.

He'd crossed the Astroturf pitches, following the yellow balloon floating high above a car showroom on the edge of town. He'd come out near the community gym, which doubled as a business centre. He ducked inside to get rid of that energy, and work on his guns. They'd been getting bigger, he was sure of it.

He hit the gym for a solid thirty minutes, avoiding the leg machines because he'd never be caught dead in anything less than three-quarter-length pants anyway, even when swimming. He didn't care about getting big hench legs. He worked his triceps twice, his biceps four times and his shoulders once, flexing in between and having regular water breaks. He knew how important it was to be hydrated when working out. He paused by the chest press but didn't give it a go. He suspected he couldn't press as much as he could lift, and he didn't want anyone to see that. So he polished his guns some more.

He had so much energy, and now so much time to kill, that he went for a swim. He hated the breast stroke, that stupid dipping and scooping that made you look like a proper bell-end, so he went with front crawl, but he was out of practice, and ended up thrashing in twenty-yard bursts before chilling out. That prick of a lifeguard had taken him out of the fast lane, and put him in the slow one with the mash heads, not knowing he'd already done a monster workout. He'd spent some time relaxing in the shallows, before swapping into the middle lane when the lifeguard wasn't looking.

Moston hung about for most of the next half hour or so, until it began getting closer to half two. He'd need to get home at the usual time before his mam caught wind of what he'd been up to. He took one last sit in the Jacuzzi and had a quick scope for any birds. When none appeared, he leaned his head back, dropped his ears below the surface, and listened to the soft drum of bubbles.

Holy *shit*, what a weekend. The absolute high of ripping off that cash point – nobody else at college had ever come near to any of that – to the crap-yourself low of Connor's disappearance… and then the news breaking of his body being found.

Moston didn't know what the hell Connor got up to in his own time, what his family were involved with, but he knew that he, Darren Moston, was smarter than to get himself into something that would get him killed.

An ATM was a big do for a young lad, but not big enough to get yourself iced into an early grave. Besides, it was most likely a serial killer, Connor taking a wrong turn after they'd stashed the cash point, and nowt to do with anything more than bad luck. The cash bonus he'd been given was probably a happy accident for the sick fuck who killed him.

He saw the pool clock read 2.55.

Shite. He'd have to run.

He legged it for the showers – not the public ones, mind you, not where any paedo or perv could take a gander at your bollocks and save the image in a wank bank so old it'd have to be played back on cinefilm. No, he ignored the signs and went straight through, on to the showers past the bogs. Ran it hot, nipped back to his locker for his clothes, and back in the cubicle in time for the steam. Good for the pores, it said in *GQ*.

He threw the cubicle door shut, checking the Casio he kept in his shoe – *2.58, shit, shit!* – but it didn't bang shut. Turning, Moston was faced with a man. He was bald, broad, between his mam and his gran in age, and had a twinkle in his eye.

The first thing that crossed his mind was how relieved he was he wasn't naked. The second thing was pure outrage that one of the old pervs he'd been worried about actually had the gall to get in a cubicle with him.

He started to say, '*Fuck off, sicko—*' when he noticed the third thing – the knife. It travelled so fast it split the air between them with a hiss.

It hit just below his ribcage, dead centre, with a sound that reminded him of one time a while back when he'd kicked a dog in the head. He remembered that dog's whimper, that look of species-to-species betrayal in its reaction, as something bloomed in his chest – an apple bursting with nothing but hot sauce, before things felt weird and distant. He dropped to his knees suddenly and began to tip forward.

'Ah, bollocks,' said the man in a broad Liverpudlian accent, as he looked down at the boy slumping into his shins with his face resting against his hip.

'You all right in there?' said another man, his voice equally Scouse but muffled beyond the cubicle partition.

'Aye, mate.' But things weren't all right. The lad was leaking red all over his new trainers. He moved to one side, and the boy folded forward again, bouncing his nose off the cubicle door – not that it caused any reaction. He was on his way out. 'Sorted.'

The man looked down at his shoes. He knew he shouldn't have worn them, but because they were following the kid to the gym, he'd chosen them so he'd fit in. Now they were already halfway to ruined. Pristine Nike Airs in neon green, with bloody streaks all over the laces. But at a glance it didn't look like blood, more as though he'd river-danced in dogshit.

He pulled the kid up from behind, two arms round his waist, which forced a final-sounding exhalation from the kid's mouth. He dumped him in the shower, landing with a dull thump.

'How's Dixie?' he asked the lookout, who was outside sitting on a bench, pretending to write a lengthy email on his phone.

'Grand, but you need to get a wriggle on, lad.'

The man looked down at the kid, who was staring back at him, breathing in shallow little bursts, his gaze all glassy shock and end of days. He didn't like doing the kid, but he didn't altogether totally dislike it either.

Rules. We all had them.

The man had them. He stuck to his.

Darren Moston had them. He hadn't.

'Go on then,' the man said, and after a few scuffles on the other side, a huge cricket bag was passed over the top of the cubicle.

The events of the past few days were forcing them all to be a bit more inventive. He was enjoying the variety.

'Ta,' he said, as he took the bag. It was enormous, but perfect for the job.

The boy looked at the bag, then looked back at him, just as he unhooked the shower head, yanked the shower on, and angled the jet at the blood pooling beneath the kid's body.

'Naughty boys,' the man said in mock admonishment. Then he sprayed the boy's blood down the plug hole.

CHAPTER 21

MIM WAS STILL sitting in the front window, waiting for Dan to come home. Her usual coping mechanism in crisis was to keep busy, but with Mick around, she couldn't do anything except babysit. She knew she shouldn't call it babysitting when she was looking after her own child (that's just *parenting*), but as the hours wore on, and she heard nothing from anybody, she felt less and less like she had a purpose. She was nothing more than a grief pillow, waiting for someone to come and cry into it.

Siobhan hadn't got back to her. Some people united unexpectedly with grief, and she'd half thought this might happen. Not so far.

Mick was by the sofa, jumping in a free-standing baby bouncer – the ever-present Bun Bun throttled in his left hand. He was happy for hours in there, and it was probably her favourite development in the baby-care world in the fifteen years between the infancies of her two children. She could leave him and get on with things. Sometimes, when he'd been in there a while and she'd almost forgotten about him, she called it the circle of neglect.

His blond curls were bouncing as relentlessly as his little pumping legs when Brendan's car pulled up and she felt a rush of hope and elation. She'd got to a point midway through the afternoon where she'd refused to believe how much she wanted him to be home. She didn't want to be one of those women who were nothing without their husbands, and she knew deep down she wasn't. But she needed him. And it infuriated her.

She watched him get out of the car. From the look on his face, she knew immediately that something had gone wrong. She left the living room, Mick's neck twisting to follow as he bobbed up and down, and met him at the door.

'Brendan, what's happened *now*?' she said as the front door opened. He was distant, his mind clearly turning over.

He kicked his shoes off. 'No hello?' The words stung, and he caught himself immediately. 'I'm sorry, I'm sorry. It's... How are you? How are the kids?'

'Fine and fine.' She shrugged it off as quickly as she could. 'Why are you home?'

'I'm…' He paused, and a curious weight seemed to build in him. 'I'm all right. But I'm off Connor's case. I'm on a sort of leave.'

'You what?' Mim said, but she knew she'd betrayed a little relief in her tone. She pushed on quickly. 'What did you do?'

Unexpectedly, Brendan laughed. 'I had a scrap with my dad, and we both fell into the empty pool we call an office.'

Mim's jaw sagged.

'Apparently it's bad form when you're SIO,' Brendan clarified.

Mim hugged him; she had no clue what to say. A fight, at work? She felt an acute stab of guilt when she realised that the altercation must have happened after Art had been to see her.

'Is he OK?' she asked into his shoulder.

'Yeah, he's fine, the stubborn old git.'

Mim sensed that he was holding something back. 'Dan should be home soon,' she said. 'I'm sure he'd love to see you.'

The thought of his own teenage son seemed to shake Brendan back into the moment. 'How's he doing?'

'I honestly don't know. Numb, I think.'

'You told him?'

'I had to. Do you think I could hide something like that?'

'It should have been me. I'm sorry. Maybe Dad was right, after all. What time will he be back?'

'Should be in the next half an hour, or so. Mick's through here.' She led the way into the living room.

'There he is! There's the big lad.' Brendan picked the boy up and kissed him on the bridge of his thimble nose.

'If you're home, we could really do with some family time tonight.'

Brendan paused, and Mim knew her suggestion wasn't going to happen.

'What?' she asked.

'I can't.'

'Why not?'

'I have to see Madison.'

'Why? You're on leave!'

'I'm on *sort of* leave. I can't let this go, baby. She'll keep me in the loop.'

'What am I missing here?' She wasn't ever the jealous type, but she could feel anger rising. 'You know, lesser women might be a bit disturbed by their husband going off to meet another woman at a time of family crisis.'

'Oh, don't, Mim, please.' There was a flatness to his tone. 'You're not like that, and you know full well I've never given you reason to be.'

'You've not answered my question.'

'I need to keep an eye on this, and she'll be able to help me do that. The case was just breaking. I need to know what's going on.'

'Why? What good will it do?'

'Jesus, because I don't trust Wainwright, and I don't trust him to get this right either. He's a career man, he's not invested in this. He's not Connor's godfather, he's not his uncle. I can't let this go. Not yet. Don't make me, Mim, please.'

Mim knew her husband inside and out, and his dogged qualities both attracted her and frustrated her in equal measure. His intentions were always honourable, at least in her experience.

She sighed. 'I know you wouldn't listen even if I told you not to.' She sat down, and it was only then that she noticed Mick had gone quiet, his eyes big as saucers as he looked from face to face. Brendan caught it too and squeezed the little boy close. This always happened when blood ran hot and thick – you forgot what it does to your kids. That steady erosion of trust and innocence.

The front door went. Brendan passed Mick over to Mim and walked out into the hallway, to find his son. His eyes were puffy and his cheeks raw.

'Why?' he said, and his backpack tumbled to the floor. He started to shake.

'Come here, son,' Brendan said, as he rushed to his elder boy.

CHAPTER 22

SAFIN DIDN'T WANT to be under this goddamn pier at five in the evening, peek-a-booing with the maritime authorities. But needs must, and prices were worth the risk.

Brexit had boosted trade in the dark underworld markets miles from either London or Brussels. Safin had left his homeland of Lithuania for the northern shores of Wales, where his skills as a trawlerman working out of Klaipeda applied just as nicely in the Irish Sea.

But then, like a thief in the night, Brexit sneaked in the back door. The tightening of customs and the OTT checking protocols that existed immediately after Brexit sent most of the local fishermen out of business in less than a month. If your freshly caught live product ends up stuck at the border for hours, it tends to die – and the market turns elsewhere.

Local fishermen had to adapt, and they did. Consequently, ports were dead during the day, but vibrant under the cover of darkness. North Wales had always been a tourist trap for the north-west of England, and those visitors loved a good polystyrene goblet of whelks, cockles or fresh crab. And Safin knew just where to get them.

Health and safety dictated he shouldn't be anywhere near the north pier between the dark hours of 5 p.m. and 7 a.m., but needs must. He couldn't sell what he used to, boat opportunities were lower than ever, so hide and seek with a bucket and fishing net was what it was. Pillar seventeen on the left was a magnet for sea life, thanks to its proximity to an active oil pipe on the bottom. It offered an unseasonal pocket of warmth. Safin had two kids in a half-decent school getting an education that was leagues ahead of his own. So off the struts he hung, dangling where the disused pier boards had given way to allow his body to slide through. He hung, like a sea-blown, bearded Spider-Man, throwing his net in, and slowly pulling it out.

It was cold, very cold. Another two weeks and he wouldn't be able to do this. Keep throwing, keep pulling.

First few throws offered a couple of barnacles, a few bottle caps. Some kelpy dregs. Not a shred to get excited about. Another chuck, another tug, while the sun started its freezing tilt into the icy horizon. Safin started to pull his net when it caught on something. Confused, he gave it a couple of fierce tugs, but it was stuck fast. *Shit.* He couldn't lose another net. They weren't cheap, and it would mean going home with less than he came for. Not an option.

He took a second to assess whether he'd actually latched onto something worth trying to haul in. He braced against the weight beneath the surface, and tried to hold as still as he could, feeling for any kind of movement.

Nothing.

The water was a pale greenish-blue, with visibility down to a handful of feet at most. He knew it wasn't deep here, maybe ten feet tops. He had a mad thought about diving down there to pull his net free from the snag. It would soak him to the marrow, but at least he'd still have his net. He looked into the bag over his shoulder. He was always dragging fish about in it, from market to stall to mongers. Today, though, it was barely half full. He couldn't go home yet. He hadn't caught nearly enough.

He lowered himself as far as he could, wrapping his legs around one of the slippery crossbeams, tightening his thighs and praying he wouldn't slip. He peered into the murky water, his nostrils filling with the scent of brine. He still couldn't see anything...

Wait.

A shape, unnatural. A perfect, shining straight line below him. It was an edge, a box, part of something that was receding into the blue fog. He could see a smaller yellow rectangle below it, faintly, but couldn't get a proper fix on it thanks to the churning waves. But this thing was what his net had caught on, he felt sure. The sea was full of garbage, and he was always sifting through it. It had never beaten his ability to provide for his family, and he wasn't about to let it start now.

He tugged sharply on his net, and while he felt no give, he certainly saw the shape below shift slightly. It gave him encouragement. He stretched his arm out as far as he could and gave another sudden yank. The same result, except for a thin trail of bubbles from just below where the shape began to fade. Safin felt that same sense of wonderment that had characterised his relationship with the sea ever since he was a small boy. He was fascinated with the deep blue, and the fact there were things down there in it he couldn't see. He started yanking rhythmically, and the bubbles started to grow in size.

Then it happened all at once.

One pull brought a sudden release of movement. The shape moved, dragging a smaller yellow one with it. As soon as Safin saw the yellow rectangle with its black lettering, he realised it was a number plate. A cloud of bubbles burst out, boiling up to the surface – accompanied by two bloated corpses, breaching less than a foot from Safin's horrified face.

CHAPTER 23

SHE'D NEVER BEEN there before, but that didn't stop Madison from getting to the Plough early. She ordered a sparkling water and took it to a booth, ignoring the barman's look of open surprise. The booth faced a flat screen showing a darts tournament. Football played on another screen behind her head. Down at the far end of the bar, where the pub's only fruit machines lingered like boxy ghosts, a handful of men in dodgy suits and limp, de-noosed ties were loudly ordering another round. They were giving a crude commentary to the barmaid, one that that would have earned each of them the right to dine through a straw if they'd spoken to Madison like that. The barmaid, however, was clearly used to it, returning flirty smiles along with their pints. Madison sighed, as her mind drifted back to Foley's message from earlier:

I've been binned. W now SIO. Keep it quiet but can u meet tonight? The plough, hg – 8 p.m. BF

When she read it she'd had to do her breathing trick to calm down, wondering what on earth was going on. But she'd done as he'd asked and now, here she was. She sat watching the darts, marvelling at how times had changed. Gone were the sips of beer between arrows, each player now with a glass of water on the table behind them, and behaving respectfully to one another. As a toddler, she'd crawled all over her dad on Saturday afternoons watching *Grandstand*, enjoying the belligerence of Eric Bristow. He had the confidence and swagger of an elite boxer, despite practising a whole different form of pugilism. Maybe that's where she got her love of that sport from too.

She took off her suit jacket and dropped it on the seat next to her. What a day it had been. And now this. Meeting her boss after hours, even though he wasn't her boss anymore. At least not at the moment. It all made her uncomfortable.

After Foley's fight with his dad, Madison had stuck behind, along with Hoyt and Christopher. Brendan had assembled his team personally, favouring youth and local knowledge. They'd all had raises and career progression because of it, and he'd proved himself

107

a fair and determined leader. He placed faith in them, and they returned it. Nevertheless, Madison hadn't told Hoyt or Christopher about her meeting with him tonight.

And now, here he was. Brendan carried a pint of Guinness towards her.

'I saw you had a full drink,' he said, as he got to the table, 'but if I'd known it was water I'd have shouted.'

He paused for a second at the head of the booth.

'It's sparkling, I've really pushed the boat out,' she replied.

'Oh, you shouldn't have.' Brendan sat down and pulled his Guinness in front of him. He stared into it, watching the white horses race in the glass as the pint settled.

She watched him, waited for him to speak.

'I'm sorry about today,' he said eventually, 'and I'm sorry for letting the whole team down.'

Madison had a quick look around before speaking. The bar was quiet. One older man in the booth next door but he looked more interested in his pint than anyone else. Still, she lowered her voice.

'I'm amazed you lasted as long as you did. Brendan, these are *not* normal circumstances.' She took a gulp of sparkling water; her stomach groaned in reply. She was starving. That prep meal at lunch felt a long time ago. She was nervous. In fight week, she needed to be eating regularly, and on schedule. Not just to keep on weight, but to make sure she had enough energy for the fight itself. Everything she consumed now was building to peak on fight night, and she'd measured it out diligently. And now one prep meal sat in the fridge at home, *Monday night* scrawled in Sharpie up the side.

She suddenly realised she'd called him Brendan and her face coloured. 'Sorry, sir.'

'Don't be daft, Iona. You're off duty, and I'm not a cop – for now. Arsing about with formalities seems a bit OTT, don't you think?'

Madison tried to settle into the new dynamic. It was like breaking in a new glove at the gym. 'How are you doing? Stupid question, but I'd feel even more stupid if I didn't ask.'

'Family's gone to bits, if I'm honest. I haven't seen my brother since I told him, but I know it's bad. His wife's gone down to stay with her folks in Cardiff. Mim seems solid—'

'That's your wife, right?'

'Aye. She's devastated, but she's levelled about it. Then you've got my son, Dan, who's a mess. He wasn't even that close to Connor, not recently at least. They'd become different lads. Probably a blessing considering how bad he is tonight. And my dad, well, you saw what happened there…'

'I bloody well did. Tensions running high?'

He took a long sip of his Guinness, watching her over the rim of the glass. He wiped a hand across his mouth. 'Look, I'm just going to come out with it.' The change in direction caught her cold. 'I need you to keep me in the loop, Iona.'

Straight away, that unnerved her. 'You just said you weren't a cop at the minute.'

'I know.'

'That could properly screw up my career. No offence.'

Brendan shifted in his seat and leaned forward. 'I know what I'm asking of you. I'll protect you if it comes out – tell them I pressurised you into it, used some senior cop force.'

'Now you're talking about messing up your own career too.'

'Iona, my career is the last thing I'm thinking of at the minute.'

'I assume you're going to look into this on your own?'

'I have to. Your sister, she's got kids, right?'

'She has.'

'Then imagine it… just for a second. You wouldn't be able to give up either.'

She hated the image he'd just put in her head. 'OK, I get it.'

'And let's face it. Neither you nor I think Wainwright's the one for the job here.'

Iona clinked her glass off his pint pot in silent agreement. 'We spent the rest of the day bringing him up to speed. Literally the whole afternoon. Hours lost.'

Brendan felt frustrated, even though he had no right to anymore. 'First forty-eight hours of the case are the most important, blah blah blah,' he said, repeating the old cop adage that was drummed into them. Brendan would have hated the cliché if it wasn't so damn true. 'It's quid pro quo. Whatever I find, I share with you. Whatever you find, you share with me. Please. I don't care who catches these fuckers first, I just want it done.'

Iona could see both the hopelessness of his position and the drive he still retained despite it. She didn't know why, but it didn't take her long to consider. 'OK.'

'Thank you.' He sat back, exhaling in relief. 'Now. What's the latest? Did anything change this afternoon?'

'Not much. Wainwright's keen to put his own stamp on things, so he's shifted things around, changed all the team roles. I didn't realise he was so methodical.'

'By methodical do you mean slow as hell?'

'Murderously.'

'What about the video? Did Jordan come up with some workable pics?'

'Yeah.' She pulled out her phone, scanned her emails and picked one. A grainy male face dominated the screen – sturdy jaw, weathered features. His bald head bounced a soft shard of moonlight. 'First one.'

His eyes flickered. 'Any ID?'

'Karthik's on it.'

'What avenues you going down?'

'The usual, with markers for organised crime. And it's going around the station like you suggested.'

'Good.' Brendan was thinking, she could tell.

'What?' She took a sip. 'Spit it out.' She liked these new terms of their relationship 'Do you recognise him?'

Something shut down in his expression and he shook his head, quickly taking another sip of Guinness. 'Nah. I thought so maybe... but no.'

She saw it instantly. He knew the bastard. And she knew he was hiding something.

So much for quid pro quo.

MY FUCKING GOD, thought the man in the next booth, his back to the couple talking. He wore a beanie hat, his faux-fur coat collar pulled up to his ears.

It had been a really unproductive day, but at least he'd managed to down a few pints while he got sod-all done. The scene was different, as he knew it would be, and the old faces had all either moved on or got old. As a last resort, Sandman Steadman had dropped into his local for one last pint before going home. While ordering, he'd noticed the fit bird sitting by herself with a face like a dropped pie.

He'd gone to sit in the booth behind her, not caring about the obvious age gap. Even young posh birds liked a bit of experienced rough from time to time, is what he told himself. He hadn't had sex in two years, not since a year before his divorce had even been mooted. She'd have been a hell of a way to break the drought. He bided his time, waiting for an opening, but cursed himself when some younger bloke beat him to it – and worse, he seemed to know her. He was about to call it when he was abruptly hit by a pang of recognition.

The voice.

Looking in the mirror, he couldn't believe he was seeing his mate's older brother, Brendan. The rozzer. He looked almost as harassed and beaten as his younger brother had earlier in the day. But that's where the lack of energy ended. This guy was buzzing, fit to burst, and spilling his guts to this girl. Turned out she was another rozzer. His day was looking up.

He leaned back and listened. He might be getting on, but his hearing was still spot on – he wasn't totally past it. By the time the two of them had finished blabbing, it was getting on for nine. For the first time all day, he felt hopeful. He still had time to get to the farm club and tell the rest of the gang all about it.

CHAPTER 24

ROSS WAS IN a bad state, and he knew it. At some point during the day, the fire of his rage had turned into a molten form of mania. He sat on the swings behind the farm club, and brooded.

The image of Connor's body on that steel counter was tattooed behind his eyelids, ready to stay with him forever.

He kicked the wood chips at his feet.

Ten to nine, he'd said. The kids' play area at the far side, he'd said.

A minute later, right on cue, a dot of white light started swaying towards him.

'Over here,' called Ross. The light stopped swaying, made a straight march to the swings and clicked off just a few feet from where Ross's feet were dangling. With the sudden glare gone, Ross could make out the familiar form of Whittle, with his old puffer jacket hood up too tight, pressing into his wild beard.

'Don't often hear from you on a school night,' said Whittle, taking the vacant swing next to Ross.

'This ain't any night,' Ross replied.

'No stories. No info. The less I know and all that.'

'Give over, you've been selling to me for years.'

'Best practice is best practice. You after the usual?'

'Not tonight. I just want control and focus. You get me?'

Whittle smiled with a sly spread of chapped lips. 'You working undercover for your brother? Seeing what you can fit me for? Class As look better on the balance sheet than a bit of skunk?'

'Fuck off, will you? What can you do for me?'

'Want to retain lucidity? Know what's going on around you?'

'Yeah. Edge off, but fully focused.'

'What are you used to?'

'Just some weed and the occasional 'E'. Need something to up my game.'

'Spit it out then. You're after white, aren't you?'

'I think it would probably work.'

Whittle pushed back on his feet and began swinging.

'You'd have to swear you ain't in league with your brother. And you'd have to do strip off to show you're not wired up.'

Ross was suddenly on his feet. 'Fuck off! If you think I'm working with that samaritan, you don't know me at all. Come to think of it, I don't really know you at all either, and now you're asking me to get me bollocks out in the park for you. Going funny on me?'

'All right, then you'd have to do it in front of me. That way, if you are informing to drugs squad, you'll be sharing your use of Class As too. That's a no-no in the force, so I'm told.'

'Fuck it, I'll just do it here then if you're gonna be a twat about it. How long will it take you to get it?'

'Abracafuckindabra.' He dug his heels into the ground and the swing abruptly stopped. He dropped his hand to his coat pocket. 'Get your phone out. PayPal me twenty.'

'Usual account?'

'Usual account.'

Ross did exactly as he was told, the phone screen casting cold blue light up his exhausted features.

'All right, there's no camera looking over this end of the property, but you can never be too sure. Now, nice firm handshake between old friends, feel it in your hand, into your pocket.' They shook hands. 'There you go, got it?'

'Yep.' Ross felt a little sliver of plastic on his palm, which he pulled back with his hand.

They stood for a moment, and Ross looked at the hulking shadow of the farm club in the dark.

'In front of me, remember,' Whittle reminded Ross – not that he needed reminding. He abruptly opened the tiny baggie with trembling hands.

'I need this now, anyway,' he said, and stuck his nose straight in the bag, snorting as if his grief would fizz up and sail away with it. The hit was slow at first and then instant, ice cubes on a hot stone, and the pain fell into the distance, if just for a glorious moment.

CHAPTER 25

'ANOTHER GUINNESS, salt and vinegar McCoy's and some of that ibuprofen you've got hidden away behind the till.' Art was balanced on the bar stool, but by God was it killing him to do so. No wonder those old swimming baths hadn't fallen over yet. They had clearly been built to last.

'I've not got owt like that back here, Artie, lad,' said Buzz. 'You'll have to nip to the offie, they'll have some.'

'Buzz, I'm on me last legs here. You've got a first-aid kit, right?'

'Health and safety says we do,' Buzz replied with undisguised sarcasm.

'And what's in it?'

Pam's voice drifted in from the back kitchen. 'A sling, a few safety pins, some antiseptic wipes, an eye patch and a handful of Peppa Pig plasters.'

'So, if we get a young pirate with a broken arm and a knee graze in here, we'll be just fine.' Ross had appeared out of nowhere, speaking slightly too quickly, smiling a little too widely. 'Guinness please, Buzz.'

With difficulty, Art turned around on the stool to look at his son. 'What's up with you?'

'Nothing, nothing, fine. The Guinness, Buzz – please.'

Art looked at him for a second more. Ross was on something. No one should be this perky when their son had just been murdered.

He turned back to the barman. 'On my tab, please, Buzz.' He handed his untouched pint to Ross. 'Take this one and head on over.'

Art watched him saunter to their usual booth, where Steadman was already sitting, the first to arrive.

'He's had a rough couple of days,' said Art.

'Not half. Tell you what, I'll get these,' said Buzz.

Despite the generosity, Art couldn't resist one more crack. 'All right. Considering your lack of painkillers, it's the least you can do.'

By the time Art arrived at the table, Ross was halfway through his pint, and hadn't even sat down yet.

Art leaned in close. 'What have you had?'

'Nothing, let's crack on.' Ross hadn't even looked at him. 'Where are the others?'

'They'll be here,' Steadman said, his eyes dancing with excitement. Art hadn't seen that look in his eyes in years – not since those old days.

'You've got something, haven't you?' said Ross, grinning. 'You lovely bastard, what have you got?'

'How are we doing?' Guppo had arrived, and immediately caught the vibe at the table. 'What's going on?'

'Steadman's got something,' said Ross. 'Where are the others?'

Guppo nodded to the bar. 'Earl's getting them in. I'm guessing Murray's kids aren't behaving.'

'We'll crack on without him, bring him up to speed when he lands,' Art decided, taking a seat.

As soon as Earl arrived, Steadman began talking fast.

'I've just been in the Plough. I saw your other son, the copper. You didn't tell us he was off the case.'

'There goes my bit of news,' sighed Art, genuinely a little put out.

'He's in there meeting another copper. Posh bird. They're discussing where they are up to with the case. Looks like she's going to be helping him from the inside. He's going to look into things on his own time.'

'Oh shite, that's all we need, that high-horse-riding twat going off on his own,' seethed Ross.

'Not necessarily. You see, we might have the edge on them.'

The group drew closer, hanging on Steadman's every word.

'They've got a couple of pictures from some bloody drone footage of the bastards burying Connor.'

'How'd they get that?' Ross interjected.

'That's not important. The bit you want to be paying attention to is the faces on the tape. She didn't recognise either, but he did.' He nodded at Art, whose heart chilled.

Art couldn't breathe for a moment. He found his voice again. 'Did you see it?'

'Nah,' Steadman said. 'If either of 'em realised someone was listening, let alone me, they'd have clammed right up. But when the totty went to the bog, he rang his wife – asked her where some old boxes were. My money says he definitely knew whoever was in that picture.'

Ross's face was volcanic.

'Looks like we need to have a good think here,' Art said quietly.

'Did they describe them in any way?' asked Earl.

'Nope. Your lad moved swiftly on,' replied Steadman, who leaned back in the booth.

'And this guy killed twenty-seven?' said Guppo. His only answer was the silence that stretched between the group. 'Then your pig son knows some fucking horrible people, Art.'

Before Art could respond, a thin stream of dark liquid was spouting across the table at Guppo, splashing in a line from his forehead, between his wide shocked eyes, and down to the middle of his belly.

Ross leaped forward and clamped a hand around Guppo's windpipe, pulling him towards the middle of the table. 'Did you do anything worthwhile today, you worthless sack of shit? Did you?'

Guppo didn't fight, but didn't bend, and stared stubbornly into Ross's wild pupils. He looked like he'd rather suffocate than relent, his cheeks beginning to redden.

Art placed a hand on Ross's arm. 'Let him go, Son – now.'

Ross threw Guppo back in his seat. Their eye contact never wavered.

'Let's keep it productive,' Earl said, giving everyone a chance to compose themselves. 'Task at hand and all that.'

'We went to Culliford,' he said, flicking his thumb between himself and Guppo. 'Had a look at that hole in the wall, had a mooch. Wanted to see if we could work out if events there had anything to do with Connor. Asked about a bit, you know.'

'Go on,' said Art.

'We're pretty sure Connor was there. Well, I'm a hundred per cent, but I won't speak for Guppo.'

'He was there,' said Guppo, wiping the Guinness from his face with a hand. His voice was scratchy.

Art nodded.

'We seen what they'd done too. Blew the whole thing out of the wall. Inventive, you'd have to give them that.'

'How'd they do it?' asked Steadman.

'They left nothing,' Earl said, 'but I saw the scuffs in the car park where the thing landed. Twenty feet easy. They blasted it out.'

Art couldn't help feeling a little proud. He'd always seen Connor as the one to take over the family name. Too late now.

'Who bankrolled it?' asked Guppo, his glance flickering to Art.

The job that Connor had been involved with must have involved resources like transport, materials and time, and that's before you get anywhere near something that could blow a cash machine out of a wall.

'Fitz couldn't have put that cash together, could he?' asked Earl. None of them were idiots, and though the game for them was cold, the taste of it was still in the back of their throats. They remembered the cut and thrust, the dirty thrill of everything they did. It was like having sex with someone you shouldn't – too shameful to admit to, but too exciting not to do. And above all else, they knew how those things worked.

Art felt growing discomfort. 'Fitz is a good lad, and a smart one too. I think he could have had the means if he put his mind to it.'

'All right, let's forget how it was done, for a minute. Why would Connor end up dead because of some cash machine job the night before?' asked Guppo. 'That's where my head is at. And if your pig son's right and it was someone you know... Is this something that needed to be sanctioned by big fish in the cities?'

Heads turned to Art. Nobody had voiced this yet, but Art's mind had been wrestling with this since it happened. When Art and the boys had been more active, organised crime in the area had been divided into patches, and you never pissed on anybody else's.

'Culliford's a Warrington spot, isn't it?' Guppo asked, his voice almost back to normal now.

Art stayed silent. Culliford was definitely a WA Warrington postcode, but it was on the periphery. It was an easy one to get wrong if you weren't totally clued in to the area and its territories.

'Yes, that's right. Dad?'

'Traditionally, yes,' Art answered carefully. He had to get this right. He could wrestle with the truth internally but couldn't handle blame from anybody else – let alone the son who was suddenly sonless. 'It's always been a bit up in the air, that one, because of where it is.'

'But it's Warrington?' pressed Guppo. 'Because if it's Warrington, it's ours. And nobody can touch it.'

Art sighed. 'Things aren't like how they were. The big Manchester and Liverpool organisations were very definite about what was or wasn't territory, and we carved out the middle, didn't we? I think Culliford is one of those grey areas, which is why Fitz may have thought he could go for it. Assuming that's why this happened.'

Art didn't mention that he'd instructed Fitz to go for it. Test the waters of Culliford's ownership with a small but well-executed crime. Art would find out whether any of the big boys still saw Culliford as belonging to them, because if nobody cared, there was an opportunity. But Art thought he had his answer now. The big fish did care, and he had one boy dead and two others missing because of it. All that blood, all on his hands.

Guppo rattled on. 'So, we can assume that Manchester or Liverpool saw Culliford as theirs, and one of them is responsible for killing the boy, right? And if we make that assumption, we can damn well assume that Fitz and the other kid are dead too.'

'That sounds about right,' Ross said in a quiet seethe.

'But,' said Earl, 'if it's one of the really big boys who did that, we can't tackle them.'

Guppo put a hand out into the middle of the table and it brought quiet. 'If Connor was killed and dumped in a hole by some gang or other, why are they doing it here? If Connor is retribution, then what are the other twenty-six doing in that hole? That hole on *our* turf?'

Art didn't like it one bit. Why here? If this was a territorial crime thing, and people were being killed because of ills over who owned what, then those same people were crossing those very borders to bury their corpses here. Why?

'I don't know,' he muttered.

'Assuming it's them, who are the big players in Manchester and Liverpool these days?' Earl wasn't letting this go. 'Hypothetically, what are we up against?'

Art didn't think he'd like the answer to that question either.

CHAPTER 26

MADISON STEPPED OVER the takeaway wrappers that littered the lobby. She lived on the third floor and took the lift, using the moment of solitude to get her head straight.

An insider. A mole. That's what her boss was asking of her.

The words were synonymous with corruption, and that wasn't what she was about. Yet she'd agreed.

This was a personal compromise. Her principles were at stake.

But were they? Her moral code was vital to her. By following Brendan Foley in his pursuit of a very pure justice, wasn't she simply backing up her own code?

The lift arrived on three, her door directly opposite it. She keyed the lock wearily.

It was too much to wade through, off the back of two unfathomable days. All she wanted to do was escape into a book, listen to some Michael Giacchino and drop into bed. If it weren't fight week, she'd chin some gin.

'Welcome home.' Hoyt was sitting on the couch, holding a half glass of red, his shirt collar pulled loose. He raised a second empty glass and gave her a smile of encouragement.

A half glass wouldn't hurt, surely? Seeing the way Hoyt read her needs like a book, she melted.

This. *This* is what she'd been missing.

'Shall we forget the shit for a bit?' Hoyt said.

'I can't think of anything better.' She went to him on the sofa and kissed Hoyt as hard as she dared without spilling the Tempranillo he was still holding.

THE HOUSE WAS pitch-black. The only creatures awake were the spiders and Brendan. He had his torch for company, and realised that if he'd been an arachnophobe, he'd never have made it any higher than the door. The attic was a mess, old boxes surrounding the rear eaves and chimney breast, newer boxes strewn everywhere else.

When they had moved in, they'd had the best intentions of avoiding a loft space that descended into disarray, but every time they came up, whatever needed storing was just put in the nearest available space, and the available gap into the room was getting smaller and smaller.

Mim had pointed Brendan in the right direction, so he knew roughly where the box he needed was. They had stored their keepsakes and childhood things in the same box. It was the pictures he was after.

In among the stacks of cardboard, there was a large, clear plastic storage box that had clips on the lid. That was the memory box he was looking for. He climbed over the plastic bags on the floor, wondering why they'd decided to keep any of this stuff in the first place, and made it to the stacks of old belongings. They were covered in dust, and a sprinkling of something darker. There was the soft ammonia scent of animal urine. Mice, rats, squirrels.

He saw the box he was searching for, its contents visible through the grime. He pulled it free but couldn't find a clean box to sit on to go through it, so he sat on the bare attic floorboards cross-legged like a schoolchild.

Unclipping the lid, nostalgic smells floated up to tug at the corners of his memory. Piles of photographs and little keepsake boxes looked up at him.

Twenty quiet minutes later, he'd got the fucker.

BRENDAN PULLED THE Audi in behind his father's, watching the headlights wash across the front of the house he'd grown up in. Everything was how he remembered it. The faux pillars either side of the front door, the bay windows and the front path lined with animal statues all facing oncoming visitors like a bizarre porcelain woodland army. He marched between the toads, badgers, geese and foxes, as the security light pinged on.

The door opened before he reached it and his father edged out in a dressing gown.

'Don't,' he said in a hushed voice. 'Don't disturb your mother.'

Brendan kept his mouth shut and stopped before the step. He wanted to play these next few moments very carefully.

Art gave him a hurt look and whispered again. 'I'm surprised you'd come here, but if you want forgiveness, I'll give it.'

Brendan nearly burst out in dark laughter. 'You think that's what I'm here for? For sorrys and slaps on the back?'

Art's face took a meaner shape. 'Then what? Haven't you done enough for one day?'

'Not nearly enough, I'd say. I'm off the case. That please you?'

Art held his palms up in supplication. 'That's not a fair question, and you know it.'

'Oh, give it a rest, Dad. I'm not on the case, but I'm not giving it up. And the man in my sights is you.'

Art's nostrils flared. 'You still want to accuse me of that abomination out in Peel Hall woods?'

Brendan stepped forward. 'Who's this?' He offered the six by four print. The man in the photograph was bald, nonplussed. There was a resignation to his posture that suggested he unequivocally did not want to be in the photograph. That he wasn't exactly comfortable with children's parties. He looked different from all the other adults in the picture, posing by the barbecue as kids splashed in a red blow-up paddling pool.

He had a gravitas about him. Shirtless, like everybody else in that captured summer afternoon, he was solid around the shoulders, his body taut, only giving way to a soft roll of flesh around his midsection. Even the way he sat in a chair, reclining like a low-rent emperor, elevated him above the rest of the scene.

While Art stared at the photo, Brendan scrutinised his father, looking for some sort of reaction. Nothing. If his father was acting, he was doing a damn good job of it.

'Any ideas?' Brendan asked, unable to keep the point from his voice.

'None, why?' replied Art.

'You're sure about that?'

'Why are you bringing me old pictures?' Art's eyes scoured the street.

'He's not here, if that's what you're wondering. Come on, Dad. This looks like it could be Ross's fourth, maybe fifth birthday party. Why would this bloke be at a family event like that and you not know who he is? I know the name of every person in the photograph except for the man in the chair, right there.'

'Why has this come up? Is this man supposed to have something to do with Connor?'

Brendan stared back cold. 'Never mind that. Tell me who this man is.'

'I'd tell you if I could, but I don't know.' Panic was edging into Art's voice. Before anymore words could be exchanged, the front door opened behind them and an elderly woman poked her head out. She was wearing a long white nightie with her hair in rollers.

'Brendan?' she said, her voice frail yet inquisitive. 'Is that you?'

'Hi, Mum.' Brendan hugged her gently.

Art stepped to one side and ran a hand across the top of his head. 'I wish you hadn't…' said Art, but didn't finish.

'Is it Sunday tea?' asked Brendan's mother.

'No, Mum, it's not – it's night-time now. Let me get you back inside.' Brendan began guiding her.

'If it's not Sunday, what day is it?'

'It doesn't matter, Mum. Come on, let's get a cup of tea.'

Brendan took her inside the house while Art stayed on the porch. The last thing Brendan saw as the front door closed was Art rooting in the pocket of his dressing gown, pulling out a packet of Silk Cut.

Brendan was struck by how much older his mother seemed. It was difficult to believe there was only a couple of years' difference between Art and his wife Moira. Art was a buoyant and jovial seventy-two years old; Moira was only seventy-four but had the look of a seventy-four that might have been seen twenty years ago, when lives were harder. Genetics had dealt a kinder hand to one parent than it had the other.

Moira's grasp of recent memory was faltering constantly, and she kept regressing to anchor points of recollection from the past. Because of this, Art had kept the house just the same since the early nineties to make things easy for his wife. Her surroundings often confused her, so he had made the home her sanctuary. Consequently, Brendan knew where everything was, but this offered the painful side effect of acute nostalgia every time he came back. It forced him to relive his childhood – never a bad childhood, just… false. His dad had put on a front of clean white-collar living, when behind the scenes his livelihood was anything but. Brendan found out at seventeen, when Art made the first tentative steps to coax his eldest into the folds of business with him. Brendan had been horrified. Since that moment, Brendan and his father's relationship had been sour, with only a recent thaw. That was until Connor had been murdered and Art regressed to a scant concept of the truth.

He noticed his mum's bare feet under the kitchen table. 'Where are your slippers, Mum?'

'I've got them on, you daft boy,' she said.

Brendan smiled. 'Of course you do, my mistake. Busy, busy, working hard, makes me dizzy.'

Dementia. Dementia seemed to attack every sufferer differently – but no matter the sufferer's plot on the curve, it hit them and their loved ones with such unforgivable might. With Brendan's mother, it had been a slow fading of lucidity over fifteen years, picking up grim pace in the last four. Clarity, recollection and a true sense of place had all slowly dissolved in Moira's mind, while quiet dignity had not. Meanwhile, Brendan's head was filled with guilt – guilt that he didn't do more, guilt that he felt like he couldn't handle it, guilt that he put his career ahead of spending more time with his mum while she still remembered who he was.

'Is it a normal tea?' he asked.

'Oh yes, it is,' she said, sitting at the kitchen table.

He busied himself while the elephant in the room got to work. He didn't know whether Art had told Moira about her grandson's death. If not, he didn't want to be the one to tell her and he knew that it was partly out of an embarrassing backbone deficiency. But that didn't stop an even more selfish thought from entering his mind.

'Mum, while I make this could you take a look at this photo?' He put the photograph down on the table in front of his mother. 'Do you know who that is? I can't remember.' He filled his tone with joviality, pretending this wasn't a loaded question.

'Ah, what a day that was,' she said. It amazed Brendan that his mum still had a perfect pachydermal memory of what had happened some three decades ago. 'It took me ages to make that cowboy cake, with all the Indians' camps made up and tepees made with chocolate fingers.'

'I remember that, Mum. That was the best cake of a whole childhood. Do you know who that is? I just can't remember. I recognise everybody else.'

'Which one?'

'This one,' Brendan said, as he put a sugar cube above the mystery man's head and the mug next to the photograph.

'Oh, Mal?'

Brendan froze. 'Who's that, then?'

'We haven't seen him for such a long while nowadays, but back then Arty and Mal were thick as thieves.'

Brendan struggled to keep the tremor from his hands. This was the true 'break-in-a-case' moment all detectives have. Pure excitement at a concrete step to resolution. But this also meant that his father had lied to his face again. So easily, so freely and so confidently. And, most damningly, the answers to the case lay much closer to home than he had been prepared to admit.

And then he was faced with another black thought of his own. Maybe it was good that his mum had dementia and she wouldn't know anything about the revelations Brendan was sure were coming.

'Thanks for that, Mum,' Brendan said.

'It's all right, son,' she said. 'We used to have a lot of parties for you kids when you were growing up. We were always so proud of you, always showing you off to whichever poor souls could tolerate it.'

'And Dad's works colleagues? Did they come too?'

'Oh yes, you know what used car salesmen can get like! There's always characters down that street.'

Brendan hadn't heard him return but he saw his father suddenly loom in the doorway, bringing in a cold haze of cigarette smoke. Their eyes met and a charge passed between them, which was full of pure knowing and the weight of revelation. Moira had told Brendan the truth.

Brendan looked over his mother's head at his father. He shook his head, then mouthed a message that came from his heart: 'I'm coming for you.'

CHAPTER 27

THE CENTRAL BULLPEN was a lot quieter today, though the atmosphere still fizzed with energy. If it weren't for a major investigation in their midst, Madison was sure that the nick would never have stopped talking about Brendan's fall from grace, but as things stood, his family troubles were shoved right down the list of priorities.

'As I outlined yesterday, we're going to do things my way. By the book. All Is dotted, all Ts crossed, checks and balances checked and balanced. Crimes are solved in the admin. They always have been and always will be. The facts don't spin us dodgy yarns, so we work off the facts, collate data and get results. This is no Wild West rodeo, throw your dad into an empty swimming pool communal balls-up. This is hard, clear, *dedicated* police work. And that's how we're going to bring these people to justice.'

Wainwright had moved Foley's desk away so that his own stood in majestic isolation at the head of the bullpen. Madison thought it absurdly petty given the crisis state of the investigation, and in her eyes only served to underline his lack of authority – and even seemed to bolster Foley's in his absence. Wainwright was sitting on his desk, legs splayed like Wyatt Earp, looking like he was trying to instill confidence, swagger and loyalty to himself as their leader. Little did he know that he simply looked like a twerp in a shit suit.

'We are one unit in here now – only one. Let's see out the investigation in that fashion.'

Another night, another day closer to the fight, and still Madison hadn't slept properly. Not since they'd started dragging bodies up from the undergrowth. Obligation and duty weighed like the two forceful hands of insomnia, and it seemed to hold the whole team in a similar grip – and no matter how much Wainwright wanted to bind two CID units together, they still sat apart, wary of each other like a pack of dogs abruptly thrown together at the pound.

'DS Karthik has spent the night on a social media campaign and public awareness efforts,' Wainwright continued. 'The images of these two men from the toy plane video will soon be national.'

Toy plane. It pissed Madison right off, the DCI's insistence on showing everyone just how many more years of experience he had on all the whippersnappers around him. It was obtuse, deliberate and unnecessary – and just what this investigation didn't need. Papers were fanned around, passed between the detectives across the two rows. Karthik didn't look all that pleased. The projector screen behind Wainwright's desk blinked to life showing a montage of Facebook ads, Twitter ads and Instagram pictures – each one showing those same grainy grey mugshots. Madison found herself with a hand up in the air.

'Sir?' she said. 'Have you notified airports, ferry ports, Eurostar? Any possible exit points from the country.'

'DS Madison, these campaigns aren't live yet. They will be in the next hour or so, to coincide with a press conference.'

'What press conference?' All Madison could think about was Brendan's hunches and clandestine investigations. They'd be scuppered by Wainwright's very public preening. So soon after the previous one, this had all the hallmarks of being masturbatory on the part of the new SIO and very little else.

'The press conference I have called to announce our two main suspects.'

'With due respect, sir—'

'And with equal respect, DS Madison,' Wainwright interrupted, 'I wasn't inviting discussion on the topic. I don't know what relationship you had with your former DI, but it is not the one you'll have with me.'

Hoyt and Madison swapped a look, while Christopher gloomily sipped from a coffee cup. Madison checked for her colleagues on the other row, who looked immediately all too used to this kind of behaviour.

'While I'm out giving the press conference, Karthik sits here and presses the big red button, or whatever the vernacular is. Those are our national efforts. Here in Warrington, we have two vans emblazoned with these pictures on either side. They have a route around the town centre that they will follow all day and every day until we catch these villains. The *Warrington Guardian* is also behind it, and this morning has printed an appeal with a confidential telephone number for tips. That number winds up here.'

Wainwright pointed to the back of the two rows of tables where a further table had been set up with three telephones. 'When this goes out, the phones will ring, we'll collect the data and we'll catch these bastards.'

Christopher let out an audible sigh.

'Something wrong, DC Christopher?' asked Wainwright.

'Those phones are going to be full of cranks.'

'For every ten cranks, there'll be one half-decent nugget. Numbers, statistics, data – the key to all good policework. Are we clear on that?'

'Yes, sir,' replied the DS, although his expression suggested otherwise.

'I need someone in charge of the hotlines, to separate the wheat from the chaff and forward the promising tips through to Karthik and myself. Any volunteers?'

'I'll do it.' To Madison's surprise, the voice belonged to Hoyt, who caught her look. In a low voice he whispered to her, 'Better than doing nothing.' He raised his voice to the rest of the group: 'The line's up and running?'

'Yes,' replied Billings. 'Four dial tones.'

'Excellent, DC Hoyt,' said Wainwright. 'Give Karthik a shout as soon as anything comes in. I'll give you two other detectives of your choosing to man the phones.'

'Not regular police constables?' Madison couldn't help herself.

'As I've said, DS Madison, these matters are not open to discussion. I want a trained detective speaking to each possible tipster. I think you lot will have a better chance at spotting someone pratting about than a regular bobby wondering when his next lunch break is. OK?'

Madison had to concede his logic, but that was the only part of his plan that carried any merit.

'You'll have to forgive me then sir, but have you informed—'

'*Enough*, DS Madison. That is enough.' Wainwright reddened. 'DC Hoyt. Who would you like on the phones with you?'

'I'll just go with your two. Billings has got a head start after all.' He pointed at Dean and Billings, who held back surprise.

'Perfect. Madison and Christopher, please crack on with any leads you had yesterday. Karthik, you stick with me. The presser is at nine, and I'm sure we'll solve this case in a matter of hours. Warrington Police will be the talk of the country. In the meantime, get to it.'

Madison, Hoyt and Christopher turned to each other. 'Why didn't you pick us?' asked Christopher. 'For the phones, I mean?'

Hoyt loosened his tie. 'So you're not stuck in here on the telephone equivalent of a wild-goose chase. You can go out, get loads done.'

'You're a genius,' said Madison. 'And a generous one at that.'

'Besides, I'll keep an eye on our fearless leader – because he's fucking this one up royally.'

'I'm glad I'm not the only one who thinks so,' said Christopher. 'You two are also from Warrington, aren't you?'

Madison nodded, while Hoyt said, 'Long enough.'

'Then we all know that no bugger from town is answering anything from the police. They'll know who these guys are, but they'll never tell a soul. Remember when they wasted thousands trying to get the public to give up Dofty Mason?'

The Dofty Mason debacle was a sore point for the entire Warrington Constabulary. A local drug dealer was wanted by the police so they employed this exact tactic, lorries with a wanted sign driving round town. They didn't have a single call, presumably because Dofty was no paedophile or serial killer. Moreover, he was a bloke providing a service to people who wanted that service. Nobody grassed him up and Warrington retained a strong line of cocaine right through its heart. If Dofty had been shopped, Warrington's coke supply would have been decimated.

'You never know,' said Madison. 'The violence in this case might provoke a reaction. But I'm with you, Christopher – no Warringtonian is going to stick his neck out. Especially if this is about organised crime. These guys have been able to get away with it for years because of the fear factor. You dob them in, you can look forward to tight-fitting plastic and a shallow grave.'

'Agreed,' said Christopher.

Hoyt set his jaw and pointed his index finger at her. *You're on to something.*

Madison was pissed off now. 'And that means that as soon as these pictures are up, these boys are out of here. I expect them to be on a beach in Marbella on the sangrias by five o'clock tonight.'

'Jesus,' whistled Hoyt.

'So, what do you think, Madison? IDs?' asked Christopher.

Madison nodded. 'I think that's where our answers lie. Find out who the victims are, you're closer to working out why they died. Find out why they died, you're closer to finding out who did it.'

Hoyt pulled out his chair. 'Then you guys best get to it,' Hoyt said. 'I'll make sure you're in the loop from here, regardless of what Terry Ten-Men is doing.'

Madison stood up and gave a single curt nod, before departing with Christopher.

'We're going to get no support from here, are we?' said Christopher as they left the MIR, more of a statement than a question.

'You can bet on that.'

'So we're on our own.'

Not quite, thought Madison.

CHAPTER 28

BRENDAN HAD GRABBED an extra-large Starbucks coffee and a bacon and cheese bagel on his way to the M62. On the other side of the motorway, it was jammed going into Manchester, but on his side of the carriageway, heading towards Liverpool, it was almost breezy.

That was the thing about Warrington – you were only ever twenty minutes away from either city, traffic allowing.

The sport chat radio station he usually liked to listen to interrupted its regular programming to bring the breaking news that two suspects had been identified by Detective Chief Inspector Wainwright of Warrington Police. Listeners were being urged to visit the station's website, Twitter and Facebook pages for pictures of the suspects, and the announcer reeled off the number to call to share information anonymously.

Brendan couldn't believe Wainwright would be so stupid, and he toyed with calling Madison ahead of schedule for an update. After a sip of cold coffee, he decided to keep his powder dry on that one – he had something they didn't. He had a name, and on top of that? Some scant childhood memories on which to build a bigger picture.

He'd racked his brains overnight, clawing at the tattered edges of his memory, pulling back anything about this man Mal he could remember. In the end it wasn't memory that jogged something loose – it was something in the picture itself that he had missed. And it was all down to a bit of manspreading.

They'd laughed about it, himself and his CID unit, when Madison asked whether it was a real thing or a subconscious territorial power play. Christopher had then come out with the immortal line: *You try sitting in a hot meeting room with a sweaty, itchy clutch purse dangling between your legs.*

In the photograph, Mal's choice of posture looked animalistic and territorial – his legs were splayed apart so that you could clearly see what was on the floor under the chair. A Liverpool Football Club cap. It triggered a memory that one of Art Foley's friends was an avid Liverpool fan who had a knock-off souvenir shop somewhere in Bootle. Brendan pored over his recollections of the man, looking for anything in his memory to add to the picture, arriving at one brief exchange. In 1992, when Liverpool won the FA Cup against Sunderland, Art had promised his kids tickets through the guy with the scarf shop, although they never materialised. Now, Brendan was convinced that the man he was thinking of was the man in the photo – Mal.

He took Edge Lane as far as Low Hill, turning right in front of the new hospital, then dropping down past the central library to angle through Vauxhall to Bootle, just north of the city centre. Before long, he had the docks all along his left-hand side, with the Irish Sea just beyond. Warehouse after warehouse, with a number of shiny car dealerships, his view constantly interrupted by the lorries that were everywhere. It was a hub of import and export. Everything straight off the boats and into warehouses, or onto waiting goods vehicles to serve the north of the country and beyond. It was a gateway to all sorts.

Brendan turned into Benbow Street, little more than a back alley off the main drag, with its original cobbles. Both sides of the street were nothing more than the back ends of warehouses, save for a couple of glass-fronted shop facias, one of which was the very shop he was looking for. He remembered it having a very distinctive name, one that he didn't quite get when he was a kid. This meant that when he researched Merseyside souvenir shops in the wee hours, he found it very quickly, even though it had closed a good number of years before and been replaced with something else. Rome 77 was a phrase that carried a lot of weight in those parts, and it was well remembered on a number of online locally based discussion forums, with a lot of fond remembrance for that scarf and badge shop down where the ships came in. The perfect name for a shop that Brendan began to suspect was a front.

The retail unit was just as it had appeared in the old pictures, although the signage was new. It looked quiet. It wasn't like he was expecting to find Mal sitting there behind the counter, but if he did it would be a bonus he'd be prepared to accept. He locked his car and crossed the cobbles, looking firmly like he'd left his career in authority far behind. He wore jeans, brown leather trainers and a red downy puffer jacket. He'd gone unshaven again too, a look he was already growing fond of, as he caught his reflection in the window to what was now called Aardvark Trophies. Beyond the glass were rows of fake gold trophies. He tried the door, found it open and went in.

The rest of the shop was sparse, with the main stock all pushed to the front windows for maximum pulling power. There was little more than a threadbare brown corded carpet over which some shelves and a few trophies were littered. The counter stood on the right, housing a glass case containing the more serious prizes. The place looked post-apocalyptic, if the apocalypse had brought about not just a shortage of food and provisions, but of vital cheap-looking sports awards as well.

Never mind Rome 77 – Aardvark Trophies looked like the biggest front in town. The back door to the shop was one of those beaded affairs, all in red on this occasion, and softly swaying. They'd been parted recently, and considering there was nobody out front, whoever it was must have been going the other way. Had they seen him coming?

He checked the bare shelves, something deep making him think. Instinct caught fast. His suspicions were true: the shelves had only been made bare recently; there were rows of dusty rings. The trophies were being shifted. Whoever was here was doing a runner.

He thought about hiding behind the counter but spotted the CCTV unit mounted high. Whoever was back there could surely see him. That made the decision for him, and without pause, he ran for the beads and flung them aside with a loud skitter. A figure in a blue tracksuit jacket immediately darted from a side room and belted towards the doors at the far end.

'Police! Stop!' Brendan shouted the lie as he raced after the figure. He looked to be in his mid-twenties, thanks to the rangy frame fleshed out by a decade of beer. A thick black mop of hair that was as lustrous as a teenager's. Brendan had the edge of urgency, forward momentum and every damn thing he'd felt those last few days, and was suddenly only a pace behind the stranger when he burst through the emergency door. He found himself in an alley, where a VW Transporter was suddenly taking off in reverse.

The tracksuit-wearing sprinter was not in it though – he was banging on its front bonnet with his palms, screeching, 'Go! Go! Fuckin' *go!*' in a Scouse accent thick as rice pudding. Brendan didn't feel like he could take out the van or its driver (who he could barely make out), but he could definitely take out the self-sacrificing martyr who'd given the shout to help it make its escape.

Brendan felt a pang of regret, thinking of just what was in that van aside from trophies. If it really was a front, it could be anything – drugs, guns, organs. He rugby-tackled trackie-man with a stiff shoulder to the right hip, dumping him wheezing into the walls of the alley, before reaching for his phone to call in the van plates – before he remembered, yet a-god-damn-gain, that he was suspended and not acting as a police officer. He committed the registration number to memory. Maybe Madison could do something with it.

'What's the rush?' he asked the man, as he hauled him back to the fire escape door. 'Let's have a seat, take a load off. Have a natter.'

He marched him back down the corridor to the trophy shop. When Brendan dumped him in the ratty desk chair behind the counter and spun the man round to face him, Brendan saw the effects of shock and fear.

'Why the sudden exit?' Brendan asked, hitching up to sit on the glass cabinet, rattling the trophies inside as he got settled.

The man facing him had the quality of the recently bereaved, all set in a lean, sallow face with sunken eyes, his black fringe draped over his forehead. Brendan had last seen a face like his on the side of the motorway when he'd attended a particularly shit-grim accident. There were grades to shock, however, Brendan had learned. Initial shock was guttural and followed no reason. At another accident he had dutifully attended, the driver of one of the vehicles had psychologically snapped with shock and pelted into the roadside woods. He was found two days later, eight miles away, dead from exposure.

This guy, however, was getting a handle on his, so this shock didn't just happen. A couple of hours ago maybe. The spectre of Mal loomed, and dots began joining in his head.

'I'm not sure I even have to ask you a question, do I?' he said. This made the man look at Brendan for the first time. 'Can I take a guess?'

His opponent stared.

'I'll take that as a *yes*. You've seen the news, you recognised one of the blokes all over it and remembered him as the previous owner of this place. You thought it would bring an unhelpful scrutiny to whatever you had going on over here and decided to jet this pony. Is any of this ballpark correct?'

The man gave a juddering nod.

'Then let me ease your mind. I don't give a shit about what you were doing here, how long you've been doing it, who you've been doing it with and how much money it's made you. I just want the man in the picture on the news. That's all. You give me a concrete way of finding him, or anything even half useful, and I'll send you out that back door with a pat on the back. I don't even care about your name. Just give me something.'

The man licked his lips, then spoke. 'Is it true? Is it him?'

Brendan circled a finger at the man, urging him to continue.

'Is he the Trench-Packer?'

'Jesus, is that what they're calling him? Bloody hell, some bloody serial killers need a leg-up in the PR game. But, yes. *Yes*. Mal was spotted filling in the grave the night the last body was deposited. So that would make us all believe he's got a fair idea about it, or did it himself. You'd agree with that, wouldn't you?'

'Yeah.'

'So. Did you ever meet him, what was he like, did he tell you anything? Do you know where he is?' Brendan went heavy on that last part.

'No, no. Nothing like that. I met him. Yeah, I met that mad bastard.'

'When?'

The man's eyes seemed to pull focus, and when he spoke, his voice was a grade stronger. 'Hang on, who are you?'

Great question, Brendan thought. He considered pulling his warrant card out of his pocket, which he was still carrying out of habit, before realising that if he did so while suspended, he could be charged with impersonating a police officer. There was too much grey area that he didn't have time for, so he went a different route. He stuck out his left foot and swung his heel back as hard as he could into the glass of the cabinet below him, shattering it into long shards.

'Answer the fucking question,' Brendan commanded, putting the man right back in his box.

'All right, all right, it was when we took it on.'

'When was that?'

'My dad took over the shop ten years back. I was helping him.'

'Where's your dad now?'

'Dunno.'

'You bought it? The shop?'

'No, no, it's on lease.'

'And Mal? He the owner?'

'Previous tenant. His shop was here before ours. I only saw him a couple of times, because there was a bit of a fuck-up with the changeover dates.'

'Do you know why he sold up?'

'No idea. Didn't seem like he wanted to. Dragged his feet a bit. I thought he kept leaving stuff here on purpose, to have to come and get.'

'What about his character? Anything strike you about him?'

'He was a stubborn git.'

'Did he leave anything here?'

The man thought.

'I won't tell anyone you helped the police.'

The man laughed with empty sarcasm. '*Police*, right.' He got up and went to the beaded doorway. 'A few of the rooms back here were full of proper crap. If we'd have needed them, we'd have got a skip in.'

Brendan followed him through the doorway back into the corridor, lined with four doorways on either side. It was quite a big industrial unit, for what was a fairly small shop front.

'Is there anything else you know about him?' Brendan asked.

'Fuck all. I'm serious.'

'Then do the shutters at the front and piss off. And if letting you go comes back to bite me in any way, I'll find you and give you the kind of hiding you'd piss your bed over.'

The man looked at Brendan for a second, but when it was apparent that the instruction was serious, he legged it back to the front. Brendan listened to the front door clang, then the motorised shutters whirr from outside.

He grabbed his phone and called Mim.

'Where are you?' She sounded harassed and fed up.

'Hello to you too,' Brendan replied. 'I was just checking in.'

'Checking in, Brendan, you're supposed to be at home. With us. We are supposed to be supporting each other.'

'I'm doing my best, Mim—'

'No, you're not,' she interrupted. 'You're doing the best for *you*.'

'That's not fair.'

'Where have you been all morning? Your family needs you!'

'Don't talk to me about family. All of this, every heartbreaking minute of it is all for my family.'

Mim turned softer. 'Brendan, you just don't see, do you?' He was suddenly more aware of the toll this must be taking on his small family unit. 'You're chasing after your nephew but you have two very alive sons here, who need their dad. I don't have to point out the irony in that to you, do I?'

Brendan couldn't answer. His eyes traced along the corridor. 'Look, I love you, but I have to go.' It killed him, but he had to do this.

He snapped off the call, staring at the doors ahead of him. He just hoped he'd have enough time to go through everything before the official investigation caught wind of this place.

CHAPTER 29

MUCH TO HOYT'S dismay, Wainwright was bang on the money. Once the suspects' pictures had been beamed all over the country, the phones hadn't stopped ringing.

His team of three sat at the hastily arranged telephone station, the three knackered old handsets bellowing non-stop. He could feel the eyes from around the rest of the pool watching them eagerly, knowing the potential importance that just one of those phone calls could carry – and as the person managing those calls, he felt a pleasing swell of importance in his chest. Too often in their CID unit it was all about Foley and Madison.

Hoyt wanted to show his own credentials as a leader. He'd delegated as much as possible, standing over the other two detective constables as they took quick notes and passed them to him, their handwriting getting ever more ragged. The first detail at the top of every sheet was the phone number of the caller (so much for the supposed pure anonymity – it was just too valuable to let go) and a name if they'd chosen to give one. Beneath that was a potted history of the call. Most of these notes revealed that Christopher was correct, too: none of the calls so far had come from Warrington. And most were from landlines.

Warrington was clearly sticking together so far. Hoyt smiled despite himself.

While two of the phones were occupied, the other started bleating. Hoyt grabbed a small tub from his suit jacket pocket labelled Beard Pomade, fingered out a small wad of the gum and smoothed it through his long beard, then picked up the nearest ringing phone and took a seat.

'Hello, you've reached the anonymous tip line. How may I help you?' he said, in as clear and friendly a voice as he could, while cheekily taking a note of the number that was flashing on the phone unit's LCD screen. A landline. Not local.

'Hi. Yeah… I've seen these guys around a few times. They've been knocking about in my local.' The voice sounded old, almost brittle, distant and heavily accented.

'Where are you calling from, sir?'

'Draycott.'

'And where's that, sir?'

'Somerset.'

Hoyt could have hung up there and then. 'And you saw them where, sir?'

'The Flapper and Firkin, it's an old boozer, real place, not one of those square plate places. A proper pub.'

'In Somerset?'

'Aye, that's right.'

'And you're sure it was them?'

'Ninety-nine per cent. It was them all right. But the lights are always dim in there, so you'd probably have to take that down to eighty per cent. Maybe even seventy, just to be sure.'

Hoyt's hand went to his forehead.

It was going to be a long day.

THE DOCKS OF Liverpool had always conjured so many images in his head. Mal savoured this last look; he wasn't sure how long he'd be away for. This might be the last time he'd stand on home soil. He'd been all over Europe so many times with no such fear about stepping on any of those planes or ferries, but he always knew he was coming back.

He looked at the vessel below him. The tired-looking Sea Hunter 450 lolled just under the quay heading, with Ger standing on its deck throwing their duffel bags into the tiny front cabin. It was, in essence, a dinghy with a fibreglass roof over one end. Only a two-seater, with barely even two berths in the cabin, and wasn't really designed for overnight stays. Still, this boat was big enough for the pair of them – they'd done this type of trip enough times – and small enough to avoid radar detection. With a favourable wind, and taking it in turns to sleep, they'd reach mainland Europe in a few days.

'Untie us when you've finished moping, Mal,' said Ger, with typical directness.

'I'm not a runner. I've never run away from anything in my life. Rats run, not dogs. Dogs run *to* the problem.'

'Who said anything about running? This isn't a usual case of keeping our heads down and ours noses clean. National manhunt, this. I'd be proud if I weren't pissed off to be leaving too.'

Mal didn't reply, but Ger forced it. 'You getting on, or are you sticking around to face the music? Because I promise you, dogs have to face the music just like anybody else. And this is one tune I'm not sticking around to hear.'

Mal looked at his colleague and saw the dependability that had got them through countless scrapes. They'd known each other years, since they were part of a gang of knockabout doormen in the early seventies. From there, their mutual love of Liverpool Football Club gave them a cause to travel, and as the football team conquered Europe, Mal and Ger conquered Europe's less salubrious corners. Liverpool got drawn to face Hertha Berlin? Off they went, blending in with the travelling football fans, turning over as many illegal rocks and going down as many dodgy avenues as they could find.

Soon they had something akin to a girl in every port, only it wasn't girls this time (of which there were always plenty, anyway), it was dealers. They had contacts all over the continent, and did constant import/export runs all over the place, using boats just like the one Mal was looking at that very moment. Only half masquerading as die-hard football fans who'd follow their team everywhere.

These contacts also meant that whenever shit got very tight, they always had somewhere to hide away from their home turf – which is what they were doing now. They had boltholes in most north European ports and they'd decide what ones to use when they got there. They just had to get on their way, and Mal just had to get on the damn boat.

He thought about what the city meant to him, catching a glimpse of the Liver Birds on the Cunard Building about half a mile south. The sight gave him a dull ache in his stomach. All the times he'd walked this city's cobbles. All the goals he'd seen at Anfield. The memories, hopes and fears of a life lived beyond any normal barriers of expectation. The rewards he'd reaped, the blood he had spilled. The people he'd worked for, in buildings just like the Cunard itself. They wouldn't be happy about any of this, but they'd be happier if he and Ger did the decent thing and skipped the country. You can't tell stories to the police if you can't be found – and knowing his employer's traits, Mal would rather be absent than the only real alternative. Which was dead.

So, they understood why Mal and Ger had to go, although it posed other problems, because replacements for men like Mal and

Ger didn't grow on trees. When Mal had told the family, who sent money into their accounts every month via standing order, they'd reluctantly seen sense.

Ger pulled a Snickers from his pocket and bit half of it off in one go. 'Come on, eejit. Let's hit the high road,' he said.

Mal undid the mooring rope, took one last look at his home town, seagull calls echoing off the brick warehouses, and lowered himself down the ladder to the boat.

As the boat puttered away, Ger chucking his chocolate wrapper up over his head to be gusted away by the wind, Mal blew a kiss to Liverpool and said a silent goodbye.

CHAPTER 30

CHRISTOPHER MARCHED OUT of autopsy room one, taking a lengthy suck of air. He shook his head. 'Shit,' he mumbled. 'That's just grotesque.'

'Still not used to it?' Madison asked.

'I'm sound with a cadaver. I've just not seen so many of them at once, and definitely not with so much... variety.'

Christopher straightened and walked over to the small mortuary waiting area, where Madison was kneeling on the floor, with papers all around her, on every chair in sight, across the coffee table, even on the floor, a procession of neat stacks.

'They wouldn't give you an office?' Christopher asked, his hobnailed boots stopping just short of the first pile.

'I didn't ask, but I'd rather be scrabbling about on a morgue floor than be in the major incident zone Wainwright's got going on,' she replied. 'A pile for each victim. I just wanted to get everything out in front of me, where I could see it. And each stack is everything we've got on them.'

'And this one here?' Christopher pointed his toe to a single sheet of paper by his feet.

'John Doe. We've got nothing on him. As if he didn't have a life before ending up in a hole in the ground.'

Christopher cast his eyes around. 'And there's more than a few just like him.'

'Yeah. It's given me an appreciation for the task at hand. Who's she working on in there now?'

'Thirteen. A woman, looks to be mid-forties, roots suggest brunette. No face, no jaw, for that matter.'

Madison let that information rattle. 'No jaw... I keep thinking back to the methodology of these killers – as in there really isn't one. Save for the plastic wrapping and the big hole, there is no real consistency between each of the murders. Sometimes it's guns, sometimes it's knives, sometimes blunt force trauma. All of them seem to be intact in terms of their extremities.'

'Of those opened up so far.'

'Right. Serial killers with a psychopathic slant tend to have a strict code they follow. They are satisfying a particular fetish or urge. That doesn't seem to be the case here. This just seems to be a dumping ground for the wild and weirdly killed.'

'We don't really have the most experience in the world when it comes to serial killers.'

'No. But I've watched enough Netflix specials to recognise something if I don't see it. And while I'm seeing a lot of bloody horrible things, I'm not seeing the MO or agenda of a psychotic killer. Foley had a hunch it was organised crime, and everything I'm seeing here backs that up. But because there's no consistency, it's so hard to establish a pattern. Without a pattern, it's hard to find who did it.'

'We've got their faces though.'

'And now the country has too. They'll have gone, I'm telling you. We've just got to hope we find out enough about them so we can see if they have any known contacts abroad, or any foreign property. That's our best bet.'

Christopher chewed this over, before brandishing a report of his own. 'This just out from in there. Prelims on thirteen – or M as they're calling her.'

'Anything that stands out?'

'Appears she's also from the well-heeled side of life. Track marks showing years of on-off hard drug use, but not so far as abuse. She's chased the dragon more than a few times, but never let it bite her back so hard it held on for good. With the lower jaw gone, they're getting a dental cast of the top set, as per the others. See if we can track her down that way. Mackie says she's getting the hang of measuring decomposition using the scale of deterioration of the organs. From what I saw, her chest cavity looked like a bowl of beef broth, so God knows how she can work it out from that. Anyway, she thinks we're close to seven years for her.'

'She died seven years ago?'

'Give or take. Mackie says her method ain't exactly perfect.'

'Any other giveaways on the body?'

'I'm going to put this sensitively – a lot more sensitively than Mackie put it – but the condition of her lower extremities suggests she was a fairly well-established sex worker, and had been for over twenty years.'

Madison mock shuddered, while Christopher rolled up the report.

'I'm off to check missing persons and VICAP again, see if anyone comes up when I punch in the criteria. Anyone else you've got here you'd like me to check while I'm at it?'

Madison cast her eyes about at the varied paper mounds around her. 'Yeah, if you take the four biggest piles, they should be enough to go on.'

'Cool.' Christopher stooped and grabbed the four stacks Madison pointed out. As he straightened up, Madison felt his eyes on her. 'Foley's not letting this go, is he? He's out there doing something himself, right?'

Madison thought about how to answer, but knew that, if Brendan were here himself, he'd tell Christopher the truth. His loyalty and trust to his team were absolute. She nodded at him.

He looked satisfied to at least know the truth. 'Say no more. I'd be doing the same. But if he comes up with something concrete that'll blow this thing apart, please, bring me in.'

'I will.'

'All right. In a bit then.' Christopher headed off down the corridor.

Madison stayed on her knees, looking at the scene around her. She was a visual person. She could look at stats and patterns in her head just as easily as she could if they were in front of her. Sometimes one triggered the other, so if she couldn't reach something she was trying to process, she tried to pull a picture together by questioning herself as she went.

A picture. What you're looking at. *What was she looking at?*

A lot of dead people who had been murdered in a number of different ways, yet, in almost every case, something fairly obvious was missing.

What was missing? Almost all the time, faces or jaws.

Why the face? Why the jaw?

Psychotic ritual. The ultimate dehumanisation.

Take out the psychotic.

The removal of identification.

They were removing things that could identify them. They'd assumed this was a maniac getting his jollies doing the sickest things imaginable, when actually it was more a code of best practice.

Before she knew it, Madison was up and sprinting after

Christopher. Down the corridor, round the bend and out into the sunlight.

'Christopher!' she shouted across the Tarmac parking bays at the front of the morgue.

He paused from climbing into his car. 'Yeah?'

'They're removing identifiers. When you're looking for M's identity – if she's been a sex worker for a long time, she must have had the odd brush with the law. Look for a record, and when you do, look for a brunette of the appropriate age with something significant dentally. Maybe a fancy tooth, or no teeth, maybe some extra-special dental work, anything. Anything that would help us identify her, that they felt they had to get rid of.'

'Got it. Adios.' He dropped into the car, started it up and pulled out of the bay.

Madison watched him go, but then the car abruptly stopped. Madison walked over and bent down to the open passenger window.

'What?' she asked.

'If they were getting rid of markers, why did they leave Connor completely intact?'

'I don't know. '

'It's that lack of consistent pattern again.'

'I know what you mean.'

'I'll keep thinking. Nice work, boss.' He sped off around the side of the hospital.

Madison started walking back to her stacks of papers. Her mind was twisting again, and she found herself walking at a slower than usual pace while she tried to work things out.

Why had they left Connor intact? They'd been so methodical.

If one were to assume that every choice they made was on purpose? They wanted Connor to be identified.

Why would you want to show someone who you've killed? To hurt them.

The penny dropped so heavily in Madison's mind that she could almost hear it.

Connor's death was a message. A message to the Foley family.

She ran back to her paper stacks and grabbed her phone.

CHAPTER 31

BRENDAN WAS KNEE-DEEP in crap. His jeans had gone a stonewashed grey from his thighs down. The two rooms that still contained some of Mal's stuff were each a different beast – one was ordered boxes, stacked in a back corner, maybe twelve of them in a little block, while the other looked like somebody had emptied a skip into it. With no other option, he'd rolled up his sleeves and got stuck in, although it didn't take him long to wish that he was still an active detective and could call in forensics.

The rooms were not big. Three metres by three metres, both painted in a weird choice of baby-pink wall, baby-blue wall, back to baby pink, then back to baby blue. It was the kind of room you'd paint for a baby who you wanted to make sure was gender fluid or just plain confused. It made them feel unbalanced and tatty. On the back wall of each was a high fire window, with frosted glass over which hung a rusted grate. There weren't any radiators, but there were a couple of high wall fans. The floor was bare concrete in one, and, well… He couldn't tell in the other. He started in the one less challenging.

He took each box and placed it on the floor, to get a better look at them. There were labels written on the top of each one, black marker on weathered cardboard. *Old stock. Hats. Cup Final 91.* Nothing that appeared so obviously out of place, but why would you write the true contents of a secret box on the lid? To be sure, he opened each in turn and found a Christmas morning array of goodies that any Liverpool fan would go nuts over. Again, nothing incriminating, nothing out of place. He liked the look of one of the souvenir hats – a flat cap in grey and red with the liver bird crest – and pocketed it.

His phone rang in his pocket, the shrill cry puncturing the cold quiet. Brendan checked the screen. Madison. He needed to call her in a bit anyway, so he took it.

'Morning.'

'Morning. Decent night?' asked Madison. The phone line was

scratchy, inconsistent.

'I can't lie, it's been better. How are things your end?' Brendan moved as he talked, out into the corridor where the line was better.

'As fine as can be. Wainwright's got us all marching to his beat with this idiotic move to share the suspects' faces without putting any retaining precautions in place.'

'I saw. They'll have skipped, won't they?'

'My thoughts exactly. Me and Christopher are still trying to put together a full set of victim IDs but it's taking time and there's only the two of us. Our fearless leader's got everyone else manning the tip lines or feeding him grapes. Listen, I have to ask you something. I've been looking for a pattern in the victims, their lack of faces in particular, which stops with Connor. I think the killers wanted Connor to be identified. I think this is a message to you and your family.'

Brendan stopped dead, his blood running cold. 'You're a bloody good detective, Iona. Do you know that?'

'I don't follow, sir.'

Madison was no fool – no fool at all. She had got to the same place he had, with barely a thread of the information Brendan had. 'I can trust you, can't I, Iona?'

'I hope we'd already established that.'

He walked into the other room, the one filled with rubbish, and let his eyes wander. It was more of the same kind of crap – hats, flags, T-shirts – except it was all unboxed, disordered and uncared for. 'Can you meet me tonight?'

'Umm. Sure. Same place?'

'No. Different. I'll text you.'

'OK.'

Brendan took a couple of steps into the room. Why would anyone just dump stuff in here? What purpose did this have, other than covering the floor?

Covering the floor.

'Hang on, Iona.' He started sweeping his feet through the rubbish, to see what emerged. Nothing obvious. He carried on, moving into the centre of the room, when his foot clattered painfully against something solid.

'Bloody *hell.*' He winced, before dropping onto his hands and knees to find whatever it was he'd just kicked.

'What's going on?' Madison asked, but Brendan was oblivious as

146

his hands touched metal. He tossed the rubbish to the side.

'My God,' he whispered.

'Sir? Sir?'

On the floor in front of him, held in place by four thick metal bolts, was a chunky iron ring. Like an anchor ring you'd find on the docks outside. The perfect place to tie something, or *someone*, in place.

'Iona, you might need to take this as an anonymous tip... but there is a shop in Liverpool you really need to send forensics to.'

CHAPTER 32

ANOTHER DAY, ANOTHER faceless chain coffee shop, the kind that had sprung up in every spare unit in every city centre going. It didn't appeal remotely to Hoyt's sensibilities of individuality, and never had. He'd always been on the upper-outside edge of every curve, right from the off. He was into Ren and Stimpy when all his classmates were going nuts for Ninja Turtles. In his teens, when music became a bigger and altogether more commanding feature of his days, he'd been all about the Manic Street Preachers while everyone was still discovering Oasis. Identikit coffee shops did his head in.

He was still amazed that this venue was the choice of the person he was meeting. So public, so open. He ordered a black coffee and aimed for a spare table in the back corner. If he had to meet in public, he'd be damned if he was going to sit in the window. He sat down, pulling his skinny suit trousers up just a touch as he did, to make sure his grey socks with the fluorescent pink piping really stood out. He put down his coffee mug and a copy of the arts section of *The Guardian* on the table. He was confident. He was the cop. He had the upper hand. His role was make or break.

Truth be told, the juggle was properly doing his head now. He had two phones, which helped. One for personal and one for work. Now that Madison was bridging the gap between the two compartments of his life, he'd had to be careful – but because Madison had started through work, he could keep her on that phone. His other phone was for everything else, and it was the one that had rung twenty minutes ago, with a place and the no-nonsense instruction of 'ASAP'. He'd made his excuses to the other dopes on the phones and nipped out. A quick jaunt over the road, and into the Golden Square shopping centre where this Costa stood by the escalators. Now, he watched everyone riding up them.

'Hot pink, bold as brass,' said a voice in his ear, causing him to start. 'That what the cool kids are wearing these days?'

The woman came round the side of him and pointed at his

outstretched legs. 'Give us some room, Flashdance.'

He shuffled across in his seat.

'Don't shit your kecks, hold it steady and embrace me like I'm your beloved auntie.' The voice carried a softened Scouse twang – not that urgent nasal Liverpudlian spit. She was that type of middle-upper-class Scouse, rooted over the water in Heswall, or north of the city in Formby, where all the footballers lived. Hoyt hopped up and gave her an obedient hug.

'Hello,' he said with a smile. 'Can I get you a drink?' Hoyt was flustered now, unsure of which role to play. The surprise entrance had punctured his confidence.

'No, I'm all right thank you. I was unaware ASAP meant nearly half an hour, so I've already drunk my bodyweight in tea.'

Hoyt flushed at that, as the woman sat down opposite him.

He'd met her once before, about ten months back, on the pretense of a shared ancestry. She'd emailed him, tracked him down, she said, thanks to some help from ancestry.com. Shared distant relatives in the old country over the water on the Emerald Isle. He'd bought it hook, line and all the rest, thanks to the strength of pride in his roots, so away he'd gone to meet her in Liverpool. Things had felt off as soon as he'd entered the pub where the meeting was to be held, in the city centre – not the kind of place he'd expect to meet a middle-aged woman on a rainy Friday afternoon. She'd carried herself as though she were the landlady – except the landlady was there, behind the bar, unmistakably brassy and loquacious, like every landlady worth their salt should be. But this lady was different.

She'd come alone, much like she was this day in Costa, but she had a man off on a side table, filling in a crossword with one eye on her – and him. Hoyt looked for him now, a not-so-sneak peek that the woman immediately caught.

'Dogs are elsewhere today, I'm afraid,' she said. She was in her late forties, to Hoyt's best guess, with dirty blonde hair chopped into what looked an expensive bob. Her skin had a faint spray-tan muddiness, and her eyes were almost unnaturally green, glowing like a bobcat's, frosted by thick black mascara that sat in occasional clumps on her eyelashes. Physically, she was heavyset yet cinched in at the waist, as if she had a rope wound tight underneath the dark coat. She wore a pair of brown cowboy boots, so authentic that the only thing missing were spurs.

The fact that she was alone made Hoyt feel better. 'How are you doing?' he asked with a smile.

'Don't take the act too far. Things are fucked,' she replied with an equally beguiling smile, throwing Hoyt right back onto his toes again. Charlotte Culpepper was nails. Nine inches, railway-compliant, steel-shafted, tungsten-tipped *nails*.

'What can I do?' he asked.

'What are you doing? We'll start there.' She folded her hands in her lap, demure body language completely at odds with what she was saying.

'I'm head of the tip line. Anything that gets called in, goes through me.'

'Well, that's a start. Anything coming in?'

'Most are the kind of ambulance chasers who hope that we're going to tell them something, like we give out key case information as a matter of courtesy when you've had the good grace to ring the tip line. But there are a few bits that sound genuine. Your men haven't exactly been keeping their heads down, have they?'

Charlotte smiled. 'They do have a taste for the theatrical, one more than the other.'

'I assume they've gone to ground?'

Charlotte nodded. 'Yes. As soon as their faces went national, they hit the road. How in God's name did those pictures come about anyway? I know those boys checked for things like wildlife cameras and so on, but something caught them out.'

'A drone. A scorned housewife keeping an eye on her estranged husband, shacked up with a woman half her age on the other side of the woods.'

'And she was spying on him with a drone?' She smiled again.

'Welcome to the twenty-first century.'

'God, that's military-grade jealousy. Go on, girl.'

'You don't seem worried.'

'What those boys were up to was their business. They were taking care of things, but how they went about it was up to them.'

'Pretty sick though.'

'The sicker the fuck, the slicker the shuck.'

Hoyt had no answer to that, mainly because he hadn't a clue what it meant, but he was quite sure it hinted at a moral ambiguity Charlotte was more than au fait with.

'So, tell me, bearded whizz-kid… if you've got the tip line all sewn up, if you're in control, then why are your boys and girls pulling up the floor at Mal's old shop in Bootle?'

'Mal one of those boys who've flown the coop?'

Charlotte nodded, her eyes sticking pins in Hoyt's.

'It hasn't come through the lines.'

'That isn't answering the question.'

'I don't know where it's come from, but it wasn't from me.'

'Because that would be suicide, wouldn't it?'

Hoyt's breath caught somewhere round his epiglottis, and his arse felt like it might drop.

'It's not what we pay for, is it?'

Hoyt tried to give his voice strength but failed. 'If that's what you were getting from me, then no. But like I said, it didn't come from me.'

'So, where? You're our eyes in the cop shop. Where did this line come from?'

It's a question that had bugged Hoyt since he'd heard that Wainwright, Karthik, Christopher and Madison were overseeing the tossing of a suspected crime scene in Liverpool. He didn't know why it was happening, but because it was the four of them, he assumed it was to do with the case. And because he had made such a commanding gesture in taking control of the tip line, he was out of the loop. Maybe that had been a mistake.

'I'm going to guess good, old-fashioned police work.'

'Who?' She sounded more dangerous by the minute.

Hoyt could think of only one possible answer. 'The old DI. He's taken a personal interest.' As soon as the words left his mouth, he wondered what he'd done.

'Ah yes, the kid in the grave. A relative?'

'Yeah, nephew.'

'That'd make you want to take notice.'

'Did they have to off the kid? Was it really necessary?' He felt the sudden bubble of nerves again.

Charlotte looked at him heavy and hard, but suddenly softened in what looked like a troubled sense of understanding. 'Mal and Ger had instructions, and they were trusted. If they felt that boy should be in a hole in the ground, then there must have been a reason for it. He must have been doing something he shouldn't. Might have offended a family interest.'

Hoyt thought about this. 'What can I do?'

'Get a grip on CID. Get off the phones or siphon off a little juice to somebody on the phones you trust. Anyone else in the unit who might be amenable?'

He thought of Iona Madison, then immediately thought, nope. And he didn't know about any of the others. Didn't know them well enough.

'Maybe,' he said. 'If you had a word with them the same way you had a word with me, that might inspire them to lend a hand.'

Charlotte's gaze dropped several degrees in temperature and leaped several notches in malice.

'I meant no disrespect,' Hoyt quickly added, with a palm raised. 'You just… make a compelling case.' He remembered the offer and the money of course, but what really stuck in his mind was the threat. Of violence. They had indeed tracked down his family in the old country. They had indeed tracked down his sister and his nieces and nephew. They knew exactly what time they went to school and exactly in which part of their quiet community they could dig four neat little graves.

'Stand up and hug me,' Charlotte said, now with a sweet smile. Hoyt rose with all the brio of a man ready to take a cold blade between the ribs.

The hug, when it came, was warm – but the words weren't.

'Control it,' she whispered. 'You are paid a fee that I consider exorbitant. Get a handle on things, or your sister's family will be going bed-bos for a long sleep. Now, hug me like it's Christmas and get the fuck back to work.'

CHAPTER 33

TUESDAY WAS A day of familiar routine for Art and Moira. The local health centre offered a sensory room for sufferers of deteriorating neural conditions, and Art took her down, sticking with her until it was too much for him to bear. It was far from easy for him, watching the shell of his wife crinkling crepe paper with her fingers, her memories skittering across the landscape of her mind like ash in a swirling breeze. Brendan had been there with his mum once and admired the thought behind it: that touching familiar textures from your past would reignite a memory in your mind. But it was so harsh a reminder of what his mother was going through, so sad to watch.

Art and Moira attended regular as clockwork, each Tuesday morning. Which meant that right now, the house was empty.

Brendan had a key. It wouldn't look strange to the neighbours seeing their son popping over. This was Brendan's chance to find any evidence of Mal among his father's things – and to see if anything looked suspiciously different since he came waving a photo of Mal around last night.

The pottery animals watched his approach once again as he marched straight to the front door and opened it. The house was bathed in cold grey daylight and looked much different from the previous evening, when every corner was illuminated by softly glowing lamps. He took stock for a second. Nothing immediately sprang out at him.

He decided quickly to start the search downstairs, before going upstairs, to where the potential goldmine of Art's spare room-cum-office lay. Moving along the hall, he looked at the family pictures with fresh scrutiny, to see if Mal appeared again, or even the other face from the drone footage. This second man was still a spectre, but with the advances towards Mal's capture, he was happy to let him stay that way for the time being. One would surely beget the other.

Nothing sprang out amid the hanging roll-call of the all-too-familiar images of himself with a bowl cut, and the same for his brother. There were a couple of them at school together, posing back-to-back.

As boys, their similarities were obvious, mostly around the eyes. Both blue, expressive and undeniably happy. They looked thick as thieves in treacle, as all brothers born so close together should be. He felt a pang of regret at how they'd gradually grown apart, even though he understood why it had happened. Why couldn't things be simple, like those days against that pale blue textured backdrop in the cold school assembly hall?

Growing up.

Growing up, something had happened that made Ross follow their father's every move. For Brendan, it had had the opposite effect.

He wondered whether, if they were to relive their lives, the results would be the same. His eyes came to rest on a school portrait of Connor, and he realised with steel and a leaden thump in his chest, that, *yes. Yes, the result would be the same.*

It was a couple of years old, the photo of Connor. Taken outside at school, the formal backdrops now long since dispensed with, now that cameras didn't need pitch-perfect lighting to get a half-usable image. He was in the woods at school, the fair-haired boy, still with that near-Scandinavian mop of hair, standing out like neon against the thick green foliage behind him. He looked happy. *We all looked so happy,* thought Brendan.

Then he remembered where he was, and remembered the one person who could have done something to change the family's fate. His father.

Mind refocused, he kissed his fingertips and placed them on the photograph of his godson as he passed, on his way through to the kitchen. He stood in the doorway. It was neat, orderly, exactly how he expected it. The cabinets all stood shut, the worktops freshly wiped. The sink was empty. If it weren't for the giveaways of normal wear and tear, and the outdated country-style kitchen, you'd be forgiven for thinking that the kitchen had never been used.

In the far corner, the frosted-glass back door was dark and gloomy because it only led into the garage. Brendan remembered there were boxes there, and boxes meant possible remnants from his father's history. He went for the door.

Immediately on opening it, something wasn't right. Art's gleaming Audi was sitting there, blue and beautiful to those with an appreciating eye. It was a one-car garage, with bare ceiling beams eight feet above the floor, hanging over the roof of the Audi like old scaffolding. Boxes lined the breeze-block far wall, while the nearside wall housed a chest freezer that was as omnipresent in the family as any actual family member of the last thirty years. So what was causing that feeling at the back of his head? The one that urged him to look again…

He was in touching distance of the freezer, so he popped the lid. Bags of frozen veg and a shoal of cellophane-clad trout looked back up at him. A cursory rummage revealed nothing buried in there any more sinister than a mint Viennetta from 1992.

He closed the lid and sat on it, to try to take in the room. He couldn't shake what was wrong, but was hooked now. The boxes didn't look especially inspiring, but he didn't feel that they were the reason for his disquiet. He drummed his dangling heels against the belly of the freezer below him, catching sight of the reflection of his swinging feet in the polished wing of the car.

Of course. The Audi.

What was it doing here? His mother's car, a fifteen-year-old Renault Clio that was still in good nick despite its years, should have been there in its place. It hadn't been driven by Moira in at least two years, maybe even three. Why had they chosen to go in it today? Especially in light of Art taking his wife out himself?

Why had the Audi been left behind? It was his father's pride and joy. Why wasn't he driving it now?

Brendan thought back to the last time he'd seen his father in it. Was it the christening, at the weekend? That already felt like a lifetime ago.

No. Ross had taken both his parents to the church and dropped his car back there to walk to the Legion so Art could have a few beers with the buffet.

Brendan walked round the front grille, and could see nothing amiss. It all looked normal. His detective's mind had clicked into gear, and he was sweeping the car for anything out of place. After he'd checked all around it, he tried the driver's handle, hoping his dad would have reasoned that it being in a locked garage was security enough, but no luck. Every modern car came with two keys, yet Art only needed one now that his wife didn't drive. The spare had to still be here – somewhere. He remembered the key drawer in the hall, the one that was part of the lintel that hid the radiator, and quickly strode back to check it.

Right under Connor's nose, as if guiding his uncle on the hunt for the truth behind his death, the drawer revealed a load of old rubbish and one pristine Audi key fob.

Back in the garage, he looked at the three buttons on the fob. Central locking, boot release and the remote alarm feature. He clicked the button for the boot, which swung up. Brendan stepped forward to peer inside.

Snug tight to the boot lining on all sides, fitting so perfectly the boot could have been vacuum-formed around it, was a scuffed and dented but still perfect cash machine.

CHAPTER 34

CENTRAL MANCHESTER HAD always had the habit of unnerving Brendan – even now. Its scale and sense of history, the range of the city's impact stretched way into the distant past. As a young lad, Brendan had always carried a quiet fear of infinity. He found looking up at the stars, the endless messy twinkly morass, too much for him. It scared him, the fact that you could keep going, and keep going and keep going without ever reaching something that would force you to stop. No borders. No boundaries. Just endlessness. It made his head hurt, so instead he'd direct his gaze to the concrete at his feet. That same sensation applied to history and the big cities that carried a lot of it – there was just so much to take in, no order, no control. He was a small-town boy, through and through, out of his depth past a certain geographical scope. So consequently, Manchester was a mess to him.

He'd got over it with Liverpool, because the buildings weren't as tall there yet. It was as simple as that. Yet when he'd gone there only earlier that day, he hadn't gone into the centre. He'd stuck to the docks and kept his head down.

Now, crossing the main artery of Manchester city centre, Deansgate, he had his eyes glued low, on his phone, following the directions on Google maps to the Rising Sun. The pip-pip of horns, the steady rumble of traffic, the clatter of a distant tram, were rising to a throb, until it all stopped when he pulled open the door to the pub, and practically fell into its comforting embrace.

Dark wooden floors and the same panelling up the walls, bedecked with fairy lights, and a bar that wrapped around both sides of a central column of optics and whiskey bottles – Brendan liked it immediately. A barman in an unbuttoned black shirt approached, took one look at Brendan and pointed to his left, into the wider side room. Surrounded by Manchester United memorabilia, shirts and signed photos, most of them featuring George Best, sat a man in a crumpled suit and wild black hair. He had five-day stubble and wore glasses. Brown eyes so bright they almost looked golden. He stayed seated, and Brendan recalled the story of Jeremiah Salix, a young policeman.

Jeremiah had botched something known as the changing of the doors – that is to say, the rights to sell drugs in a certain club were being exchanged from one gang to another, and the unwritten rule was that the police had to witness it so that they knew who was where and what was what… Only Salix had tried to intervene, unable to watch such brazen criminality without trying at least to stop it some way. For his trouble, he was held down by one of the parties, while the other beat him senseless with a pillowcase full of bricks. He ended up in a coma for nine days and woke with a burning desire to take down organised crime where he could. The price? The use of his legs.

'I'll take a pint of Timmy Taylor's while you're there,' Jeremiah said. Brendan nodded with a smile, then nodded at the barman.

'You heard him – and make it two, please,' he said, walking over to Salix and shaking his offered hand. 'How are you, mate?'

'I keep rolling forward,' Salix said with a grin, causing Brendan's to broaden. His sense of humour was always strong and acerbic, something that had only grown despite the obvious hardships life had thrown at him. 'What brings you to this neck of the woods?'

'I wish I could say it was just old mates catching up, but I'm not gonna dick about trying to have you on. I need some info.'

'Well, I guessed that. I saw your name on the news the other day, and then your spot was taken by someone else. Trouble at mill?'

The two pints appeared, deep amber with a fizzed cream head. They clinked glasses and supped. 'Yeah, you could say that.'

Jeremiah spoke, even though the hair on his top lip was covered by foam, giving him an austere moustache. 'And the Foley on the news, the one they got out of the hole. I assume that's a coincidence?'

'No. My nephew.'

Salix wiped the froth from his face and lowered his gaze. 'Shit, I'm sorry.'

'Me too.'

'You off the case? Conflict of interest?'

'Let's call it that.'

'Any closer to catching this killer? I saw there was a suspect.'

'Is the National Crime Agency involved?' Brendan countered. He had to know whether Salix had a vested interest in what they were about to discuss.

Brendan and Jeremiah had met as student officers being trained up by Greater Manchester Police, and spent two years together in and out of Sedgley Park Centre in Prestwich, five miles north of the city. After that, Brendan had transferred to the smaller climes of Cheshire, but they'd kept in touch. Brendan was a police constable when Jeremiah had been confined to the chair, and visited him in hospital while he was out for the long count. The police, when one of their officers is in a bad way, tended to look after their own, and Jeremiah had been offered the building blocks of an office career – which he had grabbed with both hands. His operational sense, understanding of the criminal state and desperate burning desire had combined to make him a considerable force – and it wasn't long before he was head-hunted to spearhead the National Crime Agency's Organised Crime Command. If there was anything going on in Manchester, Jeremiah knew about it. But Brendan had to tread carefully.

'None. As far as I know, of course. Mass murder isn't really under the remit of the OCC, unless it's got a particular characteristic.'

'Can we go off the record?'

'We always are, mate, unless you say otherwise.'

'It does have those characteristics. Of those pulled out of that hole and IDed, most have an organised crime connection. Or at least all those we've pulled out so far have.'

'You say *we*. You still involved?'

'I'm still looking into it. It's a family thing.'

'And your nephew? What's he doing in there?'

'That's what I'm trying to work out.'

'OK. What do you want to know?'

Brendan thought how best to phrase the question. But his curiosity was too great, so he went straight at it. 'I need to know about cash machine theft.'

This caught Salix by surprise.

'The practice, the methodology… and if the north-west is missing any.'

Salix had a mouthful of beer. 'The whole machine, I assume? Not just cracking one open and grabbing what you can?'

Brendan nodded.

'Well, there's a number of ways you could get your hands on one, but you need the hardware. It's one that requires planning, so it's very rarely a crime of opportunity. Usually, the perps have picked one and watched it for weeks, monitoring as and when it's refilled to work out the most profitable time to strike.'

Already, Brendan was thinking of his father, picturing him sitting in that damn Audi watching some cash point with pound signs in his eyes.

Salix continued. 'Once you've narrowed down your target cash point and the theft window, you need to pick your method. A lot of these robberies take place within a couple of miles of twenty-four-hour plant hire businesses, because some crims just rent a digger and drive it straight to the target. Literally dig it out of the wall. Sometimes it's a tractor, a drill and some metal hooks. Drill holes in the brick surrounding the machine, stick the hooks in on chains and use the tractor to drag it out. Manufacturers are getting more and more savvy though, and have adapted their security devices to make all this much more difficult; on the four sides of the cash machine's front panel, they've installed catches that, once in place, are a serious bugger to bypass. To get round this, it's become fashionable to blast it out of the wall, blowing the catches to bits. When time's of the essence, this appears to be much better than pawing at it with a digger claw, hoping you jar those catches loose.'

Brendan thought of that cash point, how scuffed it was. It had certainly seen a degree of impact. Maybe that one had been blasted out. 'How does that work? Blasting it out?'

'Usually, it's nothing more difficult than a garden hose jammed behind the fascia, which can be done with something like a crowbar. Hoses are usually less than an inch thick, so it's perfect. Pumping the right gas into the ATM housing will give it all the oomph you'd need. The pressure will build, before *bang*, your cash point has popped right out the wall.'

'And then what? When you've got it out, I mean?'

'Well, they're heavier than buggery, much more than a person could carry. You'd need something to hoist it into a vehicle, and then you're away. The digger or backhoe or whatever is usually left behind because the alarms will be going like crazy, and you'll have spectators – rest assured, nicking a cash machine is not a quiet pastime. Once it's in your getaway vehicle, away you go, and that would ordinarily be a van of some description – or certain sports cars.'

'Sports cars?' Brendan felt his stomach vacuum.

'Yeah. They don't match the normal description of a getaway vehicle, and the boots are often very good fits – so it's become a very popular choice.'

'What about an Audi RS6?'

'Perfect. It's known as a real crim's car, that one.'

Jesus, thought Brendan.

His dad wasn't retired at all. Not one bit.

'And as for your last question,' Salix said, 'I don't really have an answer. But I can get you one.'

'Make sure you do it quietly. Last thing I'd want to do is stick you in it by helping a suspended officer.'

Once again, Salix appeared surprised. 'You're suspended?'

'Shit.' Brendan had forgotten.

Salix sighed. 'I'll do what I can, of course. But don't let the info come back to me, all right?'

'Thanks, Jeremiah. It's Connor, my nephew. I have to find out what happened to him, and I think one of the case breaks might be a missing cash point.'

'You've got nobody on your own force who could help you out? They might have a better idea than me?'

'Nah, no one's got that kind of intel, and they're all up to their necks in the big murder case. Besides, they don't know the lie of the land out here – not like you.' The fact that his father might still be active was suddenly a big issue, one he needed to get a handle on, and Jeremiah Salix was perfectly placed to answer.

'Go on,' Jeremiah said, as he wheeled the six feet across the faded wood to the bar and held up two fingers to the barman.

'Organised crime is your baby. Who are the players? The big ones in the north-west, I mean. Who's doing what and where are they doing it?'

Jeremiah laughed and shook his head. 'How long have you got?'

'Potted history. Just give me the abbreviated version.'

'Simply put, north-west England is split in two with a number of satellites deferential to both. Manchester and Liverpool are the two main territories with smaller pockets answering to them, based on a number of factors. Most of them geographical. For example, Lancaster is part of Lancashire, which is a Greater Manchester province, so would answer to the crime bosses of Manchester. St Helens has some scope, but that's part of Merseyside, so they answer to Liverpool.'

'And once you know who you are answering to, who exactly are they?'

Jeremiah wheeled back to the table and deposited one pint.

'Off the record, OK? None of this could ever be proven in court, but between old friends like you and me, this is the absolute hundred per cent truth.'

'Of course – and cheers.' Brendan chinked his old pint glass against his new full one, in lieu of Jeremiah's, and finished it off.

'Manchester is headless. You've got a host of small-timers, all vying for the top spot, but not one of them seems to have the grand bollocks necessary to properly take it. The Berg were the top dogs, with a strong line of heroin, meth and arms, but they were dismantled two or three years ago.'

'What happened?'

'I really can't say, half because I don't know, half because what I do know would get me in a world of trouble. They were taken out from outside.'

'OK.'

'So that now leaves the O'Shaugnasseys, the Kendrick Boys, the newly reformed Plymouth Grove Massive and a couple of other smaller try-hards. But my take on this is that they're all too small, and too preoccupied with each other to be pissing about on your patch in Warrington.'

'Right. What about Liverpool?'

'A simpler question, the answer to which is extremely litigious.'

'I've heard a few names, but I don't know anything for sure.'

'The Culpeppers ring any bells?'

Brendan nodded with certainty. He'd heard of them all right.

'What do you know?' Jeremiah asked, wheeling back again with his own pint this time.

'Not a lot, but certainly that name is one I've heard.'

'Sticks in the memory, because essentially it's a name that's about to go extinct. There's fewer than two hundred Culpeppers in the country, and ninety-four of them are in Liverpool.'

'Nice stat. What are they into?'

'Anything and everything, for the most part. I know they've got your Merseyside counterparts going mad trying to get a handle on the docks. Import/export is massive for them, of any commodity you can think of. Not just guns and artillery either, but counterfeit clothes and goods. Huge markets. Extortion and protection rackets too, on land and sea. Again, that's a big earner for them. The NCA is trying its best to work out how they keep operating with such broad efficiency. We know it's them, we just can't prove it. And what we can prove won't deliver the jail time they should be getting.

'The most likely reason for it is police bribery, but to get away with it the way they are, they'd have to have nearly half the force either in their pocket or wrapped by so much fear and threats that getting caught is never really on the agenda. They are also lawyered up to the hilt, and every case that's been brought against them has been settled very quickly out of court. When, or should I really say *if*, we come to arrest and prosecute, we have to be more than airtight.'

Brendan paused for thought.

'That any help?' Jeremiah asked.

'Yeah. It is. What about growth? Manchester sticks to their patch but what about the Culpeppers?'

'Oh, they're in expansion mode, all right. The absence of the Berg in their immediate vicinity has given them all sorts of free range and an enhanced scope. A few of their enterprises are national concerns, and a number of the surrounding satellites have jumped ship to defer to them – or they've had their hands forced. Whoever took out the Berg hadn't bargained for what happens when you kill the head of the pride – that there's always someone just as ambitious waiting in the wings to take over. Better the devil you know sometimes.'

Brendan was mulling over all the possibilities. If his father was still active, who did Warrington answer to?

'What about Warrington?'

'You should definitely know more about this than me.'

'We have the usual stuff. Small gangs of Eastern Europeans pushing white powder, but nothing more organised than a few coordinated burglaries and armed robberies. There doesn't appear to be any concerted physical network – at least, there wasn't until we found this mass grave full of what could well all be criminals.'

'And your nephew.' Jeremiah tipped his glass at Brendan, causing the latter to sigh.

'I know. He was a good lad, always had been, but… yeah, it's a concern.'

'So, it looks like you've got a mob dumping ground.'

The clarity of the statement nearly knocked Brendan off his chair. That was it. Exactly correct. 'Like in the movies when the New York crime families take the poor bastards out to Jersey to off them, leave them out in the sticks.'

'You've got it in one. But why is someone doing that in

Warrington?'

'You think it could be one of the names we've mentioned today?'

'Who knows? Maybe you've got a player on your turf, you just don't know it.'

Brendan thought there was mileage in such a theory – or at least there would have been, if it weren't for a couple of small details. One? He didn't think his dad, for all his flaws, was a killer. He'd been involved in forgery, the trafficking of stolen goods and narcotics. But not murder. And two? He couldn't believe Art had something to do with Connor's death. It just stood so far against his understanding of the order of things. Grandfathers killing their grandsons? Brendan couldn't see it. But with the discovery of that bloody ATM, his father was proving at the very least unpredictable.

'If there is, they've been there for well over fifteen years. That's how long those bodies have been shoved in the hole.' Brendan suddenly felt an overwhelming desire to tell Jeremiah about his father's past, the cash machine and everything in between. Why *was* he covering for his dad? Surely he had done enough in his career to this point to have stepped out of his shadow, to have proven that he wasn't just a criminal's son who joined the police to feed information back to him?

The reality was that Brendan was not prepared for the deluge of questions and scrutiny this would rain on him. If a man is guilty, the son is often guilty by association. What was that saying? An apple never falls far from the tree. That's what everyone would think. Brendan would be guilty by proxy. The spectre of his father had never gone anywhere. His dad's poor life choices were overshadowing him all over again.

He pushed it to the back of his mind, drank his beer and thought about the puzzle that lay before him. There was a missing piece in all of this and he needed to go and find it.

He needn't have worried. Within five minutes of leaving Salix supping his fourth pint (could have been his ninth for all Brendan knew), the NCA golden boy had come up with the goods, catching him on his mobile, sending him in the car somewhere else entirely. As soon as Brendan put the postcode into the satnav and looked at the destination, he had a fair idea what might have gone on, and with it his heart sank like a stone with a weight belt.

CHAPTER 35

SIFTING THROUGH CRAP had always been among the least glamorous moments of a detective's day, regardless of rank. It was often hard to keep your brain in gear and make sure your intuition was still pushing heavy across all the info in front of you, to find the key to the case in a river of garbage.

Madison had baggies on her feet, bright blue against the dark pinstripe of her trouser suit. Her head was hammering with the amount of information she was looking at, all the possibilities around her feet.

There were four iron rings on the floor of the stockroom, each fringed with rust, wide enough to fit a fist through. Only on closer inspection, the rust was blood, dyed copper by time. Whose blood was anyone's guess – and anyone's guess was leading to a certain hole full of a bunch of corpses the papers were calling the 'Warrington 27'.

Two days in and the identity of those in the trench was now undoubtedly the hottest topic in the national news landscape, dominating the breakfast chat show magazine programmes fronted by the gobby and shiny-skinned, right through to the more austere evening news broadcasts. The red tops ran polls alongside the bikini-clad front-page glamour models, and the broadsheets wrote opinion pieces about how the discovery of the trench had only been a matter of time on these shores, the barbarism of Great Britain's erstwhile colonialism come full karmic circle. Social media was in hashtag *thoughts and prayers* meltdown while Facebook was full of custom profile photo frames emblazoned with *pray for the Warrington 27*. It was all absurd and futile, while the entire country waited for word from Warrington Constabulary.

DNA was being swabbed painstakingly from the iron rings by SOCOs with head torches, ready to be driven direct to Mackie at the morgue. She was the quickest way to confirm and correlate, but the way that coincidences work was lending the charade a lilt of inevitability. They'd put a name to one of their suspects, and he was called Malcolm Jevons. Or Mal, as Brendan had referred to him.

What was known of the man was scant, but they were learning more with every minute they stood in that stockroom, ankle-deep in the detritus of the life he left behind. Madison had counted umpteen ticket stubs of matches at home in Liverpool, around the country and abroad, which was providing a timeline of Jevons's movements throughout the years. Football fan and serial killer was the overwhelming picture, but the nag of organised crime still tugged hard at Madison's understanding of the case. She now thought Jevons was a mob killer, the kind that you'd find whacking people off in New Jersey or Staten Island, only they never got called serial killers. These were hitmen.

She picked out a particular scarf and folded it. It was red and gold with a label attached. The price read £5.99, on one of those small rectangular price stickers. It was brand new, probably old stock from the shop itself, she surmised, and there was a number of them. She paused for a moment to watch a SOCO photograph the far wall in great detail, moving closer, then pulling out.

'What is it?' she asked.

The tech didn't even look from behind his eyepiece, speaking out of the side of his mouth. 'UV picked up a stain of some kind, post-Luminol. Strangely carries the spatter pattern of an upward trajectory, as opposed to merely following gravity. Could be blood spatter.'

Jesus, she thought. 'Great work.' Stepping over the nearest anchor ring, this one almost white with print dust, she looked for herself, but could see nothing, no matter how much she squinted. 'Any others?'

'No,' came the answer, as the camera was shifted from landscape to portrait. 'Looks like it was scrubbed pretty effectively with an industrial cleaner, which made it so tough to catch but, well, they appear to have missed a spot.'

While she was watching the tech go to work, almost hypnotised by the changing iridescence of the splatter as the UV's blacklight was shifted, she heard louder voices from the front of the shop. Angry voices.

Pissed off with the disturbance, she walked through to the shop front, swapping one set of booties for another as she moved between crime scenes. The voices, one in particular, male and insistent, grew louder – and it mentioned her by name.

'Where is DS Madison?'

'Here,' she shouted as she entered the shop front, which was crowded with SOCOs and the hulking form of Wainwright. He was remonstrating with Gavigan, while Karthik meekly stood to the side of his superior, looking consumed by embarrassment. His expression on seeing her switched to a plea for understanding, as he mouthed, *I'm sorry.*

'There she is,' he said, his words thick with sarcasm.

'There she is,' Madison echoed. She felt that urge to stand up for herself. Sometimes she answered with her fists. Other days, it was sending fire back at fire, like for like. She found herself mirroring his posture. 'What can I do for you, sir?'

'The tip. It never came from the lines. Where did it come from?' Wainwright's tone was accusatory, his eyes bright.

'Anonymous.'

'Where from? What magical anonymous tip sorting facility do you have access to?'

'A tip is a tip,' she said. 'You know the value of anonymity where sources and informants are concerned.'

His nostrils flared. 'It's Foley, isn't it?'

'A tip is a tip,' she repeated.

'Say no more. He couldn't face it, could he? His ego couldn't take not being in charge, could it? Poor wee lamb.'

Madison felt a rush of white-hot anger, propelled by justice. 'Foley didn't choose to have his nephew murdered, *sir*,' she said, adding her own injection of undiluted sarcasm.

The atmosphere changed, just enough to let Wainwright know that he didn't have the backing of the whole team. Everyone was still.

'Outside, DS Madison,' he commanded.

She gave a slight nod, then readied herself. Wainwright turned and headed for the door, and she dutifully followed. Seniority or no seniority, protocol or nothing, this prick was not going to get away with this. *Keep control, Iona,* she told herself. Be the bigger person. Give them nothing that can come back to you at a disciplinary hearing.

Wainwright opened the door, strode out into the sunlight.

In a sudden rush of air, the side of his head burst in an obscene spray of bright red, bone and gristle.

CHAPTER 36

CULLIFORD WAS DOORNAIL dead, driveways empty, pavements bare. Everyone appeared out at work in the middle of what had become a fairly sunny day, the sky a crisp blue overhead. Brendan did a drive through the neighbourhood first, to assess the lie of the land, keeping his head down and a beanie pulled low. He really shouldn't be there, active suspension feeling like a lead weight around his neck, but there were a number of things he wanted to see for himself. The first thing he spotted was the most obvious. Crime scene tape curling in the minuscule breath of wind, a tiger's tail of yellow and black, and a ruddy great hole in a wall.

The village's layout was simple. A central artery and eight off-shoots feeding into the back end of a housing estate. A small lay-by in front of a Bargain Booze off-licence, a hairdresser and a post office. Next to the door of the Bargain Booze, which appeared to be closed for business, was a large piece of chipboard bolted to the brick, which still wasn't quite big enough to cover the squared-off edges of the hole.

He pulled a quick U-turn by a bus stop at the end of the village and headed back through the main drag, pulling up in front of the post office. He got out and looked at the hole. This was it all right. This was where the cash machine had come from – the light grey masonry dust that frosted the machine in the back of his father's car was identical to the edges of the hole. Unmistakable. He looked above the row of shops. An eyeball camera squatted beneath the guttering, presumably feeding images to a hard drive set-up in the off-licence. He wondered if the police had it, and if they did, which police force it came under.

This, of course, was the problem. Geography, jurisdiction. *Ownership.*

Culliford lay north of Warrington by a good six miles, give or take. Despite being nothing more than a B-road with an estate hanging off it, the village was valuable. Rumoured to be full of rum 'uns, offering an attractive market for stolen goods and drugs.

Attempts to flush it clean had come and gone. At one time, the police had worked closely alongside the local biker chapter to try to get a handle on it – a few of whose members lived here – until it became obvious that the bikers in question had decided (against the preference and hopes of their wider brotherhood) to play the police a fine tune. But who had they been answering to, if anybody? That was the question.

Not only was Culliford not quite Warrington, but it was not quite anything else either. Almost exactly fifteen miles between Liverpool and Manchester, and coveted by the key players in both cities. The satellite towns of the north-west of England all had some sort of deference to the nearest big city, particularly in terms of its organised crime and who could sell what where. Culliford, with its valuable marketplace and geographical question marks, was a much sought-after territory. Whoever's grasp it fell into would have sole power over the village.

That was how it worked.

Usually.

So why, wondered Brendan as he glanced through the window of the post office, did his father have a cash point from such a contentious location stashed away in his garage?

And what was Warrington Constabulary doing about this case – assuming the village even came under Warrington's jurisdiction? On both sides of the law, Culliford was complicated.

'You have them yet?' a stern male voice asked.

Brendan turned to see a man, most likely in his early seventies. He wore a sturdy wax jacket over grey jogging pants. Beside his green wellingtons plodded a dachshund so fat its belly sagged and dragged along the floor as it walked.

'Morning,' Brendan shouted back, taking the conversation back to a much more natural start point.

'Having a nosey? Not getting too far so you've come back to the scene, is that it?' The man had a curious way of speaking, his accent containing the giveaways of Cumbrian roots.

'You live here?' Brendan asked.

The man stopped walking and pointed at one of the two houses on the other side of the street. They were both immaculate, but one was perfectly ordered. Almost militaristic. That was this guy's, no question.

'Eight years now. It's amazing what your pension pennies can get you if you don't chase a fancy postcode.'

'Police? Military?'

'Bit of both, for my sins.' The man looked pleased to be recognised.

Brendan relaxed. Respect was everything, and Brendan could use all the help he could get. He walked over to the man and offered his hand, resulting in a shake that rattled his joints. 'It's true that we can always spot our own, then.'

'Aye, it is. I suppose your lot have enough going on with that horrible matter underground to be chasing about a bit of cash point theft.'

They stood next to each other to face the scene, proper coppers doing what proper coppers always do.

'Bet you could tell me a few stories about this place,' Brendan said, watching the tape coil and flutter loosely.

'I bet I could.'

Brendan felt a funny pressure on his right foot and looked down to see that the dog had actually shuffled over and lowered its belly onto his toes, as if to rest it there.

'Oh aye, Stella, take a load off. She does that. Means you're all right,' said the man.

'I'm flattered,' replied Brendan.

'So, you've got none of them?'

'I assume you saw them? From your house, I mean. You have the perfect vantage point.'

'Light sleeper like me, when it sounds like a bomb's gone off in your neighbourhood, you're out of bed before you know it. I gave a statement to the attending, so it should all be on file.'

'Jurisdictionally, do you know where we are? That's not a rhetorical question, by the way.'

The man turned to look at Brendan, as if wondering whether his sixth sense for spotting other coppers had let him down.

'I'm on leave,' Brendan said. 'My nephew was in that hole on the news, so I'm no use to anyone at the moment.'

The man went quiet again, his eyes lowered to the pavement, before finding his voice – but it had now changed. It was less confident, more tentative. 'You're Foley, aren't you? The detective whose nephew was pulled out of the ground.'

'That's me.'

'Then it's amazing you're here.' The man paused.

'Why? Tell me.'

'I've seen your nephew on the news. Pictures of him before it happened. And now I think about it, he looks a lot like one of the boys I gave a description of the other night.'

'He was here?' Brendan's heart felt like a ventricle had gone pop.

'A boy who looked a lot like him was definitely here. Along with another lad of similar age and a young man in his twenties.'

'You sure it was him?'

'I can't be a hundred per cent but... now *you're* here. And he's, for want of a better word, dead.'

Silence.

'Do you believe in coincidence, Detective Foley?' asked the man.

Brendan took a second. After the events of the last couple of days?

'I absolutely do *not.*'

CHAPTER 37

'AMBULANCE!' MADISON CRIED, sprinting low into the cold, salt-bitten air.

Karthik emerged from the doorway. 'Sniper!'

He rolled across the ground up tight to the wheel well of a parked police car. Instantly, the bonnet was peppered by a tight unit of four gunshots, tearing chunks from the metal.

Madison changed direction and allowed her momentum to take her to the wheel well alongside Karthik, where they braced, shoulder to shoulder.

'Where is it coming from?' she asked.

'No clue.'

All the other police were on the ground, covering their heads, except for one – a lost-looking constable who clearly didn't have the same sense of adrenalin as the rest.

'Down!' screamed Madison.

He suddenly snapped out of his trance when the top of his custodian helmet burst in shards of reinforced plastic, the high-calibre bullet carving it to pieces with a matter-of-fact ease.

Someone screamed. '*No!*' It was only after Madison watched the police officer's body fall to the ground that she realised the person shouting was her.

'From the east,' Karthik whispered in the sudden quiet, and Madison turned to where he was pointing – between the rooftops of the warehouses at the end of the street, to an even taller warehouse much further in the distance, which looked to be at least six storeys high, its sides clad top to bottom in tall windows. In other words, the perfect vantage point.

Madison reached for her radio and found that in her fall to the ground she'd managed to break it. She threw it uselessly to one side. 'How are we doing on that ambulance?' she shouted.

'En route,' came the reply, from inside the open shop door, beyond Wainwright's body. Nobody had tried to help the senior detective, his blood pooling on the doorstep. It was clear he was beyond help.

She turned back to Karthik. 'That warehouse, how far away is it?'

'Must be more than a mile. Hell of a shot,' he replied.

'We need to get there, now.'

Karthik motioned to one of the PCs cowering behind the police car adjacent. He pointed to the top of the policeman's head, then to himself. It didn't take long for the PC to catch on and roll his helmet along the floor to the two detectives. Karthik picked it up and gingerly held the domed peak up over the bonnet next to him.

With a hissed crack, the helmet was struck by another high-velocity round. Karthik rolled what was left of it back to the shocked PC, mouthing the word, *Sorry*.

'Safe to say we're pinned,' he said.

'What's that building, end of the street? The big one?' shouted Madison. 'Don't look up, but anyone know?'

A disembodied voice from beyond the cars came from one of the hidden police officers. 'It's the Titanic Hotel.'

'You're sure?'

'Yeah, I got married there.'

Madison and Karthik swapped a glance, before Madison nodded once. *Do it.* Then she listened while he called in units for a search. Nobody moved, even the ambulances holding back until word came back that their colleagues had arrived at the Titanic, and a room search was under way. Madison and Karthik jumped in the nearest available car and made tracks to join them, buoyed by the small piece of positivity that the other shot officer hadn't actually been killed. While he had been concussed from the impact and had a nasty cut on his head from a shard of split plastic, his helmet had saved his life.

Moments later, they arrived at the Titanic, which was indeed just over a mile away. The longer it took them to get there, the more Madison thought they couldn't possibly have the right place. It was absurdly competent shooting, and at such a distance, surely there was only a handful of people who could accomplish it.

Any of those doubts were put to bed when they were met on arrival by a local police sergeant, who told them they'd found the room. Seven floors up, along the cavernous brick hallways of the elegant converted shipbuilder's in room 732, they'd found that a safety window had had a neat circle cut out of its bottom left corner, big enough for a either a beer can or a high-powered rifle barrel to poke through. Aside from that, the room was spotless, and it was only because of the soft breeze from the Irish Sea that they'd been alerted to the hole in the glass at all, as the draught whistled eerily through it, like a dying man clutching his final breaths.

CHAPTER 38

ANOTHER CLANDESTINE MEETING, another bloody pub. It was nudging eleven. Last orders had been called, with favours called in soon after. Madison felt like her skin was grimed over with a sheen of pure dirt, and she carried the kind of mental pressure only a gin and tonic would sort. She hoped Joel didn't walk in. She knew he frequented these parts, and more than that she knew he'd kill her for being within six feet of booze the night before a fight – a fight she was determined would go ahead.

Brendan sat next to her, on a bar stool, the rest of the pub empty behind them. There were a couple of old hands somewhere in the back room, who'd been there since midday and seen the full four seasons of a pub throughout its working day.

They were drinking in Culcheth, out the back near the church, in a pub called the Pack Horse. The beer garden and the cemetery next door met incongruously in summer, with kids playing next to long-buried loved ones, the dead alongside the living. Life boiled to a fine essence at the back of a village pub.

'Why this pub, Brendan?' she asked, as she threw back as stiff a slug as she dared. She'd made sure it was a gin and slimline tonic, rather than full fat – for all the good it'd do her or her conscience.

'Why not?' He wasn't exactly belligerent, but he wasn't exactly priestly in his sobriety either. 'What did they find by the docks?'

Madison thought for a moment, still so aware that the penalty for sharing sensitive case information with a suspended cop would be severe, yet answered anyway. 'That room was a pigsty, but the real grimness was in the floor. Eleven different samples of DNA. Cross-referenced with the twenty-seven down at the morgue. It's going slow, getting those results – Mackie's refusing to share the workload, says she feels too obligated. But yeah, we've already got a match on five of them. This is the guy, and that was his chop shop. I expect all the other samples will lead back to victims from that damn trench.'

Brendan was quiet.

'Have you been on it all day?' she asked.

Again, silence.

'I'll be off then, shall I?' said Madison, as she dropped off the bar stool, the sudden swell of exasperation catching even herself by surprise. 'You've got what you needed from me, yeah?'

'Iona, please,' Brendan said, turning to her. The pleading in his voice made her pause.

'Brendan, you want trust, *fine*, but you know just how quickly I'd be in hot water if I was caught sharing detailed case information with someone who'd just been thrown square off the damn thing. So, if you want trust it goes both ways – what do you *know*?'

Brendan sat back, blew out hard through his nose, and with it his shoulders seemed to go *Fuck it*, and went slack. 'I fought with my father, because I think he knows something. About the case. About Connor.'

Madison couldn't believe it, but had been around enough major violent crime investigations to know that 99 per cent of the time the perpetrator was someone in the victim's family. Still, she needed Brendan to clarify exactly what it was she thought he was saying. 'Your dad had something to do with it?'

Brendan sipped the stout cream on top of his pint, clearly still wrestling with the dilemma. 'I think he knows more than he's letting on.'

'Why do you think that?'

'Because of where this investigation is going… and because of what my dad used to do in the past.'

'What did he do? Come on, Brendan.'

'Small-time crim. When I was a kid, he was always into something or other, had a little gang and a few money-making schemes. I found out when I was a teenager. By the time I hit my late teens, we'd managed to get him to clean up and go straight.'

'So right through your childhood he—'

'Fancied himself a piss-poor gangster, yeah.' Brendan reached for a dog-eared menu. 'God, I need something to eat. You hungry?'

Madison was. Famished. And she felt seasick at Brendan's revelation that deep in his family's history was a shady period that really should have come up before Brendan's passage to this point in his career.

'I've got a prep dinner sitting at home waiting for me,' she replied.

'Then do you mind me eating a steak in front of you?'

Madison thought about that sad little plastic box in her fridge, all by itself, then her own shoulders went, *Fuck it.*

TEN MINUTES LATER, two sizzling steaks were brought to their table. Madison's was a neat little sirloin on a skillet, bare, next to a little plate of greenery. Brendan's was a huge slab of spitting meat, dripping with oil from all the mushrooms and onions that smothered it. Next to that was a bowl of waffle fries, topped off with a handful of onion rings. From the jar of condiments at the end of the table, he liberally sprayed hot sauce over every last thing.

Madison watched in fascination and a touch of disgust. 'Your wife must be one bloody woman.'

Brendan didn't answer, but felt that earlier guilt ebb back – how were his wife and boys? He'd been jetting about all day and hadn't even dropped another text. Not since their earlier conversation. He started stabbing his fork into the food.

Telling the truth to Madison had been a watershed moment for Brendan. His equilibrium, the one he had honed right through his career, was suddenly skewed. He had just told Madison how he had kept the secret of his father's dealings through the early portion of his career, always fearing that it would come up at any time to derail his progress – but that was just it. *Progress.* It had been so swift, thanks to the urgency with which Warrington Police needed officers of a certain rank, that the early stages of the vetting process were rushed. Before he knew what was happening, he was a detective constable, and nobody was going to question him by that point. He had got away with it.

'It helped that Dad was never booked, never nicked, never even suspected of anything formally. As far as I know, he was only ever questioned once or twice as a witness, but never anything heavier than that. And when he cleaned up his act in the mid-nineties, it was because we were looking into careers and the future. He actually jacked it all in for us.'

'You and your brother?'

'Yes.'

'Good of him, I suppose. When did you pick up your dad was crooked?'

He spoke in a whisper. 'I'd worked out he didn't have a job like most dads. He had a used car centre and bodywork garage. It was a legit business on the outside.'

'Why is it always a chop shop?' Madison shook her head.

'He had some employees there, but they were all off. He was doing something else on that premises, and I had my suspicions about some of it. It was that lack of trust at home that led me to join the police. I'd watched my dad scrap about, lying to Mum and us kids, and it properly wound me up. I hated it. We were innocent, and I knew that if he got in trouble, we'd lose our father. I always thought, by dicking about the way he did, he was putting us all at risk.'

'And you think it might have put Connor at risk in the present day?'

'I always knew you were a gifted detective.'

'But if he's been clean for years, why now?'

'There's that question, but also the other: why did the lad end up in a grave with twenty-six others?'

They both sat there in silence for a moment, until Madison broke it.

'Your face changed when you saw the picture of the first man from the drone video.'

Brendan squinted. 'I couldn't quite place him at the time, but now I remember him from my childhood. Dad knew him.'

'He was one of *those* friends of his?'

'I've got this picture of him, younger obviously, sitting around a paddling pool with a bottle of Cinzano.'

'You sure it was him? Because if that video shows him putting your nephew in a grave, your family has a lot of deep-seated issues.'

'I'm pretty sure. There was a weird disconnected vibe to him. As a kid, I thought he was just a bit weird – you know, the way he looked at things and stuff. But now, I realise it's the same look a hundred sick crims have given me. That deadness in there when things are calm and cool, which suddenly becomes like a deranged *focus* when their blood is up. You know the look I'm talking about?'

'Yeah, I know.'

'I haven't seen him in years, since those old days when Dad was still active. Whether there's a link there is anyone's guess, but you're right. If it is him, we have big problems. And there's something else. Something I really don't know what to do about.'

He took a deep breath and started to tell her about what was sitting snugly in the boot of his father's sports car.

And he didn't just stop there.

CHAPTER 39

IN A MOMENT of once-in-a-lifetime rarity, Brendan was heading back into Manchester twice on the same day – this time on the train, and this time, most definitely after hours. He sat on a two-carriage train from Liverpool to Manchester, which stopped in Warrington to pick up commuters or revellers heading in either direction. The line was more fractious the later it got, but was always buzzing. It lumbered with a steady, almost reassuring, clunk clunk along the old railway line.

He'd stopped drinking just before you could use the term *pissed*, when a moment of clarity hit with the measured thunks of a treble twenty. His father was going down. He had a brother who worshipped Art, who might also be in the frame for God knows what. What to do about that? He felt pulled in every direction. He had no respect for his father, and no real respect for his brother… but he was his brother after all. And his son had just been murdered.

The carriage lights on the thirty-mile line were unapologetic. Brendan was forced to see the various partygoers in all the shades of burst-capillary crimson. The stations rolled by – Birchwood, Irlam, Urmston, Humphrey Park. Old Trafford, Manchester United's coliseum. As the train approached the city centre, Brendan could spot the vertical twinkling slab of Beetham Tower. There were cranes everywhere, their red blinking aircraft-warning lights dotting the skyline.

The train pulled into the end of the line, Oxford Road Station. The concourse was busy, most people ready to head home after a night at a show or in the pub, yet every now and then you could see the disconcerted look of an office worker who'd stayed late and was now positively shuddering at the thought of travelling home with the humanity around them.

Brendan made his way through the crowd and out through the automatic turnstiles after flashing his hastily bought e-ticket at the sensor. Oxford Road Station occupied an elevated spot over Oxford Road itself, which was arguably the second main thoroughfare of the city centre, and, once through the entrance, the throng poured out onto the pavement, carrying Brendan with it. Down the drop-off lane, between the old Cornerhouse cinema and a bar, down to a junction opposite a Sainsbury's. Brendan hadn't put his phone away and was navigating via Google Maps again, watching the little blue dot on the screen. He was heading to Chinatown, to Ross.

At least that's where Ross said he was. Brendan had rung him after Madison had gone to get as early a night as she could, what with her title fight the following evening. One more solo beer had given Brendan all the time he needed to get a real guilt trip going, but Ross had been more hammered than he was by the time he picked up. When he'd found out it was his brother calling, he'd thrown his phone down on the bar in disgust. After a couple of seconds of a heavy R&B bassline, a woman's voice came on the line. Brendan had reluctantly picked his mobile back up. She'd suggested his brother was in a bad way and could do with being collected. The guilt had lurched in Brendan again, and he'd asked where, only to be given the name of a strip club. The Obsession Rooms in Chinatown. Great.

Now, Brendan walked under the red arched entrance to the Chinese district. Four blocks of city centre property – more of a China Corner than town. He immediately saw the gaudy pink neon sign for the club. Two thick-set blokes on the door gave Brendan the once-over as he approached. Having apparently passed the test, he was down the stairs without breaking stride, handing a tenner over to a supremely bored-looking girl, no older than twenty. She gave him a ten Obsession Dollar note in return. On inspection, it was nothing more than a voucher for a cheap drink.

Once inside the basement club, he went straight to the bar on the left. After being told that Guinness wasn't covered by the terms of the offer, he swapped his Obsession Dollar for a bottle of Castlemaine XXXX, a beer he thought had long since gone extinct. As soon as the drink was in his hand, he was accosted by offers.

'Buy me a drink?'

'Fancy a dance?'

'Need company?'

'What's your name?'

It didn't stop until he held his hands up. 'I'm just here looking for someone.' His words had the same effect as a garlic-fuelled burp. They all left him promptly and, as the coast cleared, he finally set eyes on his brother.

Ross was sprawled on a sofa at the far end of the club, facing a dance floor no more than five feet wide and three feet deep, housing the obligatory pole. He walked straight over. The woman working the pole just feet in front of Ross stopped when she saw him and stepped down.

'The cavalry,' she said, before marching off on her stilettoes.

Ross watched her departure with alarm. 'Hey, where are you – oh, fuck *off.*' Then he saw his brother and threw himself back on the sofa.

'I don't care what you're doing, Ross,' Brendan said, holding one hand up and his beer bottle with the other. 'I just need to talk to you.'

Ross stared at the dance floor in front of him, flashing different gaudy colours, splashing them up in his face. Brendan dropped down on the sofa next to him, taking note of just how bad he looked. Stubble long past designer, hair every which way, skin pale as stale egg white, jogging pants stained with God-knows-what, yet still in a designer leather jacket.

Hard to know what to say to each other. They'd led such different lives.

Brendan started. 'I'm sorry for everything that's happened to you.' Ross's eyes were glassy, and it wasn't the booze. 'I'm so cut up about it, and if I'm cut up, I can't picture what you're going through.' The irony wasn't lost on Brendan that he had barely seen his own sons since Ross had lost his.

Ross didn't answer but his glance shifted to stare into the distance. Brendan followed his gaze and saw that he was lost in the reflection coming from the floor-to-ceiling mirror behind the pole. The two brothers stared back at them. God, they were a mess. Two pissed-up men in a seedy strip club, all neon panels and wipe-clean sofas.

Brendan knew what was coming – and had a fair idea of what it was going to do to his brother.

'I need to tell you something, Ross,' he said. He faltered almost immediately. 'We haven't always seen eye to eye, I know that. But you're my brother. It's going to get worse.'

Flatly, Ross replied, 'How on God's green earth can things get worse?'

'Dad is going to be arrested in the morning.'

That shocked Ross into actually looking at his brother. 'What? Why?'

'They're building a case at the moment. He's involved in a lot of shit.'

'I know that.' It was the most honest Ross had been with him about their father in years.

'He's going down for a while. Brother to brother, I want to make sure you've the chance to get your own house in order. I don't know what you're into together – if anything – but this is a heads-up. Man to man.'

Ross looked flayed. 'I appreciate that, bro.'

Brendan's brother hadn't used that term since they were kids. He might not have chosen to use it if he knew that Brendan was the person who'd uncovered the evidence that would send their dad to prison.

'You have to take care of yourself, OK? I don't care what you've done, but your wife needs you to—'

'She's gone,' Ross interrupted. 'She's left for good. Turns out the boy was the only thing we had in common. Her parents called me, laid it out. Her dad's been at our place all day, getting her stuff. Don't even know what I'm gonna be left with.'

'I'm sorry, mate. What can I do?'

'Take care of yours. And I'll take care of whatever I've got left.'

'All right. Can I get you home?'

'No. Now piss off so I can enjoy some tits before I have to go and face it all.'

Brendan looked at his brother carefully. He could see resignation, but also the spark of something more stubborn. Even though he'd come here to take his little brother home, he sensed he should let him be. This was his path to navigate – grief, worry, naked breasts and all. Trying to force him to do otherwise would only result in a fight. 'OK, bro. I'll see you soon.' He clamped a hand on his shoulder. 'Take care of yourself.'

Ross grunted and waved a hand to one of the girls, indicating that it was her turn on the pole. 'Hopefully not too soon.'

Brendan left him to his thoughts and headed for the door, unable to decipher his brother's parting words. Was Ross about to go to ground? If so, should Brendan be letting the police know so they could get a fix on him before he legged it?

No. *No.* He was going to give his brother the night. Because if it was proven Art was responsible in any way for Connor's death, the hurt for Ross was only just beginning.

PART 3

AND THE NEW

ROB PARKER

CHAPTER 40

BLOOD WAS ALREADY on Hoyt's hands, and he hadn't even properly messed anything up yet. Wainwright's death was on him and him alone.

So many times the day before he'd tried calling the number the Culpeppers used to reach him, but with no answer. He'd been reduced to leaving a frantic voicemail message. 'When I said the old DI, I meant the DI who's no longer on the case. Not the older man who happens to be the current DI!'

The phones were quiet and had been all morning – so much so that Hoyt had told the two dolts under his command that they could go out and follow a couple of leads in person. That had excited them, getting off the desk. Hoyt had personally selected the leads they were ferreting off to investigate. Both went precisely nowhere, which would take them some time to discover, so he had the place to himself. He needed it, because he was bricking himself. With the news that there was going to be a publicly high-profile arrest, the atmosphere in the nick was expectant and jubilant.

When the update was that they were bringing in Arthur Foley, his heart twisted. He was waiting for instructions, waiting for any kind of word of what his superiors wanted to do. Not his career superiors of course – nothing as mundane as that. His real superiors – Charlotte and her family. He'd need time and space to handle them.

On coffee number eight of the morning, which he was making stronger with each return visit to the refreshments table, he kept his spare phone on vibrate in his jacket pocket. Arthur Foley was important to the Culpeppers, that much was obvious, but he didn't know why – and he didn't really want to. *Just tell me what you want me to do so I can slip the noose from my sister's neck.* That's all he wanted to know.

As he was pouring coffee, he was approached by some uniformed gossip snake, desperate for a little something he could use to gain credo among his peers.

'What a story,' began the man. 'Are they fixing him for the mass murderer?'

'Dunno, mate. They're not telling us much.'

'You must have some idea, CID and all,' the man pressed.

Hoyt wanted to grab him by the throat. If Hoyt had been kept in the loop on every single thing, maybe he'd have a better chance of keeping the bloody Culpeppers happy.

When the phone eventually vibrated with a text, he darted back to his table.

If Art Foley talks, it's war on the Foleys, your sister's dead and it's all on you.

This was an impossible situation. The future of a copper's family lay in Hoyt's hand, while his sister's and her family sat in the other.

Hoyt didn't know what to do, how to stop Art from spilling. There was, however, a window. One chance. He got his head down and got thinking, in a bid to save his sister's family. Fuck Foley. He didn't care what Madison thought of him. It was his pig-headedness that had got them all in this mess.

Hoyt needed to fashion a reason to get a word in with Art when they brought him to the nick. He looked at the clock. They'd be bringing him back to the station for interviews, by which point he'd be met by a lawyer. He wouldn't be able to get near Art then.

Between Arthur Foley's arrival and his lawyer joining him, there was a single window of opportunity. Hoyt had to get to him then or it was curtains.

CHAPTER 41

BRENDAN WATCHED HIS father being dragged out of his own front door, writhing and bucking fiercely, bellowing his innocence to the neighbourhood.

All Brendan could feel was shame.

Shame that this was his father. That this was the life his father had chosen. Brendan had been banjaxed since birth.

Still, Brendan had forced himself to go back to his childhood home. Made himself stand across the street, while they tried to march Art Foley to one of the myriad police cars that had turned up for the event. The reason? He had to show them. He had to show his fellow colleagues that he wasn't made of the same stuff. Had to show his father that, despite everything, their shared blood wouldn't keep him safe from prosecution. And he had to show to himself that he was strong enough. Strong enough to defy all expectations of him and face his father's arrest head-on.

The secret past he had spent years keeping under wraps was now outed. Questions would be asked about him too now, for sure. Questions too loud to ignore. He had to hope that those who knew him, and those who had seen his exemplary records and performance assessments, would know what he was really made of. By being brave enough to stand here, watching over his own father's arrest, he would show how different the two men were.

It was a shocking scene, and one that would eventually take some processing. His father was dressed in a hooped woolen jumper, stripes of grey and brown wrapping his ample form. He had a pair of brown moccasins on, blue jeans and a constable on each arm, with two behind. What they thought of him was anybody's guess, but a high-profile arrest the day after the broad-daylight murder of a policeman wasn't good. It cast Art as the cop killer in the neighbourhood's midst. Or, at the very least, the person responsible for ordering such a death. To many, coincidences ran only so far. They'd see Brendan's dad as the mass murderer responsible for the Warrington 27.

'Fucking pigs,' Art roared. 'Jobsworth busy fuckin' pigs.'

A frail figure appeared in the open doorway – Brendan's mother. Moira's face sagged with shock. As Brendan watched her, he knew the horrible reality. In a couple of hours, she wouldn't remember a damn thing. But that didn't mean she didn't feel every heartbreaking moment right now.

'Sweetheart, I think it's time,' said Brendan. Mim, silently standing beside him, nodded. She started to cross the road, buggy leading the way.

'I'll look after her, don't worry.' Mim turned briefly, offering a low wave. Brendan nodded. When the chips were down – really down – the union between husband and wife showed what it was really made of. Fortunately for Mim and Brendan, it was made of titanium.

Art's arm was jammed tight up his back. He relented, and the bobbies, in a practised motion, posted him into the back of the waiting car. As Art clambered inside, the garage door behind rolled up, revealing the Audi shimmering into the daylight. SOCOs were already in the garage, and others poured through the widening doorway.

Brendan felt a presence at his side but didn't turn.

'You've had a truly shit week,' said a male voice. 'But I have to admire your chutzpah.'

Brendan didn't answer, just watched as Mim reached his mother, whose face lit up immediately on seeing her. They hugged. All ills forgotten. At least that was something. He finally turned to look at Superintendent Monroe, whose presence at an arrest would usually be out of place. Not today.

'It pains me to say, we're having a bad time ourselves,' Monroe said.

'I'm sorry about Wainwright,' replied Brendan, 'and I'm sorry I couldn't let this go.'

'You had a hunch. It takes a brave man to go against his dad – although I must say, how you managed to keep all this quiet is beyond me.'

Brendan had finally told Madison everything last night. He trusted Madison to get his words right when she passed them on, not to twist or misinterpret. He'd told her how his father had quit whatever side business he had going on because Brendan wanted a career in the police. That despite all the ups and downs of their relationship, he honestly thought that Art had done that. He'd told her how he'd hidden all aspects of his father's past ills from the police recruitment channels because he wanted the career more than anything. He'd seen what crime did to families growing up. He knew he had the drive and determination to make a difference. He'd told her his suspicions now – that Art was active again. That he'd persuaded these kids to rob a cash point in a territory he wrongly thought was unclaimed. To test the waters. And it had got them killed.

'We both know I wouldn't have had a career if I hadn't,' Brendan said.

'Probably not. So, what now?'

'I don't know, but I have a couple of ideas.'

'If your ideas are about the Warrington 27, then you can piss them straight into the breeze. Home Office have taken it off us. Wainwright's death made sure of that.'

Brendan nodded once.

'I can lift your suspension. Take two weeks and come back. It doesn't feel right to ask, but I'm a bit short in the DI department.'

His career was being handed back to him, but he didn't know if he was ready for it. He still hadn't caught those responsible – *directly* responsible – for killing his nephew. And he wouldn't be able to find peace until he did. 'Can I think about it?'

Now it was Monroe's turn to be surprised. 'DI jobs aren't just offered on a plate, you know. But, all right, if you insist. You've shown you're a detective, through and through. We need that.' Monroe started to walk away. 'Go home and rest up. And grieve, for God's sake.'

'The twenty-seven,' Brendan called after him. 'Are they still here? In Warrington?'

This stopped Monroe in his tracks, and his shoulders caught the pitter-patter of a fine spitting rain that was just starting. He turned back. 'They're here. Mackie, being Home Office in the first place, is being retained.'

Brendan stepped towards him. 'Then get *him* in there to have a look at them.' He pointed at the car his father was in, which was just setting off at a crawl through the assembled vehicles.

Monroe didn't answer, so Brendan pressed on.

'If he knows who any of them are, he might be able to connect the dots more than any of us. I can question him.'

'Let me get this right.' Monroe was shaking his head in disbelief.

'You want to send a key murder suspect over to identify the bodies before he's been formally charged and before he's got his lawful representation – and not just that, but *you* want to question him? Your *dad*?'

Brendan found he was putting a desperate hand on Monroe's damp shoulder, which he immediately regretted when his superior looked at his hand in outrage.

'Think of the element of surprise,' he said, snatching his hand back. 'He'll cave, he won't be ready for that at all.'

'You can't interview your own father. You should be nowhere near it.'

Brendan wasn't letting go. 'Come up with a reason that it has to be done now. Get his solicitor to meet him at the station.'

'You want me to pull a reason to break procedure out of my arse to suit a recently suspended officer?'

'Do you want to solve this or not? Because I'm sure you can. Right here, right now, without anyone else involved.'

Monroe paused and appraised Brendan.

Brendan felt that the window of opportunity was ajar, so he jumped straight back in. 'It would be Warrington Police's collar. I don't want any credit – I'm not even supposed to be here. But he will talk to me when he hears what I've got to say, and he won't to anybody else, I guarantee it.'

He could see that the superintendent was teetering. Brendan decided to go for it, push him over the edge with a fantasy headline.

'Warrington Police solve the case of the murdered Warrington 27, thanks to the quick actions and thinking of the station's own superintendent.'

The mocking look on Monroe's face clearly said, *Really?* But then something made him soften.

'Do you really think you can get him to talk?' Monroe asked.

'Get him in front of those bodies now before his solicitor gets to the nick. I'll get it out of him.'

Monroe sighed. 'This is highly irregular.'

'What good is being a superintendent if you can't play irregular?'

Monroe rolled his eyes. Brendan had won. 'Be there in thirty minutes.'

CHAPTER 42

MADISON HADN'T EVEN bothered trying to go to bed in the end. She had tried to put Hoyt out of her mind, however hard it had been, and how strange she found his behaviour had become. She thought, after the day they'd all had, he would be in waiting for her again, but her flat had been empty when she finally got home. She'd grabbed a shower after writing her reports, which took all night. About the crime scene the day before in Bootle, about Wainwright getting his head blown off, about everything Brendan had told her.

Every last word she'd documented, then submitted in time for Monroe to read when he got in at eight. Which he did, over his morning bowl of honeyed porridge in his hollowed-out swimming pool office. He had Madison on the phone by ten past, and by eight forty-five she knew that Arthur Foley had been arrested for possession of stolen property. The cash machine was, at this tentative stage, all they had for certain – but it was more than enough.

She had left them to it, however. To her mind there was actually the Warrington 29 to worry about. She and Brendan both reasoned that if Connor had been involved in that ATM heist, and had been put in the murder trench for it, then his two accomplices should have been there too – but the hole had been discovered before anyone had had a chance. Going on the descriptions given by retired sergeant Robinson of Culliford, they could reasonably look for the bodies of two other young men. Which is what she'd been doing. By 9 a.m., she had a match and was on the road again, the police information networks offering the information that the bodies of two young men in their early twenties were in Bangor, North Wales, as yet unidentified and unclaimed.

Madison was hoping she could take them off their hands. She'd hoped this so fiercely that she'd jumped on the A55 off the M56 and jetted straight along North Wales's hairline like a head-louse on crank, and left the messy politics back in Warrington. She'd been away before she heard the sirens. She'd kept the radio off, eager for a little mental space, enjoying the castles of Colwyn Bay and

Bodelwyddan on the left, and the rolling mucky tide and caravan parks to her right. She'd wound the windows down, and let the percussive mix of the engine, the sea and the rushing air beat back the image that had haunted her since the day before.

Wainwright, on the ground, staring upwards. One eye open. The other eye lost, part of a piece of skull that was no longer there, leaving a deep red gash and that grey sludge. All we were, all we are, and all we're ever going to be, was just an off-white bit of jelly floating about in a fragile little egg – and that jelly and egg can part ways in the blink of an eye. In summary? Life was fragile as *fuck*.

She was soon pulling off the main drag into Bangor, to a hospital she'd never been to before, to meet a detective she'd never met. This case. This case was testing them to their limits.

After being ushered through the barrier and parking, she soon found herself being taken to a side office by a PC, where a detective was waiting. The woman was thirty years further along her career than she was and had the overall patter down spot-on. She was firm, honest and straight to the point, while retaining an air that suggested any nonsense would not be well received. Madison wasn't in the nonsense business, so they immediately got on fine.

'Some mess you've got in Warrington,' said the detective by way of hello.

'Why'd you think I put my hand up for this jolly jaunt?' Madison replied.

'The John Does are downstairs in the little morgue. Which of them are you after?'

'Both.'

'OK. If this leads to any high-profile arrests, like the one on the box just now, I'll expect a mention and credit for the constabulary. In return we'll help in any way we can.'

Madison appreciated the directness. There were a number of admin weasels in the police, and this detective knew the game had to be played, but she made sure it was played her way. 'I wouldn't have it any other way.'

'Dandy,' she said. 'Detective Sergeant Stephens at your service.' She jabbed a thumb at her chest.

'DS Madison.'

'Follow me then, DS Madison.'

Iona liked her, found herself wanting to impress her. She wasn't like any female detective she'd met. She could learn a lot in her company.

They wound their way through the maze of offices and corridors down to a service area, through a locked door, where an in-house pathologist was at work on another cadaver, a man whose chronic obesity was betrayed by the pancaking effect of gravity. The smell was sharp, sickly and unforgettable. The pathologist was up to his elbows in the man's chest cavity, and nodded at the bank of freezers on the far side of the room.

Stephens nodded back and went straight over to the square doors, two of which, side by side, had their sealing handles unclipped. Both were opened, the hum of the freezer's motor filling the room, and with a whoosh of rails, two bodies floated out. Madison felt the room drop a couple of degrees, down to the cooler being left open, but in the presence of such recent death it was still unnerving.

Both bodies were grey in pallor and covered in cuts.

'Before you ask,' started Stephens, 'they were in the sea, and all that is the work of crabs. A family rock-pooling had a horrible end to their morning.'

'Cause of death?' Madison stepped forward and looked the two naked bodies over. One was in more athletic shape than the other, but both were undoubtedly of a similar age – the first sign that things weren't quite going the way she hoped.

'Knife wounds on this one, two in the back, either side of the spinal column.' It was to the more muscular of the two she was referring. 'This was a knife again, but right through the heart. One precise stroke. Rest of the body unharmed – well, aside from the obvious.'

'Done it before, hasn't he?'

'You think these are part of what you've got going on over there?'

Madison thought for a moment. 'Not this one.' She pointed at the man whose heart had been punctured. 'But definitely this one.' The other man lay there immortalised in death, his importance laid bare. This was the ringleader of the Culliford cash point job. She was sure of it. She was more sure of it with every second spent in his rather one-sided company. The description matched perfectly.

'If we can get the paperwork done, would you like me to arrange for him to be sent back with you?'

She nodded. 'Yes, please.'

Now they had the Warrington 28.

CHAPTER 43

BRENDAN WAS AMAZED at how different the mortuary looked in the couple of days since he'd last been there. The sparse cavernous space was now much busier, but primarily with the dead, who all lay neatly, shrouded by white sheets. There was no plastic any more, and beneath the sheets, the horrors of their injuries and decomposition were laid plain as day.

The hospital morgue was crammed with cadavers, so much so that a hasty partition screen had been erected on one side of the autopsy room, splitting the space unevenly. But the partitions couldn't reach the whole distance, so the last section was filled by an A-framed whiteboard, around which Brendan could see yet more cadavers. These were different, not laid quite as carefully. Six of them. Recent hospital deaths that had been scooted to one side to allow for the investigation to take priority.

He sat on the back wall, overlooking the room, as Mackie walked in with two police officers and his father in between them. His father looked terrified.

'We have an established order to the way the deceased are presented, Mr Foley, but you needn't worry about that,' Mackie said, herself dressed a grade or two more formally today, which meant those Home Office colleagues of hers were imminent. The case was being passed upwards, and that meant more pressure and more need to observe the immediate formalities of the established order. It was also a do-over, in a big sense, after the incandescent fuck-up that Warrington Constabulary had played. Best foot forward and all that.

Art looked like he was going to lose his breakfast and then some. He was cuffed, arms behind him, which made him look even more tentative and wary.

'He's not here.'

Everyone looked up to the source of the voice, except for Mackie, who'd let Brendan in. 'The ones who've been identified have been moved on. Funerals to arrange and all that. Speaking of funerals, when is Connor's?'

Death seemed to make Art uncomfortable. Brendan intended to play exactly on that.

'You seem less than happy, Art. Not so nice seeing your handiwork up close and personal?' Brendan lowered himself from the metal counter top and moved along the rows of tables into the centre of the room.

'You know I didn't do this,' Art said, spitting the words at his son. 'Look at me. You think I'm capable of this? Morbidly obese with a heart like a split apple. You think I could dig a hole and fill it with this lot, repeatedly, over a series of years?'

'I think you could have a go.'

'Fuck you, son.'

'If you didn't, maybe you arranged it.'

'You know I didn't. Let's leave it at that. I note that I'm not at the police station in the presence of a lawyer.'

Time to twist the screw, thought Brendan. 'Fair enough. I'll lay this out as concisely as I can. You are the principal suspect – the only suspect – with a definite, cast-iron tie to at least one of the people in that hole.' He neglected to tell him about what was found raiding Mal's old shop storerooms. 'Usually in these circumstances, the guilty party is shown his handiwork, and swears to Christ Almighty and every disciple he can think of that he's never seen them before. Nobody guilty, in any case I've ever been involved with, studied or even heard of, featured a killer who was eventually convicted saying that he recognised the victims of the crimes in question. That's why, when these people are shown to you and if you recognise them, you should be singing like a songbird. Because it will prove your innocence.'

Mackie stepped back and pushed her glasses higher on her nose. It was a small gesture but somehow gave the moment an air of punctuation. Brendan was gambling here, a gamble he'd never get away with in front of a legal representative, but Brendan was convinced that if his father was innocent of the bigger mass of crimes, then he would proclaim his innocence. One more squeeze on the neck should do it.

'And, when you see these faces, if you can tie them to anybody, or give us an idea of who may or may not have wanted them dead, well… Let me put it as simply as I can. If you can help put someone else in the frame here, it will be looked extremely favourably upon. It may even help you at trial, which, when you're caught with a cash point hidden in your garage, is a guarantee at this point. Handling stolen goods, if that's what they've brought you in on. You might avoid jail time. Maybe. But you have to start singing.'

Hand played, Brendan leaned against one of the tables. 'Tell us what you know about these people, why it can't be you, point us to who did it, and it just might save your arse.'

Simple.

Art took a moment before turning to his son. The whole character of his face had skewed. 'You're enjoying this, aren't you? You fucking embarrassment. The state of you. You piss on your family for a career step.'

Brendan could say anything he liked to show what an outlandishly hypocritical statement that was, but, for starters, he was just too shocked. He'd never seen his father turn like this. The man he'd called Father. After this moment, he'd never do so again. He remembered signposts on the road to this, but never this. Never the frothing ire that seemed on the dangling precipice of murder. Maybe he was capable of killing all these people. The hate in his eyes that very moment could be capable of absolutely anything. The ice-cold criminal of the past had been exposed. Brendan had been right. Right to cut this man so far out of his life that it had taken years to fix. Right to try to ease his own small family unit in another direction. His father was vile and pathetic, and he felt vindicated.

'The offer is there.'

Art started moving along the bodies and stopped by one of them. He waited a second. 'My hands are a little occupied here,' he said with angry sarcasm.

Mackie stepped forward and drew the sheet back.

Art blinked. 'No,' he said, and moved to the next one. And the next. On the fourth, the reaction was immediate. No surprise, really – the man in question was an unnatural grey-brown, and his eye sockets had sunk thanks to the vacancy within them. Top that off with the lower jaw's absence, the roof of the dead man's mouth obvious and lined with teeth, as an obscene strip of flesh lay down the victim's neck. His tongue. It was bad enough to look at, even if you didn't know the guy.

'I always wondered what happened to him,' said Art. He was genuinely shaken. This was it. Brendan looked to the far end of the room, where a mirror covered the entire wall. He nodded at it, and to the people beyond. This was going to work.

WITHIN TWENTY MINUTES, the one-time concerto of Art was ringing its final notes to the rafters, and the case was blown wider than a blue whale's carotid.

Brendan was almost overwhelmed. Art had managed, despite their lack of faces, to make strides in identifying twelve of the cadavers, and he might have got a couple more if it weren't for the rank stage of their decomposition. At the midway stage, Art slowed for a couple of seconds, as if the fact that he knew the identity of just so many of the victims was making it look like he could be the only one who'd put them in there. But by that point, the enormity of death had clearly got to him. He couldn't stop, couldn't stop naming them, like it was a duty of some kind – the boatman taking roll-call ready for the ferry across the water to the gates of heaven. By the end, he was spent, and looked relieved when he was led away by the coppers. However, he paused at the door.

'You wanted a name.'

'And?' Brendan asked.

'Culpepper. Most of those had something to do with Culpepper.'

Brendan nodded. Inside he was exploding.

'Now put me somewhere safe, will you, because I'll need it,' Art said.

Brendan nodded to his father's escort, who started to march him out of the room, but in a last act of chaotic, futile bravado, Art lunged in the direction of his son – and thanks to his sheer weight, he didn't make a bad job of it. The officers caught him as he got within spitting distance of his boy. Brendan held firm.

'And you, you fuckin' wretch,' father said to son. 'Well done, you. I hope you're dead proud. Because, more than likely, you've just murdered your entire family.'

The words caught Brendan cold. 'Take him.'

Art was bundled away, his fight snuffed out.

As soon as he was gone, Mackie slumped and loosened the collar of her white shirt, deflated with exhaustion. It was only then that Brendan realised the toll this had taken on her – the silent personal heft of wading through the nameless dead, trying to order the unorderable. To have names to those people she had got to know so intimately was a weight lifted so suddenly that it appeared to leave her bereft.

'Jesus *Christ.*' She blew the word out into the room.

Now Brendan had the sheer scale of his father's involvement in the organised crime networks of the north-west. One of the biggest murder cases the country had seen was suddenly on its way to being solved. The pieces were aligning, adapting shape, forming something solid.

Brendan turned to the glass: 'You got all that, didn't you?'

Monroe's voice broke into the autopsy room via intercom. 'Every golden fucking word.'

Brendan should have been pleased. Should have been moonwalking between the gurneys. But he couldn't.

The only thing in his head, bouncing wall to wall, were his father's words.

Murdered your entire family.

Surely he was exaggerating. He had to be. These Culpeppers had reach, but surely it didn't extend that far.

It couldn't... could it?

CHAPTER 44

THE CASTLES WERE now on Madison's right, the rolling muck-tide and caravan parks on her left, and back to mayhem she was headed. She was driving no faster than fifty miles per hour because behind her, in convoy, was a boxy seventies ambulance, all white with a red stripe down the side. It was the only ambulance Bangor had spare. This was probably its last run anywhere – it had been sitting MOT'd in storage for a year, but was due to go to a heritage centre by next summer. One last swansong for the old girl. Inside? Jamie Fitzmorris, aged twenty-four, from Orford. Number 28. He'd done something stupid when he was seventeen, so was on the system. Connect-the-dots easy.

She was half an hour from home when her phone rang. It was sitting on her dash, hovering in space on one of those magnetic air-vent mount things, so she could clearly see the name Joel as the caller. Her boxing coach.

She didn't answer immediately. He had never once, not in the three years that he'd trained her, called her. She had his number in case work dictated that she had to cancel or reschedule a training session, never in case he needed to speak to her. He was as reliable as shit northern weather – always there, always pushing you into something uncomfortable. So this call was unexpected. *The fight.* When was it? Tonight? *Christ.*

She answered. 'Hi, Joel.'

'Y'all right, Iona?'

'Fine thanks, mate. What's up?'

'Not much, what about you?'

You called me, thought Madison. 'Just out at work. I know I've missed a couple of sessions but… All OK?' This was as personal as they got, so it was shaky ground.

'It's a weird one. Can you come to the gym?'

'I'm a bit snowed under, mate. Can we chat on the phone?' He had her attention, but she could see that derelict box trundling along in her rearview.

'No. No, I don't think we can. The gym's empty now until four. Can you come in any time before then?'

'Not really. I'm halfway back from Bangor of all places. I mean, I'm in work, Joel.'

'Yeah, obviously, but if it was work, would you come?'

Madison's interest swung upwards sharply. 'That would be different, of course.'

'Right. Then, it's work. Come for work reasons.'

Madison waited. Silence. It was a tactic she was picking up. An old police trope. People who wanted to talk usually filled silence if offered it. She didn't like playing Joel like he was a suspect, but she needed an answer.

'I'm not calling a tip line, all right?' he said.

Madison was sold. She told Joel she'd be there in forty, then she called the ambulance driver with new instructions.

HOYT MADE HIS sixth visit to PC Morgan at the station front desk, who had got so sick of him that she waved him away as soon as she saw him. But he was frantic. *Where. The Fuck. Was Art Foley?*

'Are you sure nothing happened to them en route?' he asked.

'We're not in charge, DS Hoyt,' replied Morgan. She was harassed, but holding it together well with a straight-talked practice. 'They don't keep us in the loop. And you're on the team, aren't you? Well, d'you really think if they're not letting their detectives know, they'd ring in and tell their bloody secretary? No. Like I said, we'll let you know as soon as they arrive.'

'Jesus Christ,' Hoyt muttered as he started to walk back, when he caught the slick aura of a well-paid lawyer, sitting in the waiting area opposite the desk. He was in his mid-forties, hair receded almost to nothing, but what he had left was oiled back down the nape of his neck and onto the collar of one hideous brown suit – and his face betrayed opportunity.

'They're not telling you either?' he said in tones both educated and wolfish.

'We have nothing to tell, sir, please wait like the rest of us,' said Morgan.

Hoyt stammered, 'You're here to represent Art Foley?'

The man looked pointedly at Morgan. 'Well, I'm certainly trying to.'

Morgan rolled her eyes and moved on.

There was no time at all to speak with Foley Sr to relay the message – there was no window whatsoever.

Unless…

Hoyt walked over to the lawyer and offered his hand. 'DS Hoyt. I've been working on the Warrington 27 case. Would you like a coffee while we wait for Mr Foley to arrive, maybe swap notes?'

'I think I'll wait for my client to arrive, if it's all the same to you.'

Hoyt felt more adrift than ever.

'YOU KNOW WHAT makes this gym interesting?' Joel said, sitting in an age-old swivel chair in the dusty gym office.

'Tell me,' replied Madison, sitting opposite, their knees almost touching thanks to the small size of the room.

'Where it is. Warrington.'

She'd never seen Joel's body language like this, hunched and nervous.

'You're going to have to help me out here.'

'You get all sorts, from all over. But it's right between Liverpool and Manchester, isn't it? So, if you can't go to a gym for whatever reason in either of those places, you can come here. We get a proper mix. All-comers.'

'Go on.'

'Boxing gyms get the best of all worlds. You get the dedicated and you get those who like a rumble. You get people who train for pleasure and you get those who train because their life away from the gym means they have to be in fighting shape. Being able to fight is a survival choice… or gives them an edge that they need.'

Madison was no slouch, and she remembered Joel's word. *Tip.*

'Who've you seen here?'

Joel blew out. She had seen this before. People would rather die than talk to the cops. Madison got up, playing the exact same trick she had on Brendan the night before. If you looked like you were walking out, people would get it out quicker. 'Look, when you've had a think about it, let me know. I've got twenty-eight bodies and no murderer.'

'I've seen him here,' he said quickly.

Bingo. Madison sat back down. 'Who?'

'The bloke on telly. The guy who they – you're – trying to find.'

Madison quick-drew her phone out of her jacket pocket and thumbed through her gallery. 'This man?' Mal. Malcom Jevons.

Joel nodded.

'When?'

'Just the once. On a fight night. Earlier this year.'

'Why did he stick out?'

'Fighters have an eye contact thing, a problem with looking away when they end up looking at each other. They can't back off from a challenge; can't stop from sizing each other up. They can never give an inch. That's the vibe I got from this guy. A dangerous fighter.'

'What was he doing here?'

'It was an inter-club fight, so there were fighters from another gym who'd come here to fight ours across a series of different bouts and weight classes. It was a good do. But he'd come here with a dad of one of the fighters.'

'A fighter at this gym?'

'Yeah.'

'Which one?'

This was the bit that was really going to hurt Joel, she could tell. Giving a name. Suddenly, you've gone from nought to snitch in a single word. 'Mikey.'

'You'll have to help me here.'

'I don't know his last name, but Dean probably will. He's been coming here a while so he'll be on one of the junior class registers.'

'And who's his dad?'

'Normal-looking guy – proud, smart. He wasn't like the other one. Two totally different types.'

'Why are you telling me now? The shot's been out for a couple of days.'

'Because I've seen the schedule for the fights tonight, and Mikey's on it. Mikey C, it says.'

Who the hell was Mikey C? And who was his dad?

CHAPTER 45

ANOTHER CRISIS, ANOTHER cup of tea. The great British life ring. Moira sat in her nightdress with a mug in front of her, but now she had pale blue trainers on.

Mim was busying herself at the kitchen sink opposite her mother-in-law. She felt dutiful, yet impotent and increasingly bitter, as the tide switched and the revelations kept coming. There was so much going on around her that was shaping her wider family and her own family's future, except she had no control or input in any of it. She was along for the game as a spectator, except the result of the game and the way it was being played was changing *everything*.

'The girls in the kitchen, hey? Is it Sunday tea?' Moira asked. 'How are you on the veg – everything on time?'

'No, Mum,' replied Mim, as she started to shuffle some digestives onto a clean plate. 'But we'll have a nice cuppa before we settle in to watch some telly. How does that sound?' Not the news. Anything but the news.

'Sounds fine to me. Will *Shortland Street* be on, I wonder?' She looked at the wall clock. 'Yes, getting on for that time.'

Mim tried not to react. *Shortland Street* had been cancelled years ago.

She'd studied the simpler, broader aspects of the brain to an extent during her marketing days – particularly the precise factors that made a person more amenable to saying *yes*. It made her think of how suited she would have been as a healthcare professional. How suited she'd be as a nurse maybe, or a doctor of some kind. She often had such fantasies… but now wasn't the time. She was just a policeman's wife, whose career and family were truly messing up her life.

The front door opened with a distant thunk, and she checked her watch in surprise. The babysitter was paid up for the rest of the day, and Brendan surely wasn't going to check on his mum so quickly.

'Hello?' she shouted down the hall.

'Mim,' said a male voice.

'Ross?'

He entered the room. He looked like a cadaver on invisible strings, and God knew what he'd been up to since Mim had last seen him, but it couldn't have been good. He'd gone off the deep end and was still seeing just how far down the bottom really was.

'Is it true?' he asked. His eyes were bloodshot, and he wore an odd mix of joggers and a leather jacket, giving off the curious impression that he was only half there. He hadn't even seen his mum yet, but as soon as he caught her, he looked like he'd rather be anywhere else.

'Crap, Mum, I didn't know you were here,' he said, unable to make eye contact.

'Ross, love, come here, give your mum a kiss. Nice of you to be free on a Sunday like this,' Moira said, standing.

Ross looked at Mim questioningly, and she shook her head. *Don't ask.*

'Family's family. Family's family's family.'

It was an old phrase of Moira's that she always rejoiced when they got together, as a sort of glue to try to appease and calm the warring men in her family. It spoke – no, *pleaded* – that the bond of family was more important than all else, that everything could be set aside.

Ross took his mum's shoulders and steered her towards the door. 'Go on, Mum. They're in there. See what they're up to?'

'Is everyone here already? How wonderful!' She set off searching for a family that wasn't there.

Mim looked at him scornfully. 'You know how much that might hurt her.'

'She'll get over it. Very fuckin' quickly, as it happens.'

Mim was taken aback. If she thought *she* was bitter…

'What do you want, Ross? I know it's been a bad day but coming here to antagonise your mum like that—'

'Is it true?'

'What?'

'That they found a cash machine here?'

'Yes.'

Ross's knees suddenly buckled and he sank to the floor, howling into the linoleum. 'That lying piece of shit.'

Moira appeared at the door again. 'What's happened? Have you hurt yourself, love?'

'He's fine, just caught his knee on the table leg, that's all,' Mim interjected quickly.

'Always were a clumsy oaf,' she said. 'I can't find anyone.'

'Try the telly, Mum. See if *Shortland Street* is on yet.'

'*Shortland Street*? Don't be daft, they cancelled that years ago.'

'*Songs of Praise* might be on?' said Ross, from his knees.

'I'll check,' said Moira, before wandering off again.

Ross climbed back up, turned his attention to Mim. 'What's the word?'

'I don't know anything, just that it's clear Art was involved in a cash machine robbery, and that had something to do with the people who were killed.'

'Did Dad arrange the robbery?'

'I don't know, Ross.'

'Did he arrange it?' Ross was bellowing, and before either of them knew it had happened, he was grabbing Mim by the arms.

'Ross, I know this has been a terrible time for you,' Mim whispered into his face, 'but think of what your mother is going through. Think of the fear and confusion she must be feeling all the time.'

Ross wouldn't let go. 'Did he arrange it?'

'I truly don't know. Brendan might.'

'The fucking golden boy.'

He finally let her go and marched out of the room. 'Tell Mum I said goodbye.'

'You should tell her yourself—'

The front door slammed before she'd even finished her plea.

She stood for a moment, shaking, trying to compose herself, when she started hearing soft choral music from the living room.

'Found it!' shouted Moira.

Mim flexed her hands, forcing them to stop trembling. Then she picked up the mugs of tea. She heard the front door open again and went through to the hall, but it wasn't Ross who'd come back in. It wasn't him at all.

She didn't know who the man was but felt more threatened by his posture and the coldness of his glare than any brandished weapon could have imparted. The mugs fell to the carpet, as tea gushed up the magnolia walls in an arterial spray.

CHAPTER 46

BRENDAN DIDN'T EVEN try to follow Art to the nick. No point, what with the journalists outside waiting for a press conference. Too many questions if they saw Brendan entering the police station anywhere near his father. It was raining heavily now, as he sat alongside Monroe in his chauffeured black saloon, which was a tricked-out Passat with bullet-proof windows and a mounted computer in the back.

Monroe had assumed full responsibility for the arrest of Art. It was a separate case to the Warrington 27, however obvious the links. He was preparing to share the details and progress of the case with the Home Office detectives who were scheduled at the station. He grinned with the perverse enjoyment of criminality, which the most hard-skinned cops developed after a long and varied tenure on the law-enforcement front line.

'You crafty bastard, hiding your father's true occupation for years. I'm amazed it never came up. How did you keep it that way?' He was thumbing Tic Tacs like nobody's business.

'How long have we got?'

'Before what?'

'Before you'll be needed at the station. Because if you want to talk, can we do it privately?' Brendan tipped his head to the driver of the car. If he was listening, he didn't give any indication.

'You'll be fine to speak,' Monroe said.

'I'll talk, but only off the record. No budging, and no other ears.'

'I suppose we could get a little lunch while they process your father. He'll need some time to speak to his legal representative.'

'He's got one?'

'Warren Grealish, you know him? Solicitor, Manchester-based.'

Brendan smirked. 'Yeah, I know him. Long-time working relationship. Dad's been grooming him for years. Slippery shit too.'

'Hmm. That should get interesting. Know anywhere round here that's nice and quiet?'

'There's an Italian not far from here.' Brendan turned to the driver and raised his voice. 'Do you know the Villaggio?'

'The Village Hotel?' the driver asked after a moment's thought.

'No, the Villaggio. Hotel and pizza place.'

'Oh, on Folly Lane? Neon sign?'

'That's the one.' He turned to Monroe. 'That OK?'

'As long as I can get a half-decent carbonara and a bottle of premium lager, I'll be fine,' said Monroe.

WITHIN FIVE MINUTES, the two men were at a table for four, their jackets hung off the backs of the spare seats. Ice-cold Peronis were in front of them, both having vowed, *Just the one*. Antipasti ordered, they got down to it.

'As far as I'm concerned, Foley, you've earned your stripes. You're an excellent detective and an asset to the constabulary. With one caveat.' Brendan leaned forward, but Monroe put his hand up to stop him. 'Not that caveat. I don't retrospectively give two shits about your father's past. No, it's the fact that this information had to come from DS Madison, and not the horse's mouth.'

Brendan took a swig of the chilled beer. 'I'd have preferred it never came out, to be honest. But for better or worse, it is now.'

Monroe picked at the corner of the beer label with a fingernail. 'I can imagine why you didn't want it to be known, but just for those at the back?'

'I thought it would destroy my chances of a career in the police. It's what I wanted to do but I could only see three outcomes. One? My father would stop me from doing it. Two? The force would stop me from continuing if they knew who my father was and what he got up to. Three? There'd be pressure on me to be an informant on my own family. I didn't fancy any of those options, so I nixed the lot.'

'And. Again, for those at the back – what was it your father was involved with? Madison's report was brief on raw detail here, but I'd like to know the background for myself, even from a historical point of view.'

Monroe was spot-on. Madison had been furnished with some of the details, but not all, and this was the big reveal Brendan had been dreading since he first made the application to GMP. Fuck it now, he thought and went for it.

'We grew up here in Warrington. Lived here all our lives. My mum and dad before me, their mums and dads before them. I have a brother, Ross, as you know, whom I believe you'll want to have a chat with when this conversation is over. We grew up in each other's pockets but we were different – something that became more and more obvious as time went by. I didn't really know what Dad did when we were that young, but it involved lots of strange hours, trips abroad and a lot of uncertainty. Some weekends we'd be off on trips into the city for fine dining, others we'd be having TV dinners on our knees. When summer holidays came around, sometimes we went to Disneyland, other times we took a tent to the Wirral, and other times we went nowhere. The older I got, the more I came to learn that our father's work was full of peaks and troughs, yet all we'd ever been told was that he was a car salesman.

We were often at his dealership, which was out at the back of town. You know, on Farrell Street near the A50?'

'I know it well,' said Monroe.

'Well, it was a small dealership just along from the big Toyota place. There were loads of cars there, and I loved it. He had a team of staff working for him, and this team used to spend time with us at home a lot. I mean, if there was a do on, the sales staff would be there regardless, no invitation needed. I didn't know that this wasn't normal.

'I didn't really understand what was going on until Dad's stress levels began to spike and he started getting angrier at home with me, Ross and Mum. I never got it. Until I was ten, and I was playing at the dealership after school. I ran into the back workshop where the second-hand motors were fixed up in turnaround ready to go on the forecourt. Dad was overseeing some packets being unloaded from the interior panels of a Vauxhall Cavalier, stacking them neatly at one end of the garage. I was ushered out of there on the promise that I'd find out in a few years. Memories carved into me. Seeds planted.

'At fourteen me and Ross were invited to go hang out at the dealership after school, which was weird because we usually went there a couple of times a week without invitation. But still, we went down there and it was, in brief, all laid out for us. Dad and four of these men, the sales staff, but who were actually his business partners or whatever, sat me and Ross down and told us how they dished out medicine to poorly people in Warrington. They said that in big cities everywhere, there were Robin Hood-types who secretly helped out people less fortunate than them. They said that the lawmakers were trying to control what medicine was being distributed so as to keep people sick, whereas they had decided to help out wherever they could. The medicine, as I'm sure you can guess, was crystal and coke. They were the principal suppliers to Warrington, and used a network of second-hand cars to ferry them around the country. Cars change hands all the time, so it was pretty clever, in fairness.

'Now... they timed the speech perfectly to Ross. At twelve, he thought this was nothing short of amazing. But at fourteen, I found it all too sketchy. I'd already had a bunch of drug awareness lessons at high school and already fancied a career in the police. I didn't fall for it, but I was too young to act on it.'

The meals arrived – a big plate of creamed tagliatelle for Monroe, and chilli meatballs with extra chilli for Brendan – which he found he couldn't touch. It was his turn to peel at the beer label, which he did as he spoke.

'I didn't want anything to do with it, but it was there in my face. My mum turned a blind eye to it, I think through fear more than anything else, and my brother got sucked deeper and deeper. Before long, he was always at the dealership, whereas I never went anymore, despite my father constantly pushing me and pushing me to get involved. As I got older, the other sales staff – people who were supposed to be friends of mine – started questioning my loyalties, and Art was forced into some tough situations. There were a few very tense moments when I was seventeen or eighteen, when I was being questioned whenever these guys saw me: who had I told what to? Had I told anybody anything? What would happen if the police asked me?'

Monroe swapped a fork for a spoon to attack the sauce, which he sank his moustache into.

Brendan spoke over the slurping. 'It was awful, but Dad knew something even worse. That I actually intended to become a policeman myself. We fought and fought about it, in a period of time that messed up our relationship for good. So he told me he was finished with that life. Said he'd had enough, that he didn't want to put me in that position anymore, and that he didn't want to ruin my career. And I thought he'd seen sense and stopped. Genuinely... I thought he'd packed it all in. Turns out he was having me on.'

'This business with the cash machine?' Monroe threw olives into his mouth.

'Yeah. I know what happened now. He saw Connor as the new

hope for his little empire, to kick-start it back up again, and he also saw a chance to test the waters. Culliford is on a territorial boundary for organised crime and had been without ownership for a couple of years. It was Mancunian, answering to the Berg, but they went under about three years ago. When they went, nobody went in to claim it, too scared of putting a foot wrong. Dad thought, as Warrington, he would have a chance to claim it – all thanks to that WA postcode. So he tried; only someone was already there, represented by Malcolm Jevons and another man, supposed killers of the Warrington 27. By pushing Connor into the cash machine job, he sent him to his death.'

Brendan felt a prickle at the back of his eyes but held it.

'But the facts suggest that Jevons was representing the Culpeppers of Liverpool.'

Brendan didn't say anything, but as far as he was concerned the writing was on the wall. The location of Mal's shop suggested a Merseyside aspect, unless its position was a smokescreen. Wainwright's death, also on Merseyside, suggested that the underbelly of Liverpool was having a big say in things. And his father had linked that same name to twelve cadavers from that damn trench.

Brendan's phone beeped twice with a text message. What it said confirmed everything beyond doubt. 'Liverpool. Mal is representing Liverpool.' He held up the text for Monroe to see.

Tip-off: Mal's known as an associate of the Culpeppers. Does that name mean anything to you?

THE STATION WAS buzzing, even as the afternoon drew on, and overtime had been authorised where necessary. Some had used up all of theirs but stuck around anyway. Nobody wanted to miss a thing.

Hoyt, pissed off with his rubbernecking colleagues, had kept his head down, stuck between wanting to bury his head in the sand, and frantically needing to do something but not knowing quite what. He resorted to hiding in the gym room, watching from its tiny windows the throng of journalists who had been camped on the street all day. Something had to give, and the longer this went on, the more Hoyt felt that the thing that would give would be him.

As for Art Foley, the star man had been ushered in and was now in one of the interview rooms with that lawyer.

It would all come out soon. He just hoped it would be good news, and that Art would do the right thing – the only thing.

He left the gym to go back to the major incident room. Monroe would surely be angry if he wasn't on the phones. Not that it really mattered now. No tips were worth a penny anymore.

He was shocked, however, to find Monroe there already, perched on the head desk, with Christopher, the apparent hero, Karthik and the two others. His panic was quickly quelled by the atmosphere – which was somehow jovial. Monroe was passing around a bottle of single malt – one of the ones Hoyt had seen on the filing cabinet at the back of his office, a nice-looking one. The other detectives were pouring small slugs into mugs.

Hoyt joined them sheepishly.

'Where've you been?' asked Christopher. 'We've got him.'

Hoyt tried to feign pure delight but fell a long way short. 'Great! It was Foley's dad, then?'

'No, no. Tell him, gaffer.' Christopher raised his mug to Monroe, while passing a spare mug and the bottle to Hoyt.

'He sang. Foley got a name from him, the dots connected. Everything points to the Culpepper crime family from Liverpool.'

Hoyt almost dropped the bottle. His sister, and her kids and probably him too – they were all *dead*. 'Great. Great. What happens now?'

'We're hoping that lawyer of his gets him doing a full testimony and statement. He'll go down for the cash machine, but his statement will bring the murderers of the blessed Warrington 27 to account. And, because of the late break in the case, the Home Office are letting us keep it, just a bit longer. This CID unit, this time tomorrow, will be the toast of the national press. So, a little drink was the order of the day. But first… to Wainwright.'

'To Wainwright,' the voices echoed, and everyone took a sip from their mugs. Hoyt sprinted to the bathroom. He had a sudden urge to be sick.

CHAPTER 47

MADISON KNOCKED AT the service entrance to the Tetley Club with a canvas gym bag over her shoulder, her gloves tied together at the laces and dangling around her neck, a roll-up hanging off her bottom lip.

She was tired and nervous, and yet to feel the pre-fight charge of adrenalin. She'd left the nick in scenes of jubilation. They all assumed that the case was as good as solved. She'd sneaked out, half hoping Hoyt would bunk off and follow her. He hadn't looked well, and she had one of those wobbles she often got – when she felt that she didn't need anybody after all, that relationships were simply part of a greeting-card economy. So she'd left him to it, but it hadn't helped her mental preparation.

The flaked green door opened, and there stood Joel, hoodie up, tuned in to fight prep. His eyes went flat when he saw the ciggie and the state of her, and he shook his head softly.

'Come on, coach. Let's do this.' She threw the tab-end into the gutter drain and passed under his arm has he held the door open.

THE RING WAS a lot smaller than Brendan had imagined. He'd never seen any of Madison's title defences before. It was a postage stamp, with barely enough room to move. You certainly couldn't practise the sweet science in there. No bobbing and weaving – you were in each other's faces from the first bell. Madison had told him about it once, but she said she liked that. Said it made the whole thing feel even more *Kill or be killed*, an intimate battle of guts for glory.

The back windows of the Tetley Club were smeared with grease and fingerprints, but they allowed in the setting sunshine, casting an unseasonably warm glow across the main function suite of the club. It was buried in the old Warrington housing estates, only half a mile from the centre of town. There was a bowling green outside around which a few smokers loitered, little dots of orange held to their lips.

Brendan hadn't a clue how this was going to play out. Madison was already in the changing rooms at the back, getting her medicals done. Ticket holders were starting to file in.

On one hand, Brendan liked the public nature of the setting. The lack of back-up was stinging, however. No radio, save for a mobile, and Madison off duty. They didn't have anything like enough proof to go at something with too much bite – this was purely reconnaissance. He was trying to get a fix on the true villains here, with one eye on whether he recognised any of them.

A stacked guy emerged from the back, in a black T-shirt covered in sponsorship logos. He looked like he'd lived a fighter's life and devoured every moment. He made a beeline for Brendan.

'Foley, right?' His voice was local, deep and flat.

Brendan nodded. 'Yeah.'

'Iona's passed medical. Running order has her on fifth.'

'Good.'

'She's organised a seat for you.'

'She doesn't have any family come and watch?'

'Nah, they don't, do they.'

It was a statement, not a question. Brendan suddenly felt a surge of pride in his DS, the kind of pride she was being starved of by her own family unit. Come to think of it, he thought, he didn't know anything about her family. He knew nothing at all about her, despite the faith she'd stocked in him. He resolved to change that, as soon as he had a chance.

The man passed him a raffle ticket with the name 'Iona M' scrawled on the back. 'Over there,' the man said, while Brendan tried to make sense of the seating arrangement. 'Single seats are always by the bar. Lucky you.'

'Cheers.'

The man turned to walk back to the dressing room, when he suddenly paused and turned back round. 'Whatever it is you do in here tonight. Keep me out of it.'

HOYT HAD MADE a decision. He was going to have to do something drastic. He was going to have to get to Art Foley somehow, right there, in Warrington Police Station.

He'd spent the end of the day and into the evening loitering near the interview room, waiting for any kind of word from Foley's lawyer. He needed something he could use. Something he could gain an advantage with. All that was easier said than done when the problem was well past fixing.

Instead of avoiding his phone, he'd been frantically checking it, refreshing the screen for anything. Rather than dreading a text from the Culpeppers, Hoyt was now desperate for one. Masked men could be cresting a hill, right now, bearing down on his sister's little stone house, ready to collect the debt on all Hoyt's failures.

When he couldn't bear it any longer, and his behaviour had got long past questionable, he decided to enter the interview room and see what was going on. He couldn't take it. He had to work out what to do. He could only manage that if he knew what Art Foley and his lawyer were up to.

Hoyt passed the door to the interview room several times, before plucking up the courage to go in. When he did, he couldn't believe what he was seeing.

It was a small room, grey, apart from a potted rubber ficus in one corner. Art was sitting on one side of a small desk, with a handle sticking out of the centre of his chest, a crimson rose blossoming through his jumper. His eyes were open, looking at the handle in some kind of detached shock. Nobody else was there.

'Jesus,' Hoyt hissed, and immediately went to the stricken man, whose glance rose to meet his. Art's mouth opened, but only a rattle came out. Hoyt immediately grabbed the handle and pulled it out. It emerged with a horrible scraping sound as the blade grazed the old man's breastbone. As soon as the short blade – a letter opener – emerged, a jet of thick blood geysered after it. Hoyt thought about jamming it back in like a cork.

'I thought you were never going to come in. And I'm so glad you grabbed that knife,' said a voice.

Hoyt put his hand instinctively over the pulsing wound, blood pumping through his fingers, as Art lurched forward.

The lawyer emerged from behind the door. 'Look what you did!' he said with a slight smile, then raised his voice a shit-tonne of decibels. 'Officer! *Help!*'

Art hissed hot and phlegmy into Hoyt's neck, a redolent odour of mortality coming with it. He pulled at Hoyt's shoulder, and as the long breath came to its end, he finished it with a handful of strained words.

'It wasn't me.'

Hoyt had been done like a kipper, as he watched the vitality slip from the man.

All he could say in sad, weak reply was: 'I know.'

THE SEATING AT the bar was the best thing that could have happened to Brendan. It was elevated from the main floor. He could see everybody, every interaction, every single moment of contact. It was perfect, and Madison, the diamond, must have done it on purpose. He ordered a Guinness. Fortified and solid. He didn't chin it, just supped it, and watched.

There was a charge to the air, excited parents, partners and friends all filing in and ordering bottles of wine, while waiting staff flitted between tables. But he didn't know who he was looking for. The best thing he could do, in this hunt for Mikey Culpepper's family, was wait for Mikey himself to be introduced. Watch for a table that went berserk when he came down to the ring.

Until then, unless the Culpeppers walked in in outlandish pimp suits, he was just guessing. Brendan was a small-town, small-time detective. He wouldn't know grand-scale organised crime if it slapped him in the face. A giveaway like a glittering pimp suit would have been a big help at this point.

There was another bloke seated on an angle in front of him, his chair swung round to face the front. Bald and weathered, crap-suited and school-shoe-booted, he looked every inch the divorced dad who'd raced from his shit job to get to his disillusioned daughter's dance recital. Swap recital for boxing match and this could have been the truth. Swap Brendan's perception and prejudices for someone else's, and he could have been sitting next to a Culpepper.

Interesting thought.

'Who you watching, mate?' Brendan said, turning to his new friend. The man glanced over with a surprised look.

'My daughter.'

So far so good.

'She's fighting in the fifth. Lightweight police area title fight. A tall order, but you've got to back your own, right?' He was honest, earnest and deeply likeable, and, what were the chances, that was Madison's fight. If Madison's family didn't come here, this had to be the father of Madison's opponent.

'I'll watch out for her. Why a tall order?'

'The girl she's fighting, I've seen her a couple of times. She's a bloody terrier. Meanest amateur left hook I've ever seen.'

'You watch a lot of amateur stuff like this?'

'Yeah, always. Renee fights every few weeks or so. I have three other kids all fighting too.'

'You fought yourself?'

'I had a shot at the Northern Area title thirty years ago. Middleweight. Blasted out first round. It's a sport of levels, isn't it?'

'So I'm hearing. First time for me, this.'

The man looked at him again. 'Who brings you here?'

No point being dishonest. 'I'm police, too. The terrier is one of my colleagues.'

A smile erupted. 'Oh, I like it. We'll have a bit of fun then, won't we?'

Brendan smiled back. On any other occasion, he'd have enjoyed this. Enjoy drinking pints with this fellow, having a laugh, watching the night unfold. He'd make sure he'd do it one day.

But right now, there was business to attend to.

CHAPTER 48

EVERY SINGLE ONE of them was uncomfortable. Six men wedged into a Ford Mondeo. Ross was in the passenger side with Guppo driving, with the four others in the back, love handles fighting love handles for space. They'd just dropped off the M6 at junction 23, down onto the East Lancs to Liverpool, a straight shot of ten miles past St Helens on the left, Ashton-in-Makerfield, Billinge and Rainford on the right. The atmosphere in the car was dark and portentous.

'I can't believe he's been arrested.' It was Steadman, letting his mouth fill in whatever his brain was thinking.

'You need to fuckin' believe it,' replied Guppo. 'And depending on what he's told them, we could all be joining him very soon.' His eyes were on the road as he changed lanes.

Ross sat silent next to him. Under any other circumstances, he'd have leaped over the gear stick at Guppo for such a comment. But he couldn't. He didn't know what his dad had said, but for the first time ever he didn't care.

'Explain this to me again, please,' said Murray. 'We are going to Liverpool why?'

'He sent Fitz,' said Eastman, 'Connor, God rest his soul, and that kid Moston to do over a cash machine. But it pissed off the bigwigs of Liverpool. That about right, Ross?'

'That's about right,' Ross seethed.

Guppo jumped in. 'And we're off to go and piss off the bigwigs, aren't we? I mean it's the obvious course of action, isn't it? If you're a fucking cretin.'

These twats could do whatever they liked, but Ross needed a name. A name would give him focus. A name would give him something to aim at. They were going en masse to turn over Liverpudlian stones, looking for a name. Strength in numbers and all that, and it was the Foley name that provoked the loyal response of these moaning five in a car.

Murray took the reins briefly. 'We focus on the doors. That's where we start. Liverpool doormen are renowned for knowing a city inside out. We go together, we go one doorman at a time, we go friendly. The onion will open, it always does.'

Murray had only just finished speaking when a bullet took the nose clean from his face. Nobody else in the car had the time for shock to even register, before they were engulfed in a smattering of bullets, crossing this way and that, from all angles. Bodies twisted and lurched. Eastman's throat was caught and claret spurted into the laps of the others in the back — not that they had the chance to notice. They were all shot to pieces in a short, sweet spray of automatic gunfire that lasted less than two seconds.

The car slowed, because Guppo had far too much lead in his body to worry about maintaining speed. Two motorbikes accelerated on either side of the car and sped off towards the dockside city in the distance.

CHAPTER 49

THE VENUE WAS full. The MC tuxed out centre ring, ready to announce the fights. There were a couple of warnings about where the fire exits were before a rundown of the evening. Brendan watched the MC because nobody else in the venue seemed to ring any bells, and his plan of waiting for Mikey Culpepper's entrance was the only one he could think of – save for going around table to table asking the question, which seemed a damned stupid idea and a quick way to get yourself in trouble.

The atmosphere had elevated, people already baying for blood. The MC stopped talking, the lights suddenly dipped, and the room was assaulted by the opening bars of Bryan Adams's 'Summer of '69'. To the right of the stage was a pair of double doors, through which a fighter emerged dressed in a blue vest and blue shorts, his arms aloft and waving with maniacal abandon. A table in the back left on the top level lost their shit, jumping up and down. A sequin-clad granny was even trying to climb onto her chair to get a better view.

Brendan smiled. This plan of his was going to work, and he could take it from there. He ordered another Guinness.

'Who's your expert pick in this one?' he asked the bloke next to him.

'Not a bloody clue,' he replied.

Brendan felt himself grin broadly, gave himself a foam moustache, and watched the fighter enter the ring.

ART FOLEY MET death in Hoyt's arms. Stunned police officers stormed the room, hearing the lawyer's cries for aid. The first two who had entered stood in horror at the sight of one of the station's detectives holding a small knife over the bloodied body of a key case suspect. It defied belief, but there it was, happening in front of them, a picture drawn ever clearer by the screams of the lawyer: 'Oh God! He just jumped across the desk and stabbed him! *Stabbed him!*'

In no time, DC Christopher arrived, and tackled Hoyt to the ground. Hoyt was mute, dumbstruck, and in a state of pure incomprehension. He remembered having desperate thoughts of doing such a thing, but going through with it was something else altogether. He couldn't remember this last part, the really serious bit, but he was forced to accept that there was a possibility that it was the truth. And because it hadn't taken place in a formal interview room, because this was merely a meeting between lawyer and client, and certain privileges were in place, there was no CCTV record. None at all.

Hoyt was held down while Christopher sat on top of him. Christopher leaned into his colleague, a whiff of aftershave carrying with him. 'What the fuck have you done?'

Medics were called, while someone said an ambulance was coming from Warrington Hospital and would be there any moment. A doctor suddenly appeared. Hoyt watched, his nose rammed into the floor, as the doctor looked at the blood everywhere. 'Well, that man is dead.'

Monroe suddenly appeared at the doorway, took one look in the room. His head fell to his hands and he lowered to his knees like a robot on power-down. He was watching his career fall to pieces before him.

THE FIGHTS HAD progressed with a high level of drama and excitement, but Brendan had kept to his task. So far, he hadn't seen anybody who looked like any kind of crime baron.

The fourth fight was a back-and-forth slugfest over just two rounds, at the end of which the red fighter threw an overhand right that sent the blue fighter back to his childhood. It was a monster shot, and the crowd was on its feet, trying to get a better look. The fight was immediately waved off, and after a few moments the stricken man got up to a round of respectful, if wholly unwanted, applause.

As the crowd began to simmer back down and retake their seats, a voice spoke in Brendan's left ear.

'Would you like to come down the front, watch the next one from ringside?' It was a deep male voice, a whisper, with little by way of accent or inflection.

Brendan was almost too surprised to turn, but, emboldened by the drink, he spun slightly to see a middle-aged man with a deeply pockmarked face, short salt and pepper hair and a slight build. Brendan immediately felt himself relax, puffed up by the blood that was pumping through watching that last huge knockout. The air carried a frisson of danger and excitement so tangible he could almost reach out and give it a wary jiggle.

'All right,' he replied, and dropped down from his stool. He followed the man, who nimbly picked his way between tables, before reaching three rows of ringside seats. On the very front, just left of dead centre, was a solitary empty seat. His guide pointed to it, and Brendan opted to follow along. He sat down.

Immediately, Brendan couldn't believe how close to the action he was, the muddy brown speckling of blood all over the ring, as the referee came out to centre ring again, along with the MC, who up close had far too much gel in his hair. He pulled the microphone to his jaw.

'Ladies and gentlemen, it's time for our first title fight of the evening. The North-West Women's Lightweight Police Title.' There was generous applause, a few whoops and hollering. The crowd was ready for more blood and thunder. The lights dipped, the thumping bass and plucked strings of Dr Dre's 'Still D.R.E.' dropped, and the crowd went wild. Brendan was excited, undeniably, but then he felt a hand touch his shoulder.

'Harvey Culpepper,' said a voice close to his ear. He smelled breath mints, blackcurrant and lager.

Brendan's guts lurched, but he managed to keep it together. The voice was smooth as panna cotta, with a soft Liverpudlian echo. Brendan daren't look this time.

'My wife, Charlotte.' He could see the man's hands gesture to his right, and Brendan chanced a glance. A blonde woman with heavy make-up and an atomically uncompromising gaze looked dead ahead.

'You've caused me a world of trouble, Mr Foley. A fucking galaxy of trouble. Let's have a chat about that, shall we?'

Brendan wasn't all that sure he had a choice.

Then Madison appeared.

CHAPTER 50

SHE WAS ENGULFED by a preternatural calm, like she always was in the minutes before the bell rang – only this time, there was a slight crack in it. Madison masked it coolly, as fighters always did. Don't give a thing away. Joel knew, however.

'You're sure?' he'd asked her in the dressing room.

'Don't ask me that again,' had been her curt response.

He didn't say anything, but just like the fighter he was, adopted her cool confidence. Never give an inch. Fighter and trainer always gave the same front right the way through the boxing ladder – iron-clad, unified, cool *belief.*

There was always that awkward moment before you went out in crappier venues when you were both called ready for the ring walk, but because the venue wasn't big enough or didn't have enough staff, the two fighters were in the same corridor waiting to be introduced. Face to face, feet from each other, before trying to put each other to sleep. Some touched gloves, others ignored each other and saved the pleasantries till after. Madison did the former, while meeting her opponent's eyes. Her opponent looked nervous, constantly moving. Madison was still and composed – she loved Gennady Golovkin, and before fights Triple G was always cobra-still.

Her opponent went out, leaving her there, and her muscles hit tension, right across her shoulders. There was so much going on, but she had to retain focus. As the old adage went, *you don't play boxing.* It was so serious that calling it sport was almost an inappropriate category.

Joel sidled up next to her, but she said simply, 'Don't.' Whatever he had to say, she didn't want to hear it.

And then Madison's music hit. 'Fade To Black', by Metallica. She waited for Kirk Hammett's lead guitar to wail, before walking out. It was those shitty glittery curtains, stupid fronds that got stuck everywhere, especially when you were in a robe and gloves. They caught on her wrists and ponytail, as the lights and heat hit her.

The setting fixed her calm, settled it right down. She found her backbone, found her guile under the sudden warmth of the spotlights. She looked at her opponent up in the ring, being given a last mouthful of water, and found that confidence to think, I'm fucking doing you. You're getting banged out.

Winner's mentality.

Madison climbed the steps in two hops and, after Joel lowered the middle rope, she listened to the cheers, raised a gloved fist and went to the red corner. In her first handful of fights, she couldn't see anything outside the ring. Now, she quite liked looking at ringside, seeing what the excited faces were doing. Sometimes, you could give someone a determined smile or wink, and you had a new supporter.

But as soon as she glanced through the ropes, she saw her boss. Brendan. Looking at her. Eyes wide with surprise and... panic. Fear.

That same fear suddenly coursed through her.

Someone was talking to him. Someone she didn't recognise.

And then the bell rang, and she was ushered into the centre of the ring.

'HERE SHE IS. The woman of the hour, no less.' Culpepper's voice was a lullaby in a shitstorm. Brendan listened to the malevolence. 'You seen any of her fights before?'

'No.'

Madison was up there, in the ring, being dragged across to touch gloves with her opponent – and her eyes never left Brendan and Culpepper.

'She's dynamite, from what I've seen. Maybe caught three or four of her fights, but every time it's been quick combinations and a big one at the end that's got the job done.'

Brendan found his voice. 'Why am I sitting here?'

The bell rang. Brendan was strangely torn. His much-admired DS was stepping centre ring for a punch-up, while he was small-talking with the supposed leader of a crime empire. Madison took one step forward, held her hands high and bobbed her head right, then left.

'Whatever we talk about, let's keep it civil,' said Culpepper. 'Enjoy the fight and keep it friendly.'

As soon as Madison reached centre ring, she threw a left jab so stiff that everyone in the room gasped like it was a clean-landing power punch. It caught her opponent flush on the chin, sending her dark hair fanning backwards.

'The big grave,' Culpepper said. 'That dumping ground. It wasn't my idea but it served an insurance purpose. It was my mate's idea. You know him, the bloke whose face was on the news.'

Madison was following her jabs with straight rights, unleashing a volley of one-twos that were as quick and solid as anything Brendan had seen in boxing. However, once she'd thrown the combinations, she'd glance over to ringside, at Brendan and Culpepper.

'The victims all had something to do with you. Why?' Brendan asked.

'I'm not going to be obsequious,' said Culpepper, which sounded weird in a Scouse accent. 'Every single one of them had negatively affected an interest of my family's. Each one. Mal had this simple idea when it came to what to do with these people. At intermittent points in the last twenty years, the scrutiny on areas of Liverpool has been high. So why not get rid of the rubbish somewhere else. And why not get rid of it on the patch of someone who's really pissed you off?'

'This was about my dad?'

The fighter in blue was fighting back. Had bitten down on her gum-shield and was responding, chucking shots back with a determined abandon.

'He was a constant pain in the arse. Always pushing outwards, always sticking his nose in, always too big for his boots. He cost me a lot of money. A *lot* of fuckin' money. We enjoyed his supposed retirement. Mal had the idea of a long game of getting rid of bodies in Warrington and pointing it all at Art Foley when they were eventually found. One last thank-you note to him.'

'So you framed him? The cash point?'

'Oh no, not at all. He did that all by himself, but it was on our patch.'

'So Culliford was yours?'

'Who's else would it be?'

'So, you killed my nephew over a shitting cash-point heist?'

'No, no, no. Your nephew was killed because he stepped somewhere he shouldn't have. You know how it works and if you didn't, you do now. Your dad did and he organised it.' He paused. 'I wouldn't get too precious about your family.'

Brendan paused too. Then, he finally looked at him.

CHAPTER 51

SHE COULD HIT, this girl. She was no pushover, and she could bang. She was dangerous and Madison knew it. After a strong start, for every solid combination an equally solid one would come back. She wasn't being caught sweet yet, but it was surely a matter of time. Tiredness and energy were so important in the heat of a fight. You don't get your hands high enough by just half a centimetre and a big right hook can swing through and send you into next week. Madison hit back, dropped away, stepping to her right, away from her opponent's incoming right hand, and breathed.

She snatched a look at Brendan. Still there. Still deep in conversation. Too weird.

Suddenly, her head felt like an anvil had been dropped on it, and it dawned on her all too late that she'd been drilled with a monster left hook. The crowd *ooh*'d softly, and Madison felt the world tilt sideways before she righted the ship. Because it was a left that caught her, she instinctively brought up her own left guard, in readiness for the follow-up right hand. Good job too, because the straight right bounced off her glove and up over her head. Madison rolled and rose with a right uppercut straight down the pipe, catching her opponent flush on the point of her chin, sending her ponytail bouncing.

The crowd *ooh*'d again, and the atmosphere started to swell with anticipation that there was a real war brewing on the canvas in front of them.

MADISON WAS UNDER real pressure in there, but Brendan couldn't concentrate at all.

'Watch your mouth,' Brendan seethed. 'Sitting next to a cop, at a boxing event where cops are competing. I wouldn't be making threats.'

Culpepper crossed his legs, with one brogue slipping against the ring apron. 'It's not a threat at all. We're past that. You need to know that your father started a course of action, and you carried it on. If you agree to stop now, you can avert what's under way. But I need assurances.'

'Look, I've gone round the houses with enough petty criminals to know bullshit when I smell it. You talk Billy Big Bollocks when in fact you're clutching at more straws than a busy barman. You've been caught out, and when you're caught out you've got to take the fall.'

'You've got a funny definition of small-time crim. You've just opened one hole with twenty-seven bodies in it, all of whom fell foul. I think you should give my family a touch more credit.'

'You think killing my nephew as a penalty *then* threatening my family is going to make me stop trying to put you in the nick? Then you're as mistaken as it gets.'

'I think you're the mistaken one – who said anything about your nephew? And again, we're past threats.'

Brendan felt less sure of himself, and looked directly at Culpepper. He was unremarkable in almost all aspects for a man who wielded so much power.

On the backside slide of middle age, open-necked sky-blue shirt, cream chinos, charcoal jacket. Healthy tan, clean shaven, heavy laughter lines around the mouth and eyes – eyes that were grey and open wide. His hair nothing more than a frost of bristled aluminium across the top of his tanned scalp. His teeth were very white, with savage-looking canines. Harvey Culpepper looked like a man who was embracing every second of retirement, and spent four and half days a week on the golf course, dropping in to his offices for that last half a day to make sure his nest egg was ticking over satisfactorily.

Culpepper dropped his eyes for a moment, then brought them back up, boring right into Brendan's.

'You did fuck with me,' he said.

'What… what have you done?' Brendan whispered.

The crowd suddenly bellowed, and both men instinctively looked into the ring, where one of the fighters was down. It took a moment for Brendan to realise it was Madison.

THE CAR HAD rolled to a stop some forty yards after the bullets had stopped flying. Guppo's dead legs could no longer apply pressure to the accelerator. The traffic had stopped a way back and let the two motorbikes roar off along the East Lancs in the direction of

Liverpool. Everything had gone strangely quiet on both sides of the carriageway.

Ross felt his hearing come back last, after all other senses. It was like he couldn't remember at all what happened, his mind having already either shut it off or dispensed with the memory entirely. He was driving along, then suddenly he was in a cheese-gratered car surrounded by dead friends. As he started to shuffle up into his seat and saw the state of the men in the car with him, other snippets of memories returned. His glance in the wing mirror, the sudden fan-tailing of the two motorbike riders in an alarming state of unison, while both reached into their biker jackets. Ross flattened himself in an instant, screaming, 'Get down!' while pouring himself into the footwell.

As he lay there, Ross realised he'd obviously done enough – although only for himself, and not the others. The only thing he felt was rage. Rage, and then some. The horrors of what were around him were so stark, they only made his anger surge faster.

My son, my friends and now me.

Almost.

He tried the door but it wasn't working, so he pulled himself from the car through the shattered window, before landing hard on the tarmac. He saw the cars hanging back some distance away down both ends of the carriageway. Sirens would be coming, he knew that. But that would only bring more questions. So Ross turned and ran into the deep scrub at the side of the road, enjoying the cold wind on his face and down into his lungs. He felt, just moments from certain death, more alive than ever before.

CHAPTER 52

THERE WAS A huge pop and a bright flash, just over the top of Madison's left eye, then the world fell sideways for real this time.

This isn't the plan...

When she hit the canvas, the back of her head bounced. It was a bad knockdown, the worst she'd ever had. Shit, it hurt. Right after she opened her eyes, she saw the referee moving towards her, and his arms rising. She knew just how it worked at this level. Big knockdowns usually got waved off immediately. Fight's over, you've lost. No chance, she thought. Before the ref could get any closer, she threw her right glove over her body to her left side and pushed herself up. The room span a lurid zoetrope, whizzing across her eyes, as she righted herself. Her head pounded like the most vicious all-day hangover condensed to a solitary moment in time.

The ref's eyes were wide with surprise as he checked Madison.

'You OK to continue?' he asked, checking her guard.

'Believe it,' she said.

MADISON HAD JUST pulled off the most miraculous resurrection since Christ himself, when Culpepper changed everything.

'Don't get excited, but your dad's dead.' He said it like you'd tell someone they'd missed a parcel delivery.

The words blew through Brendan like a burst from an acetylene torch.

'He's in police custody. It's always bullshit with your kind.'

'We've got a man inside, haven't we? He's done a grand job.'

Brendan didn't know what to think. Possibilities whirled through his mind. Truth, lies, fact, fiction, what he knew or didn't know, mashing together to try to form a picture.

'Bullshit,' Brendan said, but the crack was there. This was more bravado than certainty.

'Hoyt. It's amazing what people will do if you give them a damn good reason to.'

It was the name Hoyt that did it. One of the detectives in his unit, who'd been working the case with him. Brendan's breath stopped. 'It was done in the station, with all your lot there. He's going to be in a lot of trouble, so you'll probably need to hire a new detective – well, two if you count the DI yesterday.'

Brendan couldn't breathe, let alone speak.

'You know, it's funny. You were the target yesterday. But Hoyt fucked that one up, something like telling us it was the old DI that was getting too close. We thought he meant old as in literally advanced in years, when in fact he meant old as in the one who wasn't there anymore. What a mess.' Culpepper started chuckling, actually belly-laughing at that. 'The japes that life offers you. Anyway, no harm done. Your brother's dead too.'

Brendan felt like all his blood had left his body. His shoulders began to shake.

'Now, like I said, don't get excited. We've got your mum and wife too, but hey.' He slapped Brendan on the shoulder like they were old bros. 'Lucky for you, they're OK for the time being.'

'My brother...' Brendan croaked.

'That dickhead. And Art bloody Foley, bane of my life. They've both had it coming, for such a long time. They were scum, the kind of scum you've pledged your career to getting rid of. I've done you and your conscience a favour. Drive-by on the East Lancs, about ten minutes ago, with all his daft goonies too.'

Brendan couldn't put two thoughts together. He was bottomed out and hollowed. His family was being eviscerated and he was at the boxing, talking to the man who'd made it happen.

'I thought she was done for then, but what a comeback she's mounted,' said Culpepper, and, again, it took a moment for Brendan to realise he was referring to Madison in the ring. He glanced up blankly and saw her bobbing and swinging, catching as many as she was throwing, and it was a truly dynamic, dramatic battle. He couldn't focus – on anything.

'I have to believe you've fed me a pack of lies. Or I'll kill you where you sit.'

'Steady on, Foley. Your father and brother got what was coming to them. It was inevitable, really. They've been interfering upstarts for years. The others are fine if you just stop. If you just let it go and look the other way. I know where you are, I know where you live, and for every Hoyt who reaches the end of his usefulness, I've got five more. I know what you're doing before you do it. So back off, and everyone stays OK.'

The hopelessness swallowed Brendan, and he felt his eyes water. Then the bell rang.

THE HARDEST ROUND of Madison's boxing career was over, and she marched back to the wrong corner. Joel was already up and diving through the ropes, shouting at her to come over to the right one. The stool had been placed down, and Madison lowered herself into it gingerly.

'I'm pulling you out,' said Joel.

'You pull me out, I'm getting a new trainer.'

'Then get a new trainer. You're getting twatted in there. Your mind's not on it, don't be stupid.'

As Madison looked up at him, taking the water that was being offered her, she kept seeing him glance ringside in the direction of Brendan. She looked herself and saw straight away that Brendan was crying. She looked at the man he was talking to, the man who carried arrogance and hostility. What on earth had been said between them?

Madison looked across the ring at her opponent, who was raring to go, and being urged on in wild gestures by her enthusiastic coach. Madison was sure that the neutral would know which fighter was in the ascendancy, just from watching the corners.

'I'm not losing the belt like this. No way. Give me one more round,' she demanded through her gum-shield.

'If you get hurt, it's on you.'

The bell rang to start round two. Madison stood up and drew her guard to her chin.

'YOU'RE UNDER ARREST,' said Brendan.

Culpepper laughed, and turned to the woman at his side.

'He says I'm under arrest!' he said incredulously. Charlotte Culpepper actually looked at Brendan this time and gave him a sneer so evil it would make a dog kill itself. Culpepper turned back to Brendan. 'You're suspended. You can't arrest me if you tried.'

'I can't, but she can.' He nodded into the ring at Madison, who'd just hit centre ring and thrown two jabs as stiff as railway sleepers.

'She's somewhat occupied, isn't she? And what would she arrest me for? I haven't done anything, my hands are completely clean. If you think you can tie me to any of the things we've talked about, you're as wrong as these things get.'

Brendan knew his testimony would count for a great deal. A lawyer would have a lot of fun turning a jury in knots getting Culpepper's case thrown out.

'Where's my wife? Where's my mother?' He pictured his dear mum, confused and terrified in the presence of whichever sick bastard was holding her captive.

Culpepper spread his palms. 'Are you open to negotiation? Can we make a deal? Man to man.'

'You say you've murdered my family, and you want to make a deal?'

'You know how a deal works, don't you? You have something of value I could make use of. I've got something of value that you want back. In case you're struggling, I'm talking about your little mum and your frankly too-good-for-you wife. Degenerative brain disease in your mum, is it? Nasty business that. I had a dog that had it once. A lovely collie. Poor bitch couldn't remember who we were, kept wandering off, and then the pissing started. Every room of the house, even the cupboards. House still carries a little soupçon of piss in the air. We had to put her down, in the end. Which is what I'll have to do to your mum if you don't play along here. So, a deal. We both possess things of value. Can we agree to an exchange?'

'What could you possibly want from me? Just give me my family back.'

The control in Culpepper's voice was preternatural. 'I'd be more than happy to, if you can guarantee it all goes away. All these links, everything coming back to my good family name. The people in that hole. It was all designed to frame Art. He wanted to be big-time; let him be big-time. Let it be Art. He can simply die as one of the most prolific serial killers the country's ever had. It's a very sad story, but the case dies with him. You go your way, I'll go mine. But... you'll always remember that I know where you live, and my little birds in your offices will always let me know what's going on. So, the threat is always there in case you ever change your mind.'

'You are joking, aren't you?'

'What do you think?'

'Too many people are involved, too much evidence already exists. My father sang like a fucking nightingale this morning, and it wasn't

231

just me who heard it. Paperwork is in, and the name Culpepper is all over it.'

'Are you saying you're no use to me?'

Brendan didn't say anything.

'Because if you are, I'd say your prospects are somewhat bleak.'

If Brendan agreed to try something – anything – this snake could make it known far and wide that Brendan was willing to cut deals with organised crime. But if he didn't accept something, he'd have his mum and Mim's deaths on his hands too.

'I can offer you nothing.'

'Then I have a phone call to make.'

He watched as Culpepper casually pulled a phone from his jacket pocket and placed a call. Brendan felt the sudden connection to his family, that whoever this call was placed to was where they were holding his mum and Mim. He waited half a second, then snatched the phone and jumped into the boxing ring.

MADISON WAS IN the fight of her life, with a deep cut over her right eye – the same spot as always, the scar tissue parting. Her vision was impaired, blood pouring into her eye, and she constantly had to paw at it so she could see – and every time she did so, her guard was out of place for a shot on the chin. Her opponent was an electric eel, never in the same spot, moving with unpredictable vim, and always quick with a sharp shocking counter.

She was finding out new things about herself in this fight. She'd never been pushed like this, with adversity just so terse and severe – and she found she absolutely *revelled* in it. As the blood poured out of her, making it even tougher, Madison found her enjoyment soaring, if only she could forget what was going on at ringside – which was suddenly all the harder to forget when Brendan belly-rolled into the ring, holding a smartphone like it was a block of silver.

All the action stopped in the ring. He was suddenly running to the empty far corner, and fumbled comically with the ropes, which everyone did if you hadn't done it before, and was down on the other side, running through those stupid glitter curtains.

She looked back at the man who he'd been sitting with, but he was blocked by the brassy-looking woman, who was staring daggers after Brendan. A hand crept onto her arm and pulled her back into her seat. The man, who she guessed by now had to be the elusive

Culpepper, was smiling. Actually *smiling*. At the far end of the room, the door suddenly flew open and another man ran out.

What the hell was going on?

The room stood still and the fighters looked at each other.

Madison stood there bolted to the spot in indecision.

My boss, or my boxing?

CHAPTER 53

THE CAR PARK HAD packed right out since Brendan had entered the Tetley Club, and was now cast in darkness, barely touched by the puny glow from the one lone floodlight.

Brendan sprinted for his car. It was the number he needed. He'd spotted it was a landline when Culpepper put it to his ear: 0151. Liverpool area code. A lifeline. Another man was now chasing him, having emerged from the front entrance around the corner from the car park, a bizarre layout feature that had bought Brendan precious seconds. It was the man who'd taken him to see Culpepper on the front row. Another bastard who'd get what was coming.

He gunned the Audi engine, which growled with the reliability he'd always come to take for granted, but would never now do again. The sprinter was still chasing, but Brendan was gone, spitting gravel chunks against the other parked cars with high-pitched tings. He veered out, through the sagging metal gate, and was out in the road, cutting through a red light, leaving the Tetley Club as a bright smudge in his rearview.

This was a race, simple and bare. *Get to the address connected to that landline before they kill your mum and wife.*

The Audi burst across the junction, veering right as the A50 joined Winwick Road, and began weaving along the dual carriageway.

Brendan pulled out his own phone and thumbed through his contacts to find Jordan Seebaruth. He picked up on the second ring.

'Jesus, Foley, I'm sorry,' he said by way of hello. Which confirmed everything for Brendan, and consigned any notions of Culpepper spinning him a yarn to the scrap heap. His dad and brother *were* dead.

Ice ran through him, but he had to park that too. 'Never mind that, Jordan. I need an address off a landline, and I need it yesterday.'

Seabreeze took one second before: 'OK, go?'

'You still at the nick?'

'Yeah.'

Brendan could picture the bedlam. A dead suspect, killed in-house by a detective. It was a national scandal. And it would be all hands to the pumps.

'Great.' Brendan reeled off the number from Culpepper's phone, and waited, weaving in and out of the traffic. Horns blared but they were fading out before they'd even finished. He was almost at the roundabout to join the M62 when Seabreeze answered.

'It's 58 Devon Road, Huyton.'

'Can you text me that?'

'Sure. Just take care of yourself, Foley, all right?'

'Thanks, Seabreeze.'

The message came through a second later. Brendan immediately fed the text into Google maps, and set it as a satnav destination – all while he was joining the motorway. He put the screen on his lap, tossed Culpepper's phone onto the passenger seat and flushed that accelerator pedal into the carpet.

Huyton was a Merseyside suburb, some eight miles from the city centre. Twenty-one minutes, according to the satnav. Twenty-one minutes to save his mum and wife.

Christ.

He stamped the pedal harder.

MADISON WENT WITH justice.

She pointed with her glove at the smiling man at ringside and spat out her gum-shield. 'You stay there!' Her opponent and the referee looked at her in stark confusion. 'There's a crime in progress.'

The man at ringside stopped smiling and gave her a look that screamed a dark venom at work. The punters in the venue hadn't a clue what was going on and were craning their necks to get a better view at what was happening.

Clearly remembering her duty as a police officer, Madison's opponent crossed the ring to her, her hands at her sides, breathing hard and sweating profusely.

'What's happened?' she asked.

'I'm not sure, but my DI was in here and this man is a person of extreme interest.' Madison walked directly to the ropes, overlooking Culpepper. 'You don't move a muscle, you understand.'

Culpepper glanced behind either side of him theatrically. 'What have you got me on?'

Madison remembered the fight had stopped. 'We'll start with disturbing the peace, and we'll take it from there, shall we?'

'Whatever you say, Detective Sergeant Madison.'

Madison froze at the sudden ice in Culpepper's words. Her opponent was directing the burly venue security staff right to him on the front, while the referee leaned back against the ropes and took in the scene with a bemused look. The crowd was still trying to get a look at the action.

Culpepper smiled. Madison felt deep down that something very bad was afoot.

CHAPTER 54

ANOTHER FAMILIAR NORTHERN suburb, another familiar northern street. The houses of Dorset Road were red brick, two up, two down, one-car garage on the right, front porch on the left, identical to the ones on either side. Brendan crawled along to 58 counting off the numbers as he went.

There were no cars on the drive, and the grass of the front lawn was a little longer than those around it. It looked long empty with no lights on outside. He was worried immediately that he'd been tricked.

He parked a few doors down, outside 44, and approached briskly on foot. He crept up the far right-hand side of the drive, in case there was a security light to blow his approach, but nothing came on. He crossed in front of the white garage door, carried on past the front porch and peered through the wide picture windows on the left – into a dark living room lit only by the soft orange glow from the street lamp outside. Couple of sofas, a chair, a threadbare carpet and nothing else. No telly, crucially, which was usually the giveaway.

Nobody lived there.

At the back of the room was a frosted glass door. He was about to head round the back, when one spot of orange on the frosted glass didn't move like the rest of them. He looked at it, hard. This wasn't a reflection; it was coming from the other side.

Filled with awful images of his wife and mother, he wasted no time in trying the front door. Unlocked. He felt he should be more careful, but – *Fuck it!* – and through he went.

Same with the interior door – open.

Straight through, and into a hallway. Layout experience suggested the kitchen was at the end of the hall past the stairs, where another frosted door stood closed – only the orange light was stronger through the opaqueness. He marched down the hall and threw open the door.

Brendan had never seen anything like it.

It was a smallish country-style kitchen – but all of it, every corner, was covered with huge floor-to-ceiling sheets of plastic. The glow was coming from the extractor fan unit floating over the hob. Even the floor was covered in plastic, and there was a round table on the right-hand side, with four chairs pushed neatly underneath it. On the table lay a couple of small knives, next to a serrated bone saw, a hacksaw and a full wood saw.

This wasn't just a murder room. It was an abattoir – and his family were nowhere to be seen.

Trap.

Before he could think anything else, Brendan was pushed violently into the room.

A gruff voice whispered in his ear. 'Get over there.'

A hand grabbed his neck roughly and shoved him down hard onto the table, and he reared back when an awful kidney punch took every bit of air from his lungs, opening a black hole in his side out of which it felt his soul fell out. Gasping over the table, Brendan heard the screech of duct tape being pulled from its roll and another pair of hands dragged his arms out across the tabletop.

As he realised that there were two assailants, he was held in place while his arms, head and shoulders were duct-taped to the kitchen table in thick strips, wrapped repeatedly round the wooden tabletop. Brendan was still gasping for breath when they finally let go of him, and his legs flopped helplessly in place. Another strip of tape was placed over his mouth.

'Don't want to disturb the neighbours. It's a school night, after all,' said another voice – as a man placed a bin bag on the table in front of Brendan's face. There was something in it, but he couldn't work out what, and the top was bunched like a black bouquet. Looking up from the bag in confusion, he caught the man for the first time. Brendan remembered him from childhood, clear as a summer's day, a recollection that was bolstered further by the grainy images from the drone video. Finally, he was face to face with Mal.

He hadn't gone to ground at all.

He hadn't fled the country, like Culpepper said – like everyone thought.

The arrogant, evil bastard – he'd been lying in wait all this time.

'You're going to help us a lot here. You're going to help us teach one hell of a lesson.' It was the other man again, who had moved behind him. A hand fished in his jacket. 'Let's see if you've got it – oh, you do!'

Brendan's warrant card was pulled from his pocket, and placed next to his face, with his police ID facing upwards so that he could see the bored-looking version of himself before all this awful shit happened. As Brendan looked up, the man who'd picked his pocket moved around the table to point the lens of a smartphone square at him. He was in his fifties, wrinkled and reddened with the sudden exertion, clad in a blue Adidas tracksuit, with an open, eager face. There was something almost child-like about him. It was the mystery man who'd been with Mal, who himself took a seat opposite Brendan like he was sitting down for supper.

'Ready when you are, big man,' the second man said, and Brendan didn't like where this was going one bit.

'What do you think is in this bag here?' said Mal. There was something acutely horrible about his manner, with his head tilted back slightly, a leer playing across his parted mouth, lips wet with anticipation, eyelids half-closed in something akin to pleasure. Brendan looked at the bag and considered it properly for the first time. Whatever was in it was bunched up, with the odd bumpy bit of something solid, but other than that it was just a shapeless object, maybe a couple of feet long.

'This is what happens if you cross us, or the Culpeppers.'

Mal reached for the bag, parted the top and looked inside – to which he gave a mock gasp with a sickly shocked smile. He reached his hand in, and Brendan couldn't halt the swelling tide of dread racing dark and clear across his mind.

Mal started to twitch his nose. And then started revealing his front teeth, to give a *'chut, chut, chut'* sound, like a rabbit would make. Mal's hand emerged, wiggling and giving life to what he held in his hand.

Mick's toy rabbit, Bun Bun.

Brendan wished he was dead.

He screamed – but all that came out was an aspirated gush of air, and his mouth filled with the acetate bitterness of the glue on the tape.

The shape in the bag. The angles and bumps against the black plastic adding form. The small round bit at one end.

His son. His *baby son*.

'You're a cop. I've never done this to a cop before, but it's the ultimate show of power, isn't it? When this video gets out, with your nice little face and that warrant card next to it, you're making us untouchable. When you're dead, which won't be long now, you'll be

239

revered as a saint round our way, making us untouchable all over again. And to think, when I knew you as a little boy, this is where we'd end up.'

As the smartphone recorded every second, Brendan begged for his consciousness to slip away, willed it all to stop and for the universe to offer another Big Bang and start everything from the beginning again. If Death had offered him a hand there and then, he'd have grabbed it. All he could think of was the face of his beautiful baby son, life long-since departed, his little hands in the bag and the sheer, scaleless, infinite horror at what had happened to him – all thanks to the actions of his supposed father figures, who should have done so desperately much better.

CHAPTER 55

WHEN MADISON PEERED through the porch door at the back of the kitchen, she saw a sight that would never leave her. She'd gone round the back for a recce, but now she had to act.

After apprehending Culpepper, she had left him in the capable hands of the Tetley Club security under the instruction of her opponent, Police Constable Renee Twist. She'd tried Brendan on the phone but there was no reply, so she'd tried the station, see if he'd called in. Turned out he had, and Seabreeze was only too happy to fill her in on *everything* – details she could scarcely even believe. Art Foley was dead. Died in custody is all she got from the garble of words Seabreeze volleyed at her, as well as an address he'd given Brendan. When she said she was on her way, he said he was coming too, before calling back moments later to say DS Christopher was joining him.

Her mobile was in her hand, the line already open, when she said into it, 'Life in peril. Storm the front, storm the front door.'

'Got it,' came the reply from Christopher, who was crouched in front of the garage with Jordan Seebaruth. As she watched inside, Brendan's torment abruptly stopped as the man with him at the table and the other assailant began barricading the kitchen door. It was clear to Madison that her colleagues were trying to get in. The man with the camera turned to the other door, the one that led to the living room, as another man tried to force his way into the kitchen through that way. The black sleeve on the arm through the door was the giveaway that it was Seabreeze, and he and the man in the blue tracksuit starting brawling, half-in and half-out of the room. Seabreeze gave away at least a few stone, and that was just belly. He was quickly overwhelmed by the bloke who'd filmed Brendan's mental torture.

Madison had to act, and she did. Swiftly and decisively. She picked up a stone rabbit that was looking tired in the abandoned flower bed of the rear patio and threw it at the plate-glass door. Enhanced building codes meant that the rabbit didn't actually break through but obliterated the first pane of the double glazing. She threw herself at the deep crack in the remaining pane and tumbled through, glass and all.

THERE WAS A loud crash in front of Brendan, coming from the patio door. His vision was blurred thanks to his streaming eyes and the pull of the tape across his face, but he could see that someone dressed in bright red was trying to push their way through the plastic at the back of the kitchen. There was a commotion behind him, which he would normally feel vulnerable about, but, frankly, enough damage had been done back there. His legs felt like blended eels. There was a hissing sound followed by a tear, and to his eternal surprise and relief, DS Madison pushed through a hole in the plastic sheeting into the kitchen, still covered in bruises and blood from her fight, in her boxing kit, holding a huge shard of glass. It was a sight he'd never forget.

Once in, she looked at the commotion Brendan couldn't see, then turned immediately to the table, and with the shard of glass sawed at the binding holding him to the table. 'I've got you, boss,' she said breathlessly.

'Fuck!' shouted the trackie man, as he ran to Madison, leaving the door barricaded at the handle by a wedged dining chair. As soon as he got near her, she stopped sawing and threw that big left hook of hers, snapping the tracksuit guy's head almost *Exorcist* three-sixty. He tumbled into the plastic over the hob, cracking his head on the extractor fan, which fell down on top of him.

Brendan's restraints were almost severed and, suddenly adrenalised by the prospect of escape, he managed to get a hand loose. He used whatever strength he could, stretching the remaining strands until they snapped. He tore the tape from his mouth. Madison and the man were grappling on the floor, blood and hair flying.

Brendan remembered the tools on the table, which were now in reach. He grabbed the bone saw and cut himself free. He turned to the commotion behind him, to see Mal heaving his weight against the door, using whatever leverage he could to keep it shut. Behind the frosted glass of the door, he could see four hands trying to force it open.

Mal saw Brendan was free and couldn't resist a leer. 'He cried a lot you know. Well, at the start…' He smiled sickly.

Brendan felt a blind rush of justice, could think only of his baby boy. Before he knew what he'd done, he'd charged at Mal and stuck the bone saw as hard as he could into his chest, bullseye central. With a deep howl, he pulled it out and stuck it in again. Mal's eyes lost contact with Brendan's and took on a blanker quality.

'You fucker,' he spat in Brendan's face, his gaze still off in the distance somewhere.

Brendan spat back in his and stuck the knife in again with another anguished cry, this time thrusting the blade up beneath his chin, smooth and to the hilt.

'Mal!' came a shout. It was the man scrapping with Madison. Brendan rushed over, yanking the bone saw out of Mal as he went, who gasped wetly and slumped against the door.

Brendan's rage and desperation were complete. He walked straight over to the other man, who was now using sheer weight to straddle Madison, trying to crack her head back against the floor tiles. He stuck the bone saw in the side of his neck, and out again, dragging an obscene arterial spray that gushed across the room. The man grabbed at the wound, but blood ribboned away in crude gouts. He fell back and slipped, his foot sliding on the blood and plastic, then landed with a crash of glass. Brendan checked on his DS, who'd saved his life.

She lay there on the floor, battered, her eyes wide.

'Thank you, boss.'

Brendan couldn't find any words, as he pulled himself shakily to the table, grasping for Mick's teddy. He held it tight, his eyes streaming, fingering the soft fabric of the attached blanket, unable to look fully at the bin bag. His grief was threatening to send his conscious somewhere far away.

The kitchen door crashed open and Christopher and Seabreeze fell into the scene, and the four of them stood there, surrounded by blood.

'Jesus Christ, what…' Christopher couldn't finish. He looked at Mal, behind the door, and all the blood. Seabreeze, his face blank, went to the man by the broken patio window, and breathed out sharply. Brendan looked at the body on the floor. It was ghastly. The tracksuited man had fallen on the remaining shards of upright glass in the pane, neck first, rendering the join between head and body tenuous at best.

Brendan and Madison looked at each other. 'I won't tell anyone,' she said, pulling herself upright. 'About any of it.'

As if guided by a deific hand, all eyes drifted to the bin bag.

Madison put her hand on Brendan's shoulder as he sat shaking on the dining chair. 'Let me,' she said. Gingerly, she took a sharp breath and peeked in the bag.

She closed her eyes.

With a blast of exhaled air, she upended the bag, and poured its contents onto the table. A few shirts, a broken coat hanger, and a mixing bowl, presumably from the kitchen itself– not baby Mick.

Brendan couldn't stop the weirdest tears – tears of grief, horror and abject, heart-bursting relief.

CHAPTER 56

NOBODY SPOKE MUCH.

The events had bonded them, fused them. Shared trauma, but also a righteousness. There was the good and right that they did in their jobs, then there was justice. So often, the two things never met. Yet here, in this shitty kitchen on the edge of a northern metropolis, they'd found it.

The conversation was short. 'Who knows we're here?' asked Brendan.

'Nobody outside of us four,' replied Madison, to which Christopher and Seabreeze nodded, the former adding: 'None of us are supposed to be here.'

'I'm suspended,' conceded Brendan.

They looked at the bodies, all processing.

'Self defence?' suggested Madison.

Seabreeze answered like he was working through a maths problem. 'Four on two. Unsanctioned police activity, with a suspended cop who's got links to organized crime. One victim pretty much beheaded, the other stabbed a number of times. This doesn't look like reasonable force. And... there's nothing in that bin bag.'

Wordlessly, over the sixty seconds that followed, they made a silent agreement.

Brendan checked Madison over. Christopher stood there in that first-on-the-scene paralysis until he quickly got moving. Seabreeze fell into activity. As a career tech, it was his first time in the field. He was a natural.

'Pull the tape from the ceiling carefully, then drag the plastic to the middle,' he said. 'Careful not to pull any paint.'

They all did as he said and took turns to walk around the circle of plastic surrounding two bodies. Before long, aided by careful direction, Christopher had come out of his funk, and Seabreeze had them arranging the bodies into two tightly packed tubes. None of them wanted to think of the similarities with the bodies in the damned trench.

Brendan watched as those bastards were pushed and pulled about like the clods of meat they'd been reduced to. They'd tried to trick him and use that awful video as a calling card for what they were prepared to do if you crossed their interests – without actually quite doing it, restamping their authority over the region with the cruelest of threats. They were clearly going to kill Brendan anyway but, in deceiving him, all they'd managed to truly do was get themselves killed in the coldest blood. He should have felt disgusted with himself, and fearful at his sudden descent to violent, bloody murder. But he couldn't.

He couldn't feel anything.

THE BODIES WERE soon in the boot of Brendan's Audi, and the kitchen emerged spotless – a true testament to the barbarous planning that went into the attack. All four police and two bodies cruised from the scene to a landfill Seabreeze knew of on the edge of Birchwood, off the M62. They went in convoy, lifted the barrier that was the only shoddy security and entered. They threw the two bodies into the deepest part of the furthest hole they could find and watched them tumble into the garbage. The weight of the parcels, from such a height, meant they plummeted deep into the assembled waste.

Brendan still hadn't said anything. He was fixed blankly on where the bodies had fallen, his slip into shock as sudden and deep as the fall the two parcels had just taken.

It was Madison who piped up, the soft glow of the M62 on her bruised face, blood crusted dry in blotches. 'As far as I'm concerned, that's case closed and the end of it. Any objections?'

'None,' said Christopher, and he spat headlong into the void.

'Not a thing,' said Seabreeze, already turning away.

Brendan still couldn't bring himself to utter a sound.

EPILOGUE

BRENDAN AND MADISON went to separate hospitals, as agreed. Madison could sell her injuries easily in her boxing kit, as if she'd been sent to the hospital by the on-site medical staff for a quick once-over. Brendan had to tell the receptionist, then the triage nurse, what had happened. His words were barely audible, but he'd never forget them.

He went home later, walking shakily, the adrenaline finally ebbing away, to find Mim in bed and his mum in the spare room. Dan slept soundly in his own bed, and after spending a long time on the floor by baby Mick's cot, just staring at him, letting his eyes empty soundlessly, he picked up the infant and took him to bed with him, slipping him in between himself and Mim – but not before tucking Bun Bun under his arm, his tiny fingers ruffling the fabric from dreamland. It turned out they'd had a surprise visit from Ross, and an even bigger surprise in a man called Mal, who Moira remembered immediately as an old friend of the family, despite the years between visits. Mim hadn't a clue. He'd left after a cup of tea and a happy little reminisce – although Mick's Bun Bun had been noticed as missing.

Mal had been there, in Brendan's house, and that ruined everything. After a while, he showered for as long as the hot water ran, took four Ibuprofen and a slug of cooking sherry from the kitchen cupboard and decided that in the morning he'd have to tell the family they'd need to move. That is, after he'd told them that Art and Ross were dead.

He lay down next to Mim, and silently wept. It had been too long coming.

She woke and held him. Over Mick's starfished, sleeping form, he told her about the death of his father and brother. Nothing else. She held him, until he slept.

When he woke up in the morning, sleeping in later than he had done in a long time, he was called by Christopher. It was Hoyt, his own team member, who'd been the inside man – and the man who'd killed his father. He also told him Ross' body was never recovered.

Nobody knew where he was.

He didn't leave his bedroom for the next two days, glued to round-the-clock news channels, watching the national dissection of what had really gone on in Warrington, between bouts of a strangely bleak sleep. A thuggish cloud of depression had descended onto him, snatching him of his will to move forward, despite the incendiary stories that were being written about his father.

If the news anchors were to be believed, Warrington was in a state of confused mourning, now that the supposed mass murderer in their midst had been exposed. Art Foley's name would be forever synonymous with prolific serial killers. Brendan had had to field two calls, from Netflix and Amazon Prime, for his inclusion in the true crime series they had both hastily green-lit on the subject. Art Foley finally had his infamy, although it wasn't for what he'd hoped. The fact he was dead, killed by one of the cops who tried to bring him in, only added to the story. Some saw Hoyt as a hero; news outlets painted him sympathetically. Brendan didn't know what to think. He just filed it all away. His angst, trauma and scars, all stored.

When he eventually left the bedroom, he made a call to a local health centre and booked himself in for a course of grief counselling. Of all the things that could beat him in the months to come, he was going to make sure it wasn't that.

LATER, THERE WAS an all-singing, all-dancing memorial service for the Warrington 27 at the town hall. The individual bodies had long since been dispatched to funeral homes arranged by the victims' nearest and dearest, so all that stood in front of the assembled crowds and press was a hastily created statue of a huge iron tree, with twenty-seven different orchids growing on it – each one engraved with the name of a corresponding victim. Standing on a roundabout at the end of Buttermarket Street, right in the middle of the town's shopping district, it would be walked under by shoppers and circled by commuters for generations to come. Brendan wondered if by doing this, and putting it here, the whole town would end up stigmatised by grief.

As the mayor was wrapping up his speech, praising the efforts of the young police force that brought this heinous matter to an end, Brendan slunk from a quiet side street and stood next to Monroe. His *think about it* period was up. This was man to man and all hell else.

They both knew the score. Hoyt was awaiting trial for murder. Art had indeed died, and had died a mass murderer – one of the nation's most prolific, most committed serial killers, brought to arrest by his own son, the hero detective Brendan Foley – whose brother was officially classed as missing. As for Culpepper? No evidence for anything. Nada for nada. Into the breeze he'd gone. Malcolm Jevons and Gerry Toyne were on the run in Europe, and the NCA and Interpol were trying to track them down. Life at the station was getting back to normal, aside from this day out.

'Your job is still here,' Monroe said, after the obligatory pleasantries. 'We need a DI. You're the country's golden boy, and the nick's best bet. Come back and run CID.'

Brendan thought about it for a couple of seconds. 'I don't want it. I tell you who's better than any of us here. Madison. Make her DI. She's the one.'

He had other things on his mind.

And he left. Back down the side street.

MADISON KEPT HER distance, watching the exchange between her boss and Brendan. She left them to it, her own confidence rocked ever since the depths of Hoyt's duplicity had been revealed. Her strength and belief in herself had always kept her, for better or worse, iron-clad in the early stages of relationships. Yet, somehow, he'd got to her. Detectives and relationships were always shocking bedfellows; you analysed your counterpart with the same code and veracity with which you'd run the personality analysis of a child murderer. But somehow, she'd managed to bypass that, and having seen it betrayed so spectacularly, it would be a long time before she opened up like that again.

She thought he might have been a bit combustive when push got to shove, but never this. Never murder. She hadn't seen him after Art Foley's death. Just knew he'd been at the cells at the nick for a couple of days, then transferred to Risley HMP to await trial. She'd resolved to erase him in an instant, as you would bath scum. The betrayal, however, would live tight for a while, an unwanted shadow.

Arthur Foley's prosecution and inquest had been taken off the department, quite rightly, so now finally it was a Home Office matter. The rest of them were on to new things. Christopher had been elevated to DS. He, Madison and Seabreeze ate often together at one of the local cafés, none of them saying much of note, but all bound without question. They seemed to take ugly comfort in each other.

Now, as she watched Brendan Foley walk off down the pedestrianised side street towards the Golden Square shopping centre, she saw him pause and turn to her. She waved and he smiled. They hadn't seen each other since that night. He started to walk over, pulling a beanie up over his head, scanning for press cameras.

As he got to his one-time DS, Brendan hugged Iona.

'Gotcha, boss,' she said into his shoulder.

'No,' Brendan said, pulling back to look into her eyes. 'You're the boss now.'

FAR FROM THE TREE

ABOUT THE AUTHOR

Rob Parker is a married father of three, who lives in a village near Warrington, UK. The author of the Ben Bracken thrillers and the standalone post-Brexit country-noir *Crook's Hollow*, he enjoys a rural life on an old pig farm (now minus pigs), writing horrible things between school runs.

Rob writes full time, as well as organising and attending various author events across the UK - while boxing regularly for charity. Passionate about inspiring a love of the written word in young people, he spends a lot of time in schools across the North West, encouraging literacy, story-telling and creative-writing.

He is also a co-host of the For Your Reconsideration film podcast, and a regular voice on the Blood Brothers crime book podcast.

Also by Rob Parker

The Ben Bracken Thrillers

A Wanted Man
Morte Point
The Penny Black
Till Morning Is Nigh

Standalone

Crook's Hollow

Follow Rob on social media at:

@robparkerauthor

@robparkerauthor

@robparkerauthor

www.robparkerauthor.com

info@robparkerauthor.com